Movement at one of the windows caught her eye, and abruptly she blinked.

It must be a reflection from the setting sun, she told herself, or the shadow of a bird flying overhead. But the sun was too low to cast reflections or shadows at that angle. She leaned closer, until her nose was pressed against a wooden slat, and stared harder through the narrow slit.

It was still there, pale and sort of oblong in shape, like a hand parting the blinds at the right height for a person to peek out, just the way—

She swallowed hard. Just the way she was doing.

Dread washing over her, she jumped back as if the slats had burned, then kept moving backward until the tile floor changed to carpet. There she spun around and raced down the hall and the stairs to escape.

D0243478

COPPER LAKE CONFIDENTIAL

BY
MARILYN PAPPANO

All the characters in this book have no existence outside the imagination of the author, and have no relation whatsoever to anyone bearing the same name or names. They are not even distantly inspired by any individual known or unknown to the author, and all the incidents are pure invention.

All Rights Reserved including the right of reproduction in whole or in part in any form. This edition is published by arrangement with Harlequin Enterprises II B.V./S.à.r.l. The text of this publication or any part thereof may not be reproduced or transmitted in any form or by any means, electronic or mechanical, including photocopying, recording, storage in an information retrieval system, or otherwise, without the written permission of the publisher.

This book is sold subject to the condition that it shall not, by way of trade or otherwise, be lent, resold, hired out or otherwise circulated without the prior consent of the publisher in any form of binding or cover other than that in which it is published and without a similar condition including this condition being imposed on the subsequent purchaser.

® and ™ are trademarks owned and used by the trademark owner and/or its licensee. Trademarks marked with ® are registered with the United Kingdom Patent Office and/or the Office for Harmonisation in the Internal Market and in other countries.

First published in Great Britain 2013
by Mills & Boon, an imprint of Harlequin (UK) Limited,
Eton House, 18-24 Paradise Road, Richmond, Surrey TW9 1SR

© Marilyn Pappano 2013

ISBN: 978 0 263 90363 8
ebook ISBN: 978 1 472 00726 1

46-0613

Harlequin (UK) policy is to use papers that are natural, renewable and recyclable products and made from wood grown in sustainable forests. The logging and manufacturing processes conform to the legal environmental regulations of the country of origin.

Printed and bound in Spain
by Blackprint CPI, Barcelona

Marilyn Pappano has spent most of her life growing into the person she was meant to be, but isn't there yet. She's been blessed by family—her husband, their son, his lovely wife and a grandson who is almost certainly the most beautiful and talented baby in the world—and friends, along with a writing career that's made her one of the luckiest people around. Her passions, besides those already listed, include the pack of wild dogs who make their home in her house, fighting the good fight against the weeds that make up her yard, killing the creepy-crawlies that slither out of those weeds and, of course, anything having to do with books.

Chapter 1

Going home alone? Are you crazy?

With her brother's words echoing in her ears, Macy Howard pulled into the driveway of the house she'd left a year and a half ago and stopped. The garage door slid up at the touch of a button, revealing a space empty but for a few tools and yard-care equipment. The lawn was mown, the hard surfaces neatly edged, the flowers freshly watered. She had no doubt the backyard looked as good, that the pool was sparkling clean, the house and guesthouse dusted and vacuumed and ready to be lived in again.

Not that she would ever live in this house again.

Hands trembling, she eased the minivan into the garage, shut off the engine and watched in the rearview mirror as the door slowly came down. If she closed her eyes, if she relaxed, she could almost believe it was a normal day back before her life had blasted all to hell.

Clary would be in the child seat in back, tired after a morning of play and shopping, and the groceries would be waiting to be carried in and put away. She would fix lunch—sandwiches, probably; Clary was in a peanut-butter-and-jelly rut—then she would put her daughter down for a nap before Mark made his usual post-lunchtime call to see how his favorite girls were.

But it wasn't a normal day.

Clary was in Charleston with her uncle Brent and his bride, Anne.

Mark was dead.

And Macy was fiercely glad he was.

The tips of her fingers began to ache. Taking a deep breath, she forced them to unclench from the steering wheel. Things she used to do without thought now required conscious effort: undo the seat belt, open the door, slide out, close the door. Her footsteps echoing on pebbled pavement, she walked across the garage to the door that led inside, then stopped.

She couldn't do this. She should have stuck to the original plan: drive up Friday morning with Clary, Brent and Anne. Check in to a hotel. Come to the house with her brother and sister-in-law. Pack what she intended to keep—nothing that would remind her of Mark. Leave and never come back.

But no, she'd wanted to be alone her first time here. Didn't want an audience for whatever emotions she might feel. Didn't want to show even the tiniest bit of weakness to people who watched her, every moment, for just that.

She fitted her key in the lock, twisted and opened the door into the laundry room. Though shutting off the alarm system came instinctively, the first step beyond that was like slogging through knee-deep concrete that hadn't yet set. The second was hard, too, and the third, but finally she reached the pantry, then the kitchen.

Stainless, stone and tile gleamed. Her lawyer must have hired a cleaning service after getting her email that she was returning. A lime-green colander filled with fresh red apples sat on the island. The sweet scent of hazelnut mixed in the air with wood polish, and a vase of rusty-hued flowers occupied the center of the breakfast table. Through the window over the sink, she could see the beds that had been her passion, bright and alive with color, as if she'd never gone away.

Home. She was home. In a place that could never be home again.

Grief swept through her, and she mercilessly squelched it. She'd done all the mourning she intended to do for Mark within the first week of his death. After that, when the truth had come out, she'd sworn to never feel one more moment's sorrow for him. Her only regrets were for her daughter and herself, and for the sweet little baby he'd caused her to lose. The life she'd lived, the future she'd planned, the past that had been nothing but lies…

A sound startled her before she realized it was her own strangled emotion. *Anger,* she named it. Anger was good. Anger would carry her through this.

Her shoes clicked on the high sheen of the marble floor as she walked through the house that Mark had built. It had been a happy home, or so she'd believed. A shared home. But all the choices had been his—the style, the materials, the colors.

She thought back to the warm, muggy October day he'd died and shuddered. *All* the choices had been his. But the question still haunted her: How had she not known? She'd lived with him, loved him, had a child with him and been carrying their second daughter. How could she not have known him for the monster he was?

Stopping at the foot of the stairs, she looked up. Despite the recent cleaning, dust motes floated on the air, scattered, slowly drifting toward her. For too many months, she'd been like them, scattered and drifting. She'd been weak, vulnerable. *Fragile,* the doctors had called her.

Her chest tightened, making each breath harder to take. She imagined the dust particles flowing in with the air, carrying the faint scent of Mark's cologne into her lungs, and with a sudden shudder, she pivoted toward the French doors that opened from the family room onto the patio.

In all her years in the house, the backyard was the one place she'd felt truly comfortable. It had been her space, her choices, her retreat. The stone patio gave way to lush grass, to the shimmer of the pool and the gardens and beds that spread everywhere.

She could breathe out here.

The only request she'd made of Brent, who'd handled her affairs for the past eighteen months, had been that he hire Bo Larkin to take care of the garden, and he'd done it. Bless his heart, he would have done anything to help her get better.

She walked across the grass, satisfied to see that Bo had been as meticulous in her work as Macy was herself. How had Bo felt, though, caring for a garden that no one saw besides her and the lawn service guys? All that time and effort…

As she neared the corner of the house, a snuffle outside the privacy fence caught her attention. It was followed by rustling, grunting and slithering, and for an instant the hairs on her neck stood on end. Swallowing hard, Macy took the last few steps that blocked her view of the narrow side yard...and saw a big yellow dog happily trampling the daylilies that grew in the corner of the bed. A hollowed-out area under the gate explained the noise.

"Hey," she said sharply, and he looked up at her, tongue lolling from his mouth, before laying his head on his paws.

"Scoo-ter!"

The shout came from the street, a man's voice, and the dog's ears pricked before he hunkered in a little more.

"You've run away, haven't you?"

Big brown eyes watched her.

"*Scoo*-ter!"

The Lab managed to make himself a little flatter, closing his eyes, for a moment appearing as if he were asleep. Then he opened one to a slit to peek at her. She stopped her smile before it could form and moved past him to the gate.

"Scooter, dang it, you know you've got to take your medicine," the voice muttered. "Do I have to chase you all over the neighborhood every time?"

Macy glanced at the dog, still pretending to sleep, then unlatched the gate. At least someone in the world was apparently having a normal day, even if it did mean chasing down his recalcitrant dog. She wondered if he knew how much to appreciate that. She would give up every dime of her fortune to learn what "normal" was supposed to be now.

When she tugged the heavy gate open, Scooter's owner was nearing her driveway. He was tall, lanky, wearing cargo shorts and a T-shirt and glasses, with his brown hair standing on end, as if he'd combed his fingers through it in frustration. A red leash was draped around his neck.

He was a stranger to her, luckily. She really would have hated for the first person she saw to be someone she knew, someone like her friend Sophy's mother, Rae Marchand, who lived three houses down, or Louise Wetherby from the end of the block. Either woman could put any gaggle of teenage girls to shame with their gossiping skills. Rae was pretty harmless about it, but Louise liked to leave her victims bleeding from the sharpness of her tongue. Macy intended to avoid both women during her stay.

"Hey," she called. "Would Scooter, by chance, be a yellow Lab with a fondness for making his bed in my daylilies?"

Switching directions, the man grimaced. "I'm sorry. He's on meds right now, and he knows I give them at noon, so he's started making his escape about ten minutes before."

Automatically, Macy checked her watch. It was 12:05. "You think your dog can tell time?"

Her dry tone quirked one of his brows. "You think it's coincidence he's taken off at the same time every day for a week?" Without waiting for a response, he went on. "If he's damaged the flowers, tell me where I can replace them or send me a bill or something."

"I'm sure they'll be fine." She stepped back to allow him through the gate. The dog was still feigning sleep, though with one ear cocked up to hear better.

"Scooter." His master—well, owner, since he didn't seem to have much mastery over the dog—crouched in front of him. "We talked about this, didn't we? You're not welcome in anyone's yard but your own."

Macy restrained a smile. For so many months, the only people she'd dealt with outside her family were so overwhelmingly serious. For that matter, with the exception of Clary, the family members were too serious, too. Now here she stood in her backyard with a man who had discussions with his dog about proper behavior and, apparently, expected the animal to understand. It wasn't normal, but it beat her usual days by a mile.

The man hooked the leash onto Scooter's collar. "Come on," he said sternly. "Apologize to the lady, then we're going home."

For a moment the dog remained motionless, then he leaped to his feet, eyes wide, looking as surprised as if he'd really been woken from sleep. He jumped at his owner with enough force to knock the man down if he hadn't been prepared, then panted and strained toward the gate as if eager to be on his way.

"Apologize, Scooter."

Happiness draining from his face, the dog walked over to Macy, head ducked down, eyes peering up at her, then rubbed his head lightly against her knee. He really did look contrite, and finally her smile formed.

"Apology accepted," she murmured, feeling silly.

"By the way…" The owner straightened, standing six inches taller than her. "I'm Stephen Noble. Scooter and I live down around the curve." He gestured toward the north, which gave her one important piece of information: he wasn't part of the Woodhaven Villas subdivision. He hadn't been one of her and Mark's neighbors.

Though he probably still knew everything that had

happened. He did live in Copper Lake, after all, and he didn't seem the least bit hermit-ish.

"Macy Howard." She watched his face closely for some reaction—even in Charleston and Columbia, in the beginning, her name had drawn some response—but not from him. "Have you lived here long?"

"About ten months. I came to work with Dr. Yates for a while and decided to stay."

Inwardly cringing at the mention of a doctor, Macy breathed deeply. "So you're a physician's assistant or a nurse or…?"

His eyes—hazel behind the glass lenses—shadowed, then he laughed. "No. Dr. Yates is a vet. So am I."

Relief washed through her. She wasn't sure she'd ever be recovered enough to comfortably deal with medical personnel. And being a vet certainly helped explain why he thought his dog could tell time and why he had regular discussions with him.

"I've never had any pets," she said as explanation why she didn't know that detail about Dr. Yates. Mark had chosen whom they socialized with, and a veterinarian had never made the list.

She had never been the snob Mark was; by his standards, her own family wouldn't have been good enough. They didn't have old blood and old money, prestige and power. They didn't rate with the great Howards.

A snort of disgust rose inside her, but she choked it down. Not now, not here.

"I've never *not* had pets," Stephen was saying. "Being a vet was all I ever wanted to do. More or less."

"So you got your dream. Good for you." Being happy was all Macy had ever wanted. A comfortable life. A husband she loved who loved her back. Kids to cherish. Stability.

You're stable now, she reminded herself, forcing even breaths. She had some unsteady moments, but they were fewer and further between. She was capable and competent. She *was*.

"What do you do?"

She blinked, then refocused on Stephen. "Do?"

"Do you work? Have a job besides taking care of this place?"

"I, uh…no." She hadn't worked since a part-time job in college. As soon as Mark had graduated, she'd dropped out and they'd gotten married. He'd never wanted her working then, and she didn't need to now. Between his death and his grandmother's a month later, Macy had enough money to support herself, her daughter and whatever family Clary might one day have for the rest of their lives.

"Well…" Stephen shifted, tugging on the leash. "I've got to get this guy home and shove a couple pills down his throat. Remember, let me know about the flowers. I'll take it out of Scooter's cookie money."

She murmured something—goodbye, she thought— and watched them leave, the dog walking quietly alongside his owner, but they faded from her thoughts before they were gone from sight.

Sure, she had money to support herself and Clary, but…what would she *do?* What would fill her days? What would she contribute? How would she show Clary how to be a kind, compassionate, responsible, productive adult?

And the most terrifying question of all: With all that

free time, with nothing to do but take care of Clary, how would she ever stay sane?

A few times on the way to the curve that marked the end of Woodhaven Villas and the beginning of the Lesser of the World, Stephen looked back over his shoulder at the Howard house. The first two times Macy stood in exactly the same position, not looking after them to make sure the flower-smashing dog wasn't coming back, but just standing there, not looking at anything, it seemed.

The third time she was gone.

She'd dressed as if she belonged in the house designed not so much to be a home but a showplace. He didn't know much about women's clothes, but the sleeveless dress and heeled sandals she wore just *looked* expensive. So did the gold-and-diamond watch on her wrist and the rubies and diamonds in her ears.

Oddly enough, she hadn't been wearing a wedding ring. Surely she didn't live in that place alone.

Maybe she didn't live there at all, he thought with a grin. Maybe Scooter had interrupted a burglary in progress. Or maybe the family was away on a trip and she'd broken in to live there as a squatter. Maybe she was the maid playing dress-up in the boss's clothes, or—

As his own house came into sight, he reined in his imagination. It had run wild for as long as he could remember, so he did try to exercise restraint from time to time. But wouldn't it be a hoot if she *were* some kind of upper-class thief?

Though the Howard house, as the last house in the development, was less than a half mile away, there was a whole galaxy in that distance. He had nine hundred square feet, compared with Macy's four or five thousand.

His backyard was big enough for a grill, a few chairs and a few swipes with the lawn mower, while in hers he'd glimpsed extensive gardens, a pool and what looked like a guesthouse tucked into the rear corner. He had wood floors and furnishings that ranged in age from ten years to way older than him. He had a living room, a kitchen big enough for him and Scooter, a bedroom, a bathroom and an office. He was a happy camper.

Even in her mansion, Macy Howard hadn't looked very happy.

Scooter took his meds eagerly—two pills slipped in side slices of hot dog—then went to gulp down a bowl of water. "You want a walk as a reward for taking your pills? You could just say so. I'd rather walk with you than chase you down, yelling that silly name. Who in the world names a beautiful boy like you Scooter?"

The dog grinned at him, water dripping from his beard, then went to his bed and stretched out.

Stephen made sure the kitchen door was locked—since Scooter had learned to turn the knob, that was his newest escape route—then went across the narrow hall to what was supposed to be the master bedroom. He slept in the smaller room at the front of the house, just big enough for a bed and chest, and used this room as his office.

Bookcases lined two walls, both packed full. More books were piled on top and on the floor and also lined the windowsills of all four windows. A few posters from favorite movies hung on the walls; magazines and papers all but obscured his computer, and two large dry-erase boards, covered with notes, took up the rest of the space. The room was cluttered and messy, but that was the way he liked it when he worked.

He'd settled in his chair, just able to see the dog through the doorway, and jiggled the mouse to wake the computer when his phone rang. Fishing it from his pocket, he answered without checking caller ID. He knew who it was; his sister was a creature of habit. "Hey, Marnie."

"What are you doing?" Her usual question.

"Working." His usual answer. "How's your day?"

"It's fine." She sounded distracted. She was normally eating lunch when she called, usually while doing something thoroughly disgusting for her job as a lab geek for the Copper Lake Police Department. "Are you busy this weekend?"

He looked to the wall where a calendar was supposed to hang, then remembered its thumbtack had come loose a few weeks ago and he'd never gotten around to putting it back. "I work Saturday morning, I think. Why?"

"I actually meant Saturday night."

"Why?" he asked again.

Marnie's sigh was long-suffering. "A friend of mine— well, a friend of a friend of mine—needs a date for a thing, so she asked if I'd ask if you'd go."

"Which friend?"

"Sophy."

The muscles in his neck relaxed. He liked Sophy Marchand—had been out with her a couple of times without Marnie acting as intermediary. "Why didn't Sophy call herself?"

"No, she's *my* friend. Her friend is Kiki Isaacs."

In the kitchen, Scooter gave a little whine. The dog had excellent hearing—and taste in women. Kiki was a detective with CLPD, pretty, whiny, aggressive and didn't know the meaning of the word *subtle*. The few times he'd seen her off the job, she'd still been armed, even though she could probably heave him like a javelin. She was an in-your-face type, and frankly, she scared him.

"Uh, you know, Scooter's been sick this week."

On cue, the dog lifted his head and gave a pitiful wail. Switching the phone to the other hand, Stephen fished a cookie from the bowl on the desk and tossed it to him, mouthing, *Good boy.*

"And you know how I always play catch-up on weekends." He set goals on Monday and worked as he could during the week, then busted his butt on the weekend to be sure he reached them.

"Would it make any difference if I told you I'd be there, too?"

"Where?"

"It's a retirement party for the police chief. We all have to go."

"How about I go as your guest and Kiki can hang out with us?" *Or not.*

Marnie muttered to herself—he caught the word *decomp* and didn't listen for more—then said, "I, uh, have a date."

Stephen's eyes widened. He couldn't remember the last time his sister had had a date. He loved her dearly, but she was…different. Dead people interested her way more than any living soul. Chitchat for her usually involved lab values, blood-splatter evidence, processes of death or similar subjects most people did *not* want to talk about over dinner.

"Does it matter to you if I take Kiki?"

Again she was silent. Probably weighing the satisfaction she could receive having her own escort at the party while Kiki went dateless against the knowledge that Kiki *would* have been dateless if not for her. "Yes," she said at last.

"Okay. Remind me Friday."

"Thanks." The line went dead. Never any goodbyes for Marnie. If she was finished talking, she hung up.

Stephen set his phone down, then leaned back, staring at the molten red-and-green world rotating on his computer screen. Slowly the view zoomed in, showing mountains and plains, deserts and seas, trees and buildings and people, then it swept out to a global view before repeating it in a new spot.

Marra'akeen. The world where he spent much of his time. The world where he would much rather be come Saturday night. But if it was important to Marnie, he would go and he would be more pleasant than Kiki deserved. And if she acted the way she usually did, he swore he would make the next villain he created a pushy, curly haired whiner named Ke'Ke.

Opening his last document with a sigh, he read what he'd written the day before. By the time he reached the last page, he was in the story's rhythm and began typing. Though there were as many ways to write a book as there were people writing them, he liked stopping in the middle of a scene, saving himself the hassle of deciding what should happen next when he came back to it.

He worked steadily for more than an hour before his gaze strayed to the south window. The roof of the Howard house was just visible through the trees. He'd driven past it hundreds of times since he'd moved here, and he'd never seen any sign of life. Of course, the Woodhaven Villains weren't the type to sit out on their porches, in the few houses that even had porches, or work in the front yards themselves. In his world, they were Lord Gentry who hired Workers to do anything remotely similar to manual labor. They lived in luxurious cocoons, surrounded by tall walls and state-of-the-art alarm systems to keep out the Lessers. It was all way too confining for him.

Macy Howard had looked confined, but there had been something restless about her, something…uneasy.

He shook his head to clear it. He would probably never see her again. Scooter rarely used the same hiding place twice. Though she might come in handy as a model for the repressed daughter of the Lord Gentry Tu'anlan, who escaped her fortress home to become one of the Warrior Women who guarded the Crystal.

Turning his back on the window, with the repressed but rather pretty Ma'ahcee forming in the back of his mind, he began typing again.

The brief interruption of Scooter and his master had eased a bit of the tension knotting Macy, a fact she hadn't noticed until she walked back into the house with her suitcase and her entire body went tight again. One even breath after another, one forced step after another, she went to the purse she'd left on the kitchen island and pulled out the list she'd made.

Go inside. Walk through the rooms. Take bag inside. Unpack in guest room. Change clothes. Start.

An overly simple list, but some situations called for a step-by-step guide, Shrink #4 had told her. *Every situation, no matter how stressful or complicated, can be broken down into manageable steps.* Time to test his theory.

Mentally she checked off the first three items, then let her gaze shift through the doorway and down the hall to the stairs. She thought of the dust particles, of climbing the stairs, of being as far from an exit as she could get in the house, and skipped ahead to the last item.

Start. Start sorting through six years of furniture, treasures and detritus. Start choosing what to take with her and what to leave behind. Start rebuilding the life Mark had stolen from her. Start over. One manageable step at a time.

First she needed packing supplies. Once in the van, she backed out of the driveway and into the street, and the tension in her shoulders eased. As she turned out of the subdivision onto the main road, it eased even more. It wouldn't go away, not while she remained in Copper Lake, but it was a definite improvement.

Her destination was the self-storage facility on Carolina Avenue that also rented moving vans and sold packing supplies. She didn't know the clerk behind the counter, and thankfully he didn't seem to recognize her, taking her cash and helping her load bundles of cartons, rolls of Bubble Wrap and heavy paper and tape into the back of the van.

She would have driven straight back home except for a wandering glance at the riverfront park while she sat at a red light. Seated there on a bench, watching two small children play, was Anamaria Duquesne Calloway. Though they'd socialized with the same people, they'd never been friends, not really. The Calloways were the one local family more prestigious than the Howards, but Mark had never approved of Robbie Calloway's wild behavior before marriage, and he *certainly* hadn't approved of Robbie's marriage to the mixed-race Anamaria, so he'd kept Macy at a distance.

However, once, while she was pregnant with Clary,

Macy had gone behind Mark's back to meet with Anamaria. She'd wanted the psychic's assurance that everything was fine with the baby, and she'd gotten it. The easing of her worries had been worth Mark's irritation—and his grandmother's fury—when he'd found out.

Once, Macy reflected as the light changed. *Once,* in the years they'd been married, she'd done something Mark hadn't wanted.

She would have driven past the entrance to the park if some bit of resentment hadn't seeped through her. Instead, she turned in, parking beside the lone vehicle there. She was being pushy. If she wanted Anamaria's professional advice, she should call and make an appointment. She shouldn't intrude on a mother's playtime with her children. She should, shouldn't, wouldn't, couldn't...

Before the argument inside her had played out, there was a tap on the window. Startled, she looked up to see Anamaria's sympathetic face. With a click, she opened the door and slid out, straight into Anamaria's comforting embrace.

"Macy. It's so good to see you."

For a moment she held herself stiff—when she was stiff, it was harder to be overwhelmed by emotion—but it took too much effort. She softened in Anamaria's motherly embrace. She felt welcomed. Unjudged.

"I'd heard you were coming back," Anamaria said when at last she eased her grip.

Macy smiled faintly but didn't ask from whom. The answer could be as simple as her husband—the lawyer who'd handled both Mark's and his grandmother's estates—or as complex as some soul on the other side, maybe Mark. Maybe even her lost baby.

A small hand gripped the hem of Macy's dress, and

she looked down to see Anamaria's daughter staring up at her. "I'm Gloriana," she murmured around two fingers tucked in her mouth. "Where's your little girl?"

Macy blinked, then looked at Anamaria. "I must have mentioned Clary to her sometime," the woman said with a serene smile.

"She's with her uncle," Macy replied, unconvinced by Anamaria's smile. According to rumor, every Duquesne woman had gifts of one sort or another. Gloriana was young, but no age was too young to use the talents you'd been born with, she supposed.

"Go play with Will." Anamaria gave her daughter a gentle push before linking arms with Macy. "Come sit. We'll talk. Are you coming home?"

"No." Macy's reply came automatically. When they reached the bench, she sat down, then shrugged. "I can't face… You know how people love to gossip. Eventually Clary would have to pay the price."

"No one blames you or Clary. How could they?"

"We lived with him, Anamaria. *I* lived with him, I shared a bed with him, I was married to him for seven years. And all that time I never had a clue that he was…"

Even now it was hard to say: he was a remorseless cold-blooded killer. The husband she'd loved so much, who'd been such a doting father, had beaten strangers to death and buried them on his grandparents' property right outside town. And to make his evil even worse, he'd learned the skill from his grandfather.

The blood of serial killers ran through her daughter's veins.

Shuddering despite the warm afternoon sun, she hugged herself tightly. "I should have known. I should have suspected *something*."

"Are *you* psychic now?"

Her gaze cut sharply to Anamaria, who was watching her closely, but not in the same way her family did. They were looking for signs that the depression was returning, the weakness overtaking her, the instability gaining control. They didn't understand how difficult it was when her every move was scrutinized: *Is this the action, the thought, the comment of a sane person? Is she rational, merely emotional or sinking back into the abyss?*

But there was nothing measuring or judging about Anamaria's gaze. A simple question, a simple look.

"No, I'm not psychic. But I should have…"

"Mark and his grandfather were very good at hiding their secrets. You couldn't have known unless he wanted you to."

Macy breathed deeply. That was what the psychiatrists, the psychologists and even some of the other patients in group therapy had told her. Somehow it sounded more convincing coming from a woman with the gift of sight.

"What are your plans now?"

Macy's laugh was rusty. She probably hadn't used it more than a half dozen times in the past eighteen months. "I don't suppose you could tell me."

After a moment, Anamaria took her hand in both of hers, her expression growing distant, as if watching a scene no one else could see. "Everything's going to be all right in the end," she said at last. "If it's not all right now, then this isn't the end. It'll come, Macy. One day you're going to realize that you and Clary are better than ever."

They were just words, but Macy knew words had power. Words had destroyed every illusion she'd ever had, and now they gave her, if not peace, at least a little hope. She did find them hard to believe, but she could embrace the possibility. She could believe that sometime in the not-too-distant future, her life would be good again.

She *had* to believe it.

Or there was no reason to continue living.

Chapter 2

In need of a break, Stephen saved his file to the hard drive, then emailed it to himself. It also went automatically to an online storage account, too, but, hey, a guy could never be too careful. Sometimes the old saying "Writing is easy; just sit down and open a vein" was too true. When words were hard to come by, he didn't risk losing any of them.

He stood and stretched, joints popping, before walking to the front door. "Wanna go for a walk?"

Scooter glanced up from his place on the couch, yawned and settled in deeper. Eat, sleep, play—that was his routine.

"Next life I'm coming back as a dog," Stephen muttered as he went out and locked up behind him.

The spring air was warm, the sun shining. He'd done cold for four years, getting his degree at Oklahoma State University Center for Veterinary Health Sciences, then another winter in Cheyenne, Wyoming. He'd be happy if he never saw snow or subzero temperatures again.

Hands shoved in his hip pockets, he turned north and walked to the end of the road, past each of the three neighboring houses. Elderly sisters and their husbands lived in the first two, and he called hello to them, the sisters sitting on one porch, the husbands swapping stories on the second. The last house was occupied by a great-grandson or -nephew who drove an eighteen-wheeler and was gone more often than not. Stephen hadn't seen him five times in the months he'd lived there.

When the road ended just past the third house, he considered taking the path that led into the pine woods, eventually reaching Holigan Creek, where he'd found a shady spot that was great for kicking back. Instead, he turned and went back the way he'd come, speaking to the old folks again, passing his own house, heading for the Woodhaven gates.

He wasn't athletic. The closest he'd ever come to a team sport was online fantasy games with players around the world, and the only weights he'd ever lifted had been in the form of dogs, cats and various body parts of horses or cows. But he liked to walk. It cleared his head and freed his subconscious to work on the current book without his conscious self having to take part. It was one of the best perks of writing.

The Ancients knew there wasn't a lot of money in it, not for a midlist fantasy author. But he loved it, and his audience was building with each title. An author couldn't ask for much more.

Though the *New York Times* bestseller list would be nice.

His intent was to turn around at the gates, return

home and shoot for another thousand words before his muse gave out, but movement just past the gate caught his attention. A minivan—the name didn't do the luxury vehicle justice—was parked in the driveway of the first house on the left, its hatch open, and the woman he'd met thanks to Scooter was wrestling out a bundle of flat boxes bigger than she was.

He went to help her because his mama didn't raise him to ignore someone in need of assistance. That was the only reason. Her being pretty in a skittish-mare sort of way, with brown eyes that dominated her face and porcelain skin that Scarlett O'Hara would have killed for, had nothing to do with it.

"Here, let me give you a—"

Before he could say *hand,* she whirled around. The boxes fell to the ground, one sharp edge landing on her sandaled foot, and she stumbled back against the van, mouth open in a silent gasp, eyes huge.

"Sorry. I didn't mean to startle you." He wasn't exactly known for quiet grace. Size-thirteen feet were never stealthy, and he tended to scuff his shoe soles when he was thinking about something. But, judging by the paleness of her already-pale skin, Macy Howard had been preoccupied, too.

"I—I—" Her hands fluttered and a shiver passed through her, reminding him of a parrot he'd once treated. He still bore the scars on his left arm. "I'm sorry. I wasn't paying attention."

Never apologize. That was the First Rule in his protagonist Lucan's life. One of these days Lucan would have to break that rule—if he didn't, Sa'arca would rip his heart out; Warrior Women were funny that way. "You're entitled to not pay attention." He picked up the bundle, not much heavier than Scooter and not nearly as unwieldy. "Where you do want these?"

A little pink returned to her face, but she still looked as if she might bolt any second. "In the garage, please."

The garage was big enough for three vehicles and so clean that his house looked like a pigsty in comparison. The walls were painted tan, and the floor was surfaced with some sort of grit in a darker shade. A worktable against one wall held the same collection of tools he had at home: screwdrivers in various sizes, a hammer, a few wrenches, a pair of pliers. Along with athletic, he wasn't exactly mechanical, either.

A lawn mower, an edger, a trimmer and a plastic cart were gathered in one corner, all well-used, unlike the tools. Rakes and shovels hung on hooks on the wall; a shelf held motor oil, extra trimmer line, paper towels and paper leaf bags. The rest of the space was empty.

He rested the boxes against the wall near the door into the house. "Are you moving out?"

"I've already done that." She deposited two giant rolls of Bubble Wrap nearby, then managed a weak smile. "I'm sorting through things. Deciding what to keep and what to get rid of."

"Where do you live now?"

She hesitated. Unsure whether to tell him? After all, they were strangers. Then, with a lack of grace that wasn't normal for anyone who could afford a house in Woodhaven Villas, she gestured. "I don't actually live anywhere right now."

Interesting answer. Ranked right up there with her blank look when he'd asked what she did earlier. Maybe she really was Macy Howard and this really was her house, or maybe she wasn't and it wasn't. It wouldn't hurt to ask Marnie.

She pushed her hand through her hair, dislodging the suede band that kept it from her face. "I've been staying with my parents in Charleston. It's time to get a place of my own. To move on. I just haven't decided where."

"Not in Copper Lake, huh?"

An expression of distaste crossed her face fleetingly. If he hadn't made a habit of studying people since he decided he was a writer, he would have missed it. "Preferably not." She left the garage to gather more packing materials, and he followed.

He'd never made a move where he hadn't underestimated how many boxes and rolls of wrapping paper he needed, but that didn't seem a possibility with Macy. Cartons and materials filled the minivan, with the exception of the driver's seat. Even the passenger seat was filled with thick slabs of paper and rolls of tape.

Already moved out. Packing up stuff. No wedding ring. Staying with her parents. He was guessing there was a very unhappy divorce in her recent past. Not that he could really imagine any other kind of divorce. He'd heard urban myths about friendly ex-spouses making a better go as friends and coparents than as husband and wife, but he hadn't witnessed the phenomena himself. His mom's divorces—from the husband who had produced Marnie, then from his dad—had left her soured on men in general. His own divorce had involved as much fighting as the marriage, and they'd had precious little to fight over.

But there was no polite way to ask where her ex was while she sorted through and packed up their house, no matter how curious he was. Instead, he returned to the van for the next load.

Within minutes, the vehicle was empty and one bay of the garage had pretty much disappeared under the supplies. After setting down the last bundle of boxes, he shoved his hands into his pockets and rocked back on his heels, seeking something to say.

"Well."

Macy's smile was tight as she folded her arms across her middle, the classic body-language pose warning others to keep their distance. Unless she was cold, and she didn't look cold. "Thanks for the help," she said without meeting his gaze. "I appreciate it."

"You're welcome." He stood there a moment longer before taking a few steps backward then pivoting to stride the length of the driveway.

Well. Brilliant comment for someone who'd ranked respectably high in his vet med graduating class *and* made part of his living with words. Animals and characters who existed only in his head were so much easier to deal with.

But not nearly as interesting as Macy Howard.

Macy made it halfway to the door before her feet automatically stopped.

Was she ready to face the monster inside?

Immediately she corrected herself. Mark had been the monster. The house had merely been his lair. There was nothing inside that could hurt her; she'd already faced the worst hurt possible when she'd lost the baby. Nothing here could scare her; she might have run away before, but she was strong now.

With a deep breath, she went through the door almost

as if life were normal. She'd managed to assemble one box, ready for use, when her cell phone rang. The ring told her it was Brent. Common sense told her he was calling because she'd failed to check in yet.

"Hey, bub," she greeted him, making an effort to sound as if she were on a relatively even keel.

"You didn't call."

"I intended to as soon as I took a break for dinner." Before he could ask, she went on. "The trip was fine, the house is fine and I'm fine. How's my baby girl?"

"Missing you. Anne and I are doing our best to keep her happy."

Macy pulled out a bar stool and eased onto the buttery soft leather. Poor Clary had spent much of the past eighteen months missing her mom, through the times when Macy had been physically present but not so much mentally to the months her absence had been physical, as well. Months in a psychiatric hospital—luxurious, costly and no place for a small child. "Give her a big hug and a kiss for me. I can't wait to see her Friday. You, too. And Anne."

"We're anxious to see you, too."

Anxious, she was sure, was putting it mildly. There were enough years between them—seven—that he'd always had a protective streak, but after Mark's death, it had multiplied ten times. Where before he may have gotten mildly concerned, now he was truly anxious, edgy, burdened with worry over her mental status, her ability to handle the slightest of stressors. If she hadn't won Anne over in her argument to come here alone, she never would have managed to leave Charleston without him by her side.

One more debt of gratitude to her sister-in-law. Anne

had had enough family drama of her own. Her older sister had been a patient at the same hospital as Macy, which was how Anne and Brent had met. Now she'd married into a family with its own share of drama.

"So you're doing okay. Really okay."

She smiled to help the confidence come across in her voice. "I am. Really. I got all the packing stuff, and I was just taping boxes together so I could get started. I'm fine, Brent, honestly. It's an empty house. It's no big deal."

Though she hadn't been able to climb one step to the second floor. Though her suitcase remained three feet away in the kitchen, and sleeping on the sofa in the family room wasn't beyond the realm of possibility.

"I met a new neighbor." She fiddled with one of the apples in the bright green colander while trying to distract him. "His name is Scooter, and he was trampling my daylilies. He was really quite nice, though, and apologized before leaving."

There was a moment's silence, then Brent cautiously repeated, "Scooter?"

"I know, awful name, isn't it? Just about anything else would be better." Her smile felt more natural as she recalled the dog feigning sleep, then innocence, then remorse. He'd been the one bright spot in her day—he and his owner.

Stephen Noble. Nice name. Nice guy.

"Okay, I give up," Brent said. "Are you teasing or did you really meet someone named Scooter?"

She'd had a sense of humor before Mark's betrayal and the miscarriage her doctor had attributed to overwhelming stress. For Clary's sake, for her own sake, she was going to get that back. "I really did. He's a beautiful yellow Lab who lives down the street and escapes every day to avoid taking his medicine."

Brent's chuckle was a reward. Just as the laughter had disappeared from her life, so had it from his. Her parents had been there for her, too, but the bulk of responsibility had fallen on him. He couldn't get back those months, but she hoped that from now on, he and Anne could have the happy, hopeful lives newlyweds deserved.

"I'm assuming since Scooter couldn't tell you about the medicine, you met his owner, too. Was she nice?"

"He," she corrected him as an image of Stephen flashed into her mind again: tall, lanky, handsome in a disheveled sort of way. She hadn't had *disheveled* in her life since meeting Mark. She would never have *rigid and dishonest*—oh, yeah, let's not forget *sociopathic*—again. "Yeah, he was. He's a vet in town."

"Clary needs a dog when you're up to—" Brent stopped, coughed, then lamely finished, "when you're settled wherever."

When you're up to it. When you can take responsibility for yourself and your daughter. When you're normal again. Once more Macy put all the everyday-average she could force into her voice. "I agree. I'd like having a dog in the house. Preferably one that would only piddle where he's supposed to." And stayed out of her flower beds, because wherever they wound up, she would have flowers.

With the awkwardness past, they talked a few minutes more before Brent said goodbye. As soon as she hung up, she missed the sound of his voice and felt the solitude closing in around her a bit more sharply. She wished she'd already gotten a dog so he could follow her from room to room and maybe bark a little or whine, just to remind her she wasn't alone.

"Okay, Macy, you're twenty-nine years old. The shrinks all agreed it was time for you to be on your own again. You're on your medication, and you know staying busy helps keep the anxiety under control. Now *do* something."

Her voice seemed to echo off the stone and tile and stainless, giving her the impetus to slide to her feet and go back to assembling boxes. When she had two dozen of them stacked on the floor, she brought in wrapping paper and Bubble Wrap, walked into the hall and fixed her gaze immediately on the Chinese vase on the foyer table. It was pretty in its own overembellished way, belonging to some dynasty centuries past, but she'd never liked it. She would be happy to give it a good home somewhere else.

She was reaching for the vase when something drew her attention up the stairs. The dust motes still floated, still smelled faintly of Mark's cologne. They reminded her she hadn't yet gone upstairs, a fact that niggled at her. It was just a house, a structure filled with nothing more harmful than memories. Yes, the bedroom she'd shared with Mark was up there; yes, his clothes still filled the closet. Yes, the nursery was there, too, waiting for a baby who'd died before living.

But her things were up there, as well, and Clary's. And she had to face it eventually.

Wiping damp palms on her dress, she climbed the first step. Her gaze dropped to the runner bordered on both sides with rich dark wood. She'd learned through all her treatment that focusing on long-term goals didn't work for her anymore. She had to take life one day at a time. Take these stairs one step at a time.

Mark's cologne smelled stronger as she climbed—too

strong, it seemed, for a house that had been locked up for a year and a half. But it was a very distinctive scent, one created just for him, and the sense of smell was such a very strong one. Just a whiff of baby lotion took her back to Clary's infancy, and cinnamon transported her to her grandmother's kitchen with an apple pie in the oven.

The stairs made a straight run to the second-floor landing, a gracious space with a sofa, built-in bookcases and a view through a large round window of rooftops, trees and the Gullah River. To the left was Clary's room, the nursery, a bathroom and two guest rooms. To the right was the master suite.

She turned right, automatically assessing furnishings as she walked: portrait of Clary at one year old, keep; prissy demilune table that had come down from Mark's family, discard. Engagement photo of Macy and Mark, keep in case one day Clary wanted it; massive oil painting of a former Howard's ship at sea, discard.

The bedroom door was closed. Doors were meant to be closed, Mark had preached, a habit that went at least as far back in the family as his grandmother. Macy wrapped her fingers around the cool knob, twisted it and swung the door open.

Whatever emotion she'd expected didn't come. The room was so distinctly stamped with Mark's personality that, even though she knew it intimately, it was as if she'd never been there. Dark woods, heavy furniture, murky palette…how had she ever slept in this space? Laughed? Made love? How had she breathed in here?

Breathing was no problem now as she walked through the room. She felt distant, removed from the moment. The book she'd been reading the day he died still sat on the lacquered table next to the sofa in the sitting area.

The jewelry chest, almost as tall as she and ornately carved, still stood against the wall, the cherrywood gleaming from its recent cleaning. She opened the bottom drawer, then closed it before sliding open the next one. Necklaces, bracelets, earrings, rings, watches—too much gold and too many gems for a woman who'd never really cared about jewelry.

The first and second drawers, peeked into on tiptoe, held cuff links, Mark's watches and a half dozen antique pocket watches. He'd known exactly which Howard ancestor each had belonged to.

She opened the third drawer last, the only one that they'd shared. This had been their everyday stuff: matching Rolexes, the first necklace he'd ever given her, their wedding rings.

She had refused to have the ring buried with him. Finding out the truth about him, learning that the man she'd loved didn't really exist—she couldn't have borne having that connection with him through eternity. The only thing she was grateful to him for was her daughter, and considering that grief and sorrow and scandal had taken her second daughter from her, she figured they were even. She owed him nothing.

Shoving the drawer shut, she continued her walk-through of the suite. His closet, his bath, her closet, her bath. There she stopped at the window, fingers parting the wooden blinds enough to give her a view of the backyard that had given her such pleasure, of the pool and the guesthouse. That had been her idea, a place for family to stay when they visited, where Miss Willa could live if she ever had to leave Fair Winds.

She sniffed. Mark's grandmother had left the family home, all right. After the funeral, she'd gone to Raleigh with her and Clary to stay with Mark's mother. A month later she'd gone to sleep and never woken up.

She never would have stayed in the guesthouse anyway. Except for Brent a few times, no one ever had.

Movement at one of the windows caught her eye, and abruptly she blinked. It must be a reflection from the setting sun, she told herself, or the shadow of a bird flying overhead. But the sun was too low to cast reflections or shadows at that angle. She leaned closer, until her nose was pressed against a wooden slat, and stared harder through the narrow slit.

It was still there, pale and sort of oblong in shape, like a hand parting the blinds at the right height for a person to peek out just the way—

She swallowed hard. Just the way she was doing.

Dread washing over her, she jumped back as if the slats had burned, then kept moving backward until the tile floor changed to carpet. There she spun around and raced down the hall and the stairs to escape.

The aromas of a thin-crust pizza with heaps of onions and cheese scattered with the best of Luigi's toppings filled Stephen's car as he turned into Woodhaven Villas. The only thing keeping him from grabbing a piece already was the fact that he was driving, and the only thing protecting the pie from Scooter was the doggy seat belt securing him in the backseat. He was voicing his mournful disapproval when Macy Howard came running out of her house.

Running, Stephen mused. In *heels.* Not very gracefully, granted; he wouldn't have imagined her body could move so *un*gracefully. It just didn't fit with the image of a Southern belle. But still, running.

She came to a stop in the driveway near the minivan, though not actually *stopping*. Her hands patted her sides, the way a person did when feeling for keys or a cell phone in pockets, but her dress didn't appear to have pockets. She looked from the van to the closed garage door, then back in the direction she'd come from, and her face, he saw, was ghostly pale.

Already knowing what his choice would be, he debated it anyway: Luigi's pizza hot from the oven or damsel in distress? Before he even completed the question, he'd brought the car to a stop at the end of Macy's driveway.

Scooter whined as Stephen unbuckled his belt. "I know, buddy," he agreed. "But this'll just take a minute, okay?"

He got out of the car and had closed half the distance between him and Macy before she became aware of him. For an instant, the blood drained from her face so completely that he was surprised she didn't fall unconscious at his feet. Then recognition came, and she took a great heaving breath. "You."

Was it a greeting or accusation? "Yeah, it's me." Again. He gestured awkwardly. "Is everything okay?"

Her cheeks pinked, and she ran a nervous hand through her hair. "Yes, of course. Well, maybe…" She stared at her trembling hand when she lowered it—her entire body was trembling—then grimaced. "Maybe not. I—I thought I saw somebody. Out back. Well, not out back. Actually, in—in the guesthouse."

So she'd startled and run out of the house without either keys or cell phone. He pulled his phone from his pocket. "I'll call the police—"

"No." Her color drained again and she reached out,

though not far enough to make actual contact. "Um, no. No, no, no. Please."

"If someone's broken in—"

"No." She breathed deeply. "If you could—could just…take a look with me?"

Stephen could say he'd never wanted to be a hero, but he'd be lying. He wrote fantasy, after all, which was all about heroics. But it would be truthful to admit he'd never been hero material. He was a bit of a geek, the total opposite of a jock, and believed in his heart that everything could be resolved without resorting to violence. Hell, the only fight he'd ever been in had ended when the other kid threw the first punch—the only punch— and bloodied his nose. He'd learned his strengths and limitations that day, and confronting a possible burglar definitely fell under limitations.

"Look, the Copper Lake P.D. is good. My sister works for them. They can have an officer here in no time, and I'll wait until…" He let his words trail off when her head-shaking became emphatic enough to send her hair swinging.

"No police. It's—it's okay. I shouldn't have asked. I'll just…" She looked as if she didn't have a clue what she would do.

Stephen sighed silently. "All right. No problem. Just let me get Scooter. I don't want to leave him alone in the car."

Her distress eased a little but didn't go away completely. He didn't know why she was so adamant about not calling the police—though there *was* his earlier theory that she wasn't really Macy Howard—but he was pretty sure she wished one of her braver, brawnier neighbors had come along. Instead, she was stuck with the king of let's-talk-this-out and a mutt who didn't know the meaning of confrontation.

He opened the rear door of the car and set Scooter free, then turned back to find Macy already halfway to the door.

"My keys are inside," she explained.

On many of his trips through the neighborhood, he'd wondered how the Lord Gentry of Woodhaven Villas lived. The inside of Macy's house definitely lived up to his imagination. With her hustling ahead and Scooter trotting along beside him, he didn't get a chance to see much—though he definitely recognized Macy in the giant wedding portrait in the living room; so much for the jewel thief or intruder theory—but what he saw was impressive. It was too big, too showy and seriously unwelcoming, but he was impressed.

She walked quickly, sweeping keys and cell off the kitchen island, marching to the patio door. There she hesitated, and he was about to suggest a call to 911 again when, as if she'd made a decision, she unlocked the door and strode toward the guesthouse.

The entrance faced north and the gardens instead of the main house. They climbed the brick-edged steps to the porch, then it took a while to unlock the door. She probably needed both hands to guide the shaking key into the little hole. Finally the tumblers fell into place, and she stepped back to allow him to enter first.

In his practice, he'd faced vicious pigs, aggressive dogs, recalcitrant horses and a huge number of cats that had tried to rip his skin off. He'd been bitten, scratched and stepped on, but that was okay. The animals had mostly been scared. They hadn't *intended* to hurt him. Except maybe the cats. But an intruder who'd broken into an unoccupied house, who, as far as they knew, could have been hiding there since Macy had moved out...

Fortunately for Stephen when he opened the door, Scooter didn't overthink situations. He sniffed the air, then trotted right past Stephen and Macy and into the living room, his nails clicking on the wood floor. He didn't seem fearful, his hair wasn't standing on end, he wasn't on alert. If anyone had been here, they were likely gone.

The living room, dining room and kitchen ran from front to back, occupying the middle third of the house. Doorways on each side led off, presumably, to bedrooms. There was a whole different vibe to the little house compared with the big one. The colors were warmer and lighter, the furniture more about comfort. Even with the blinds closed, it didn't seem as dark here as the big house did with all those windows.

Stephen followed Scooter through the room, checking possible hiding places, looking inside a coat closet and a pantry. Macy stayed a few steps behind him. "Does anything look out of place?"

When she didn't answer, he glanced over his shoulder to see her shaking her head from side to side.

"Where did you think you saw this person?"

"At the window. There." She pointed to the doorway on the right, and their odd little entourage moved that way. The bedroom was sparsely furnished with sleek pieces and a serene blue-gray color scheme. It was simple, elegant. Like the woman behind him.

He went to the window that faced the house, double-wide with wooden blinds the same delicate gray as the bed linens. There was no dust on the slats, none of them appeared disturbed and no footprints were visible on the floor. If they called the police, considering that the scene of the crime was in Woodhaven Villas, the responding officer would probably send one of Marnie's coworkers out to dust for fingerprints. Hell, Marnie would do it herself if he asked, even if Macy did refuse to make a report.

But so far, he'd seen nothing to indicate anything more than an overactive imagination.

When he looked at Macy, her cheeks were pink again and she stared at the floor instead of him. He gave what he hoped was a reassuring smile. Even if she didn't see it, she would hear it in his voice. "The good news is that there doesn't appear to be anyone here. Let's check the other rooms just to be sure."

A faint nod was her only response.

The closet and bathroom were empty, ditto the bedroom and bath on the other side of the house. The door from the kitchen to a tiny patio was dead-bolted, and all the windows were closed and locked. The house was more secure than his own.

Realizing he'd lost Scooter along the way, Stephen returned to the first bedroom, hoping the mutt wasn't curled up on the bed. He wasn't, but was sniffing the floor beneath the window instead. Strange houses were full of new scents for his sensitive nose, which was okay as long as he didn't feel compelled to leave his own. "Come on, Scooter. Let's go."

Tail quivering, the dog spun around and raced out of the room. If Stephen had been a second slower opening the front door, Scooter would have smacked into it.

"I'm sorry," Macy said as she relocked the door. "I really thought I saw…" Her voice wasn't much steadier than it had been before they'd entered the guesthouse. He guessed it was embarrassment now. People like her probably weren't used to making panicky mistakes.

"It's okay. Better to be sure, right?"

She made a soft sound that might have been agreement or could just as easily have meant nothing at all. Hands tightly clenching her keys and cell phone, she led the way back through the garden and around the pool to the patio. There she glanced at the guesthouse with such a look of dismay on her face that he couldn't help but say something.

"Hey, we've got a pizza in the car. Want to share it with us?" When she hesitated, he added, "It's from Luigi's. Even people who just pass through town know that Luigi makes the best pizza ever."

Her smile was just a little one. "I know. I have cravings for it in Charleston."

"It's an extra-large supreme. We can bring it in or you're welcome to come to our house." Sensing her uncertainty, he grinned. "Come on, it's *Luigi's.*"

For a moment, her features tightened even more, then relaxed a little. "Sure," she said, opening the door to allow him and Scooter inside. "Bring it in."

Chapter 3

The instant the front door closed behind Stephen on his way to get the pizza, Macy grimaced. The last thing she wanted tonight was to have dinner with a stranger and his dog, even if it was a Luigi's pizza.

No, the *last* thing she wanted was to be alone in this house. And with this being their third visit in one day, Stephen wasn't exactly a stranger anymore. If he were a homicidal maniac—like Mark—he'd had enough chances at her already. And she liked his dog. Scooter was sweet and cuddly, and the Lab neither suspected nor cared that she was apparently delusional.

Her gut tightened, her stomach heaving so violently that she pressed one hand to her abdomen, the other to her mouth. Had she really seen someone in the guesthouse? Was she crazy? Was she already losing the balance she'd fought so hard to recover?

Since there was absolutely no sign of anyone having trespassed on the property, she couldn't have seen someone, but she preferred to think she'd overreacted rather than imagined a threat. She was anxious about being here. Under the circumstances, who wouldn't be?

She'd let memory get the best of her and made a fool of herself, but now it was over. At least she'd had the luck to find Stephen driving past and not one of the neighbors she knew, and enough control to stop him from calling the police. She didn't know if her months in the psychiatric hospital were common knowledge in Copper Lake, but she didn't intend to give anyone reason to doubt her sanity. No panicked calls to the police about nonexistent intruders. No more fodder for the town gossips.

And she could look on this dinner as therapy. If she and Clary were ever going to have a normal life, she had to learn how to socialize again. Small talk, no anxiety attacks, just a well-adjusted woman sharing a pizza with a man who'd done her a favor.

The front door clicked, signaling Stephen's return, and she moved to the cabinets, taking out plates, glasses and napkins. An earlier check of the refrigerator had revealed that Robbie Calloway—or, more likely, Anamaria—had had it stocked with the basics, so she removed a jug of iced tea, a couple of bottles of water and a couple of bottles of her favorite pop.

The enticing aromas of the pizza entered the kitchen a few seconds ahead of Stephen and Scooter. For just a moment, Macy felt light, eagerly anticipating the pleasure to come. It was a fleeting sensation, one she'd almost forgotten, and it left an ache when her usual uneasiness replaced it.

"I should have asked…do you mind having Scooter inside? I can run him home if you'd prefer."

She thought of all the things the dog could damage—antique rugs peed on, wood floors scratched, delicate porcelain broken with a swipe of his tail—and a smile blossomed across her face. "No, he's fine. Nothing in here is that important." Not to her, at least. Anything he did damage would just be one less thing for her to find a home for.

They settled across from each other at the small dining table that separated the kitchen from the family room. Scooter took up a position exactly between them, looking excitedly from one to the other.

"He's a beautiful dog," she commented. "I'm thinking of getting one for my daughter and me."

"Your daughter?" Stephen stood and crossed the few feet into the kitchen. "Knife?"

She nodded toward the block on one counter pushed far out of reach of little fingers. "Clary. She's three. She's in Charleston with my brother and his wife. They're coming up Friday to help."

Returning with a paring knife, he cut a slice of pizza into Scooter-sized pieces, fed one to the dog, then took a bite of his own slice. "You have any particular breed in mind?"

The one time she'd broached the subject with Mark, he'd listed the breeds he would find acceptable—in other words, very expensive—before giving a flat refusal. She had been disappointed by both responses but hadn't really expected anything else. After all, an over-the-top belief in their own superiority was a defining characteristic of the Howard family, and Mark liked order. A yappy puppy would have upset that.

With those expensive, purebred animals in mind, she

replied, "Something without a pedigree. One that needs a home and is good with kids."

"There's a no-kill shelter just outside town. Unfortunately, they have plenty that meet your requirements."

Macy chewed her first bite, and the pleasure she'd briefly anticipated bloomed through her. It was almost enough to make her moan. After swallowing, she asked, "Is that where Scooter came from?"

"Nope. A client bought him sight unseen, didn't do any training, then wanted me to put him down because he didn't behave. He's been with me ever since."

"I wish I could say I was surprised, but my husband's grandmother generally turned down visits with her only great-grandchild because Clary refused to be merely seen and not heard." Miss Willa had had no patience for the baby, just as Mark would have had no tolerance for an exuberant dog. He'd killed people for no more reason than he wanted to. It was doubtful he would have spared a dog that was less than perfect.

Revulsion rippled through her, her fingers gripping her glass until the tips turned white. She took a couple of deep calming breaths and was grateful to hear Stephen go on talking, though for a moment the words were dampened by the hum in her ears.

"—is afraid she's never going to get grandkids, much less great-grandkids," he was saying when she could focus. "I tell her she should have had more than just the two of us. I doubt 'procreate' even makes Marnie's list of things to do in this lifetime, and I— Well, gotta have a wife before I have kids."

"You're not married?"

"Not for a long time. Sloan and I met in vet school, graduated together and both got jobs in Wyoming. I did small animals, she did large. I hated the winter, she loved it. I didn't want to stay, and she didn't want to leave." He shrugged as if his marriage and divorce had been that simple. No sign of regret in his voice. No heartbreak in his eyes.

She gave the obligatory *I'm sorry,* and he shrugged again, a loose, easy movement.

"Sometimes things don't work out. She's happy there. I'm happy here." He reached for a second slice of pizza. "What about you? Is there an ex-husband somewhere?"

Her hand trembled, and a chunk of onion fell to her lap. She set down the pizza, grabbed a napkin and wiped the spot it left on her dress while her mind raced. Wouldn't it be okay to lie, to simply say, "We're divorced. He's out of the picture"? It wasn't as if she were staying in Copper Lake or would even see Stephen again once she left next week. Not every person who asked was entitled to the truth about Mark. It could be her little secret.

Her dirty little secret. Just as Mark had his.

He'd wound up dead because of his.

She took a drink to ease the dryness in her mouth, then folded both hands together in her lap, out of Stephen's sight, and opened her mouth to tell the lie. But the wrong words came out. "No. He's an ex only in the sense that he's not around. He, um, died a year and a half ago."

That was the first time she'd said the words out loud. She hadn't had to tell her family when it happened because the sheriff did it for her. She hadn't had to tell Clary because her daughter was too young to ask. Everyone else had found out through the media or the very efficient gossip network.

Granted, she'd told the bare minimum just now. She didn't mention that he'd been trying to kill his cousin,

Reece, and Jones, the man she'd married soon after, after they'd unearthed a bone from one of Mark's and his grandfather's victims. She didn't try to find words to say that he'd shot himself in the head when his murder attempt failed. She couldn't even imagine telling anyone that she'd been married to a cold-blooded sociopath.

"Jeez, I'm sorry," Stephen said in a quietly comforting tone, the one he likely used when he had to deliver bad news to his patients' owners. "That must be tough."

"It would be tougher if I still loved him." Immediately she clapped one hand over her mouth. Oh, God, had she actually said that out loud? To a stranger?

Shoving her chair back with a scrape, she jumped to her feet and went into the kitchen, face burning, palms sweaty. Her stomach was knotted, making her hope she wouldn't have to dash for the bathroom. She damn well needed practice at this social interaction thing if she couldn't even control the words that came out of her mouth.

A low whine came from Scooter, followed by a soft word from Stephen, then the sounds of the dog enjoying another bite of pizza. Macy stood in the middle of the kitchen, back to them, hugging herself, wondering what to do next.

Deal with it. You made the comment. Now stop acting like a nut job and go back to the table.

Grabbing a handful of napkins they didn't need, she slowly retraced her steps and sat down. "I...I'm sorry. I didn't mean to say— I don't normally bring that up in conversation."

"Don't worry. I won't repeat it to anyone." He slipped another bite to Scooter, then changed the subject. "I haven't been to Charleston yet. Is that where you're from or did your parents move there later?"

Her breathing slowed, her fingers slowly unclenching. "I've lived there all my life, except for here and in college. My parents bought my grandparents' house after they passed, so there have been Irelands living in it for more than a hundred years." Her smile felt crooked, though she gave it her best. "Mom and Dad are celebrating their fortieth anniversary with an extended tour of Europe. It seemed as good a time as any to take care of things here and—" She considered choices: *start living again. Put the past behind us. Get away from the shame and the scandal.* "—move on." That was bland enough.

"Do you think you'll stay there? Just get a place of your own?"

"I think I might close my eyes really tight, point to a spot on a map and go there." She didn't see herself in Charleston five years from now, or even five months from now. Emotionally, she needed her family close, but *emotionally* she needed distance. Yes, she needed their support, but too much support made her dependent. Even now, when she was adamant about getting back to her life, she hadn't been able to give much thought to where she wanted that life to play out. She had to start relying on herself, making decisions and standing by them. She needed to take control again.

"Pick a spot in the southern half of the country. It gets danged cold above the Mason-Dixon line."

Again her smile was weak. "I kind of like cold."

"Says the woman who's lived all of her life in the South. Spend a winter in Wyoming. It'll change your mind."

"Where did you grow up?"

He offered her the last slice of pizza, then, when she shook her head, moved it to his plate and sprinkled it with mozzarella and red pepper flakes.

"Here and there. My mother was restless. She'd wake up one morning and say, 'Start packing, kids. We're going someplace new.' I was born in California, went to four grade schools in Arizona and New Mexico, two middle schools in Louisiana and two high schools in Texas."

"Makes it hard to put down roots."

He shrugged. "My family is my roots. Mom lives in Alabama now, and Marnie and I both wound up here. She'll stay. Me, I don't know. When I came, it was only supposed to be for four months, but I'm still here."

"What about your father?"

"He never left California. He wouldn't leave. She couldn't stay." After a moment he ruefully added, "Like Sloan and me." He took one last bite, then offered the rest to Scooter, who removed it delicately from his hand. "He still asks about her every time we talk. He wants to know if she ever wanders back to California."

"So he can try to win her back? Or so he has sufficient time to go into hiding?"

"I don't know." Stephen wiped his hands on a napkin then leaned back comfortably. "I got over wanting them to get back together a long time ago, but I think he actually misses her. He never remarried, never seemed at all interested in another woman."

A security light at the far side of the backyard came on automatically, drawing Macy's gaze outside. The settling dusk had escaped her notice, but now a faint shiver rippled through her. It was okay, she counseled herself.

So the sun had set. No big deal. Dangerous things were dangerous, whether it was daylight or midnight.

Stephen stuffed the used napkins into the pizza box then crushed it in half as he stood. "I'd better head home. You must be tired or ready to get some sorting or packing done." He went into the kitchen, automatically opening the cabinet under the sink to toss away the trash, then pulled his wallet from his hip pocket as he turned to face her again.

"'Home' is the first house to the north. It's the one with the fence that can't keep Scooter in." For a moment he hesitated, then held out his hand. "And here's my card. It's got my cell phone number on it. If you need anything…"

Macy accepted the card, murmuring thanks for the dinner and everything else as she walked with him and the dog to the front door. As soon as they reached their car, she locked the door, set the alarm, then leaned against the door frame. Slowly she uncurled her fingers from the white cardstock and stared at it.

Stephen Noble, DVM.

As the emptiness of the house closed in around her, she felt a little bit safer. A little bit less alone. Just a little, but she would take what she could get.

"Dr. Noble, if you have a minute, Peyton's here. She's got something to show you."

Stephen looked up from the chart he'd just finished, automatically checking the clock on the wall. Five minutes to eight, and he'd already seen five patients. "I always have a minute for Peyton. Tell her I'll be right out."

He'd learned early in life that there were four kinds of people: those who liked dogs, those who liked cats, those who liked both and—the ones he couldn't relate to at all—those who preferred neither. Peyton was definitely in the first group.

So was Macy Howard.

Not liking animals was a deal breaker for him. Not that he was looking for anything with Macy. She was pretty, sure, but she had a child. She had been recently widowed. At least, a year and a half seemed recent to him. Not nearly enough time to deal with the emotional upheaval.

But she wasn't still in love with her husband.

Before he got any further with that thought, he walked into the lobby, where nine-year-old Peyton was waiting. Her face lit up and she called, "Dr. Noble, did Penny tell you I had a surprise?"

He didn't need a guess to identify it as the dog standing beside her wheelchair. He crouched in front of her. "A surprise, huh? Do you have new glasses?"

"No."

"New sweater?"

"You've seen this before," she chided. "It's my favorite sweater. I wear it all the time."

He pretended to study her, from the top of her blond curls all the way down to the toes of her sneakers, then raised both hands in surrender. "I give up. You've stumped me."

Laughing, Peyton leaned over to lay her hand on the dog. "I got my service dog! Her name is Sasha, and she's just for me, even though she has to be friends with everyone. Isn't she beautiful?"

The golden retriever turned gorgeous brown eyes on him as if understanding the question and waiting for the compliment. "She is," Stephen said. "Almost as beautiful as you. Has she learned all your lessons?"

"Yup."

"Have you learned all her lessons?"

Peyton's head bobbed. "Mom and I spent two weeks at the center where they trained her. And I wasn't scared of her at all. Not even the very first time we met."

"I knew you wouldn't be. Has she gone to school with you yet?"

"Today's the first day. All the kids in my class are gonna be jealous because Sasha can come and their pets can't. But their pets wouldn't behave, and Sasha will be a very good girl 'cause she's been taught."

"And if we're going to be on time, we need to go now." Audrey King, Peyton's mother, left the counter where she'd been chatting and joined them. "Thanks, Dr. Noble. This is going to make a big difference in her life."

"No need to thank me." All he'd done was locate the service dog group. Audrey and Peyton and generous donors had done the rest.

"We'll bring Sasha back so you can get acquainted," Peyton announced as she wheeled her chair around. "After all, you're gonna be her new doctor and her new friend. See you."

Two new friends in two days. He was on a roll. Would Macy mind being categorized with a retriever? He didn't think so. She wanted a puppy for her daughter, and she'd been very tolerant of Scooter. She hadn't barred the door to him or objected to his sharing their dinner.

Was her daughter as pretty and delicate as Peyton? Did she have her mother's blue eyes, her mother's silky brown hair? Was she friendly or shy? Did she have any comprehension of the fact that her father was dead?

No, not at three. At eighteen months, she would have known Daddy, but now she wouldn't have any memory of him. She wouldn't know that he had played with her, fed her, rocked her to sleep—if, in fact, he'd done any of those things. Judging from Macy's remark last night, he hadn't left *her* many fond memories. Even if he'd loved his daughter, that knowledge was gone forever for Clary.

At least Macy had her daughter. When he and Sloan had split, everyone had told him how he was lucky they hadn't had kids. He hadn't quite seen it. He'd married with the intention of staying together forever, of having at least three kids. And they'd divorced with nothing. No kids, no love, no hope.

Of course, he'd come to understand his friends' and family's meaning when he'd packed up to leave Wyoming. If he and Sloan had had a child, he couldn't have done it. He could leave her and the state behind without ever looking back, without regret, but not his child. He'd grown up seeing his dad only on holidays and summer breaks, and he wouldn't have done that to his own kid. He'd still be in Wyoming freezing his butt off half of every year.

As he returned to the exam room, where a beagle was waiting with its floppy ears and soulful eyes, he wondered how Macy had gotten through the night. He'd kept his phone on the nightstand—though he always kept it on the nightstand. Being a vet wasn't a nine-to-five job, or in his case, six to noon three days a week plus every other Saturday.

She'd been pretty upset when he'd seen her in the driveway, and he wondered again why she'd refused to call the police. Was it some sort of innate distrust of authorities? Did it have something to do with how her husband had died?

How *had* he died?

Stephen could ask his boss. Yancy Yates had been in Copper Lake forever. He'd married into the Calloway family, Copper Lake's version of royalty, right out of school. Anyone or anything he didn't know, his wife did.

Or he could do a Google search on Macy. The internet left few secrets.

But as he began examining Clarence—yes, the name fit—he decided against doing either. Macy had made it clear she wouldn't be around long. If she chose to tell him more, great. If she didn't…well, he could find out the rest after she left.

Clarence heaved a sigh as Stephen lifted one of his ears to look inside.

"It's undignified, isn't it, buddy?" he murmured. "We just poke and prod everywhere, and you don't even get asked."

Another reason he wouldn't actively try to find out more about Macy. Technology aside, people were entitled to some dignity, some privacy.

After finishing Clarence's exam, Stephen returned the dog to the run, where he would wait to be picked up later by his owner. He stayed busy the rest of the morning, finishing up the last of his charts exactly at quitting time. His usual routine was to grab lunch from a fast-food restaurant, take it home and write through the afternoon.

Would he stick to it today, or would he be tempted by his neighbor?

Let's see. An afternoon with Lucan, Sa'arca and

Tu'anlan, wreaking mayhem on everyone, or being neighborly and making sure Macy was doing okay.

He was no fool.

Or maybe he was, because he picked up two burgers and two orders of fries at the SnoCap and, instead of driving past the Howard house and out the gates into the Lesser of the World, he pulled into the driveway beside the minivan.

Bag in hand, he rang the doorbell, the deep sepulchral tones raising gooseflesh on his neck just for a moment. The place had cost more than he'd made in his vet career, but it couldn't begin to reach the level of homeyness that his little house had, secondhand furnishings and all.

He didn't hear any footsteps through the solid door. It just suddenly opened to reveal Macy on the other side. She wore a pair of red shorts that could have been a whole lot shorter and a tank top that couldn't have been much snugger. Her hair was pulled back in a ponytail, her feet were bare and there were faint shadows under her eyes. A hesitant smile curved her mouth, though it wasn't directed at him.

"No Scooter?" she asked instead of greeting him.

"Not this time. I was on my way home from the clinic and I thought you might like to take a break."

He held up the bag, and she eyed it while taking a deep breath. "SnoCap?"

"Of course."

She glanced over her shoulder, and he looked, too, seeing stacks of boxes down the hall, taped and labeled in a neat hand. She'd been busy. She'd already packed more stuff than he even owned, but he would bet she hadn't made a dent in the job.

Since she was clearly wavering between her options,

he said, "Hey, you've got to eat. And if you'd feel more comfortable with Scooter, we can take it to my house or I can go get him."

Another moment passed before she smiled tautly. "Let me get my shoes." Leaving the door open, she went to the kitchen, then returned almost instantly wearing flip-flops and carrying her cell phone. After locking up, she slid her keys into one pocket, the phone into the other, before climbing into the front seat of his car.

Lunch with a pretty woman. Maybe he wasn't a fool, after all.

Macy wasn't sure, but she might have drooled just a little when she caught the first whiff of the hamburgers. Greasy burgers from a drive-in hadn't been Mark's thing. When he wanted a burger, he'd gone to the country club restaurant and paid a ridiculous price for an Angus burger that didn't compare in taste.

She and Clary both loved SnoCap burgers.

As they drove through the gates that signaled the perimeter of Woodhaven Villas, she felt lighter. In such a short time, she'd become used to the smothering sensation in the house. Now that it was lifted, she could breathe easier.

"While you were away, the Villains tried to put up security gates at this exit that would have kept out those of us who live down here," Stephen said. "It didn't endear them to us."

"The Villains?"

His cheeks flushed. "Uh, yeah. Sorry, but…you know, like Texas and Texans. Georgia and Georgians. The Villas and Villains."

A laugh escaped before she'd even realized it was

building. "Don't apologize. It's a good description for most of my neighbors."

"This street is the only access to the houses down here, but they didn't want the riffraff driving past their houses, though they claimed it was for security reasons. They even offered to build a new street to the north to solve the access problem, but it would have tripled the distance to anywhere we needed to go."

Macy wished she were appalled or even surprised, but she wasn't. Like Mark, some of her neighbors had a deep appreciation for exclusivity. "I assume you and the rest of the riffraff protested."

"We did, but it wasn't really necessary. The town council didn't even consider their proposal." He gave her a sidelong look before turning into a driveway. "I assume you wouldn't have joined forces with them."

She smiled grimly. "I wouldn't have. But Mark…he would've been leading their charge."

Stephen's gaze stayed on her so long that she realized at last they weren't moving, or else they would have crashed by now. She shifted uncomfortably then unbuckled the seat belt.

"Mark was your husband," he said finally, once again using the soothing tone that had probably calmed and comforted untold pets and their owners.

"Yes."

The silence stretched out again, quickly becoming unbearable. He broke it by opening his door and picking up the bag of food, swinging it gently in her direction. "We should eat before the food gets cold. Prepare yourself for an exuberant greeting. Scooter's not very familiar with the concept of company since we don't get it very often."

"I'll brace myself." As she got out, she took a quick

look around. The house and the yard were small, almost doll-sized compared with their counterparts in Woodhaven. Everything was neat, though: the white paint and green trim fresh, the sidewalk edged, the picket fence faded to a soft gray. The front porch was big enough for a couple of rockers and a half dozen baskets of brightly colored flowers, though it stood empty now, and the door was painted a rich russet that welcomed guests.

Scrabbling sounded inside as they climbed the steps, accompanied by excited panting. By the time Stephen opened the door, Scooter was beside himself with anticipation. For an instant, it seemed he didn't know which deserved his attention first—Macy or the bag of burgers—but the burgers soon won out. She couldn't blame him. At the moment she was more interested in the food, too.

Then she sneaked a glance at Stephen and felt the need to confirm that. She really, really was.

"Welcome to my castle," he said on the way to the kitchen. "Which is probably just a little smaller than the master bedroom in your palace."

Probably, she admitted. The house was compact: small square living room, double doors opening right into the kitchen with its dining table, bedroom visible from the living room, second room—office, apparently—visible from the kitchen. It was cozy and snug, the shine long since worn off the wooden floors, the walls a nice neutral buff, the furniture well-worn and actually inviting. She always felt as if she should perch on the edge of the antiques in her house, but this sofa and chairs welcomed lounging.

The place reminded her of old times, before she met Mark Howard of *the* Georgia Howards.

She took a seat at the kitchen table as Stephen emptied the bag. He didn't bother with plates or napkins other than what had been tucked inside at the drive-in, discarding the greasy outer ones. He sat across from her, pinched off two bits of burger to stick Scooter's pills in and gave them to the dog, then took a hearty bite for himself before fixing his gaze on her. "How's the packing going?"

"Slowly." She savored her first bite—a year and a half since her last SnoCap fix!—then swiped a crispy fry through ketchup. "It's easy to figure out what I want." *Nothing.* "I'm saving some stuff for Clary, but all the antiques, the family heirlooms…"

"Does your husband not have a family that wants them?"

"His mother's in North Carolina, but she has enough family heirlooms of her own." And Lorna blamed the Howard family for everything her only child had done, including his suicide. She didn't want anything associated with them. "There's a cousin, Reece, but she doesn't want any of it, either." The family had cost her too much, as well.

"So what are the options? Estate sale and invest the money for your daughter?"

Macy took her time chewing. The locals probably knew she and Clary had more money than she could ever spend, but there was no need for her to admit that. So far, Stephen had treated her pretty much like a normal person—albeit needy and a tad jumpy. But money changed people's perceptions, and she needed to be treated like any other woman.

"Probably," she agreed, though the thought of expending even that much time on Mark's possessions soured her stomach. "Or make some museum donations."

He blinked and his brows arched. "Huh. I wouldn't know a museum-quality piece if I stepped on it. And you let Scooter in the house not once but twice?"

At the sound of his name, the dog lifted a hopeful gaze, then lowered it again when Stephen snorted. "Hell, you let *me* in? I'm not exactly known for my dainty feet and grace."

"They're just things," she said with a lift of one shoulder. Hating the sound of herself callously dismissing priceless treasures, she gestured to the room on the right. "I wouldn't have imagined a vet could do a whole lot of work at home."

Not that it looked much like a vet's office. There were tons of books, but even at this distance it was obvious they weren't textbooks. Dry-erase boards competed with movie posters for wall space, and she wasn't sure what kept the desk from collapsing from the weight of the mess on it.

"Different work," he said casually.

She studied the dry-erase boards, covered with cramped writing, some items circled, arrows pointing to others, then caught sight of several small plaques hanging between them. They looked like awards of some sort. Vet of the Year? Best Neighbor Surrounding Woodhaven Villains? "What kind of work?"

He gazed into the room himself for a moment before saying, "I'm a writer."

She hadn't expected that answer. In truth, she'd had no idea what to expect. But once he'd said it, it seemed perfectly reasonable. He had a little bit of a nerdy aura about him—the glasses, the uncombed hair, the conversations with Scooter. Sort of an absentminded-professor thing. "You write for veterinary journals?"

"On occasion. My last article was on feline diarrhea." Said with a self-deprecating look.

"A very important subject to cats and the people who clean up after them."

His grin was quick, boyish. It reminded her how appealing *boyish* could be. "Mostly I write books. Epic fantasy. A universe far, far away. Villains and quests and warriors and saving the world."

She'd met authors before—professors in college who were published, historians come to speak to the local historical society, ditto a few horticulturists at the garden society. The Howard family was the subject of its very own book: *Southern Aristocracy: The Howards of Georgia.* Granted, they'd paid the author to write it and the only copies that existed outside the family were in various Southern libraries.

But a fiction writer—excluding the Howard family biographer—was different. Someone who wrote for the pure pleasure of writing, for the simple entertainment of others...that was cool.

"Have you published anything?"

A faint grimace flashed, though she suspected he'd tried to hide it.

"I'm not the first person to ask that, am I?"

"Pretty much everyone asks. I've had five books out. The sixth one is scheduled for this summer, and I'm working on the seventh." Finished with his hamburger, he pushed to his feet, went into the office and returned with a hardcover novel, setting it beside her.

"S. K. Noble." She wiped her hands thoroughly on a napkin before picking it up. The cover was rich purple, the artwork in the center an image of a mysterious man with storm clouds swirling above the mountains behind him. "How cool. I'm sorry. I don't read fantasy."

He sprawled back in his chair, reaching down to scratch Scooter with one hand. "No need to apologize. What do you read?"

"*The Cat in the Hat. Goodnight, Moon. Sesame Street* books. Anything with bright pictures, words that rhyme and messages short enough for the attention span of a three-year-old." She flipped the book open, pausing to read the brief biography on the inside jacket. Too bad there was no photo of the author. In his office, with him looking as disheveled as it did, it would be charming. "How do you manage both working at the clinic and writing?"

Paper crumpled as he scooped up the wrappers from their lunch and tossed them in the trash can under the sink. Instead of returning to sit, he leaned against the counter, his long legs crossed at the ankle. "Clinic until noon three days a week, plus every other Saturday. Write at home the rest of the time."

Guilt tickled her nape. "I've taken up an awful lot of your writing time," she said as she stood. "Today, yesterday…"

"Everyone takes a break now and then, especially for food. We don't miss any meals around here, do we, Scooter?"

The dog snuffled in agreement.

She stood there a moment, torn between staying a little longer in any house that wasn't her own and not wanting to disrupt his schedule. He'd invited her for lunch, but lunch was over. Manners won. "I should let you get to work and get back to my own work. I appreciate lunch. It was wonderful." She started toward the door, and he and Scooter followed.

"I'll give you a ride home."

Macy paused in the open door, remembering that he'd driven. Then she glanced at the blue sky, the soft white clouds, the leaves rustling in the breeze. "I'd rather walk." She liked walking and took Clary for a ramble through their Charleston neighborhood every day. But in all the years she'd lived here, she'd never walked down her own street because while gardening was an acceptable pursuit for Mark Howard's wife, exercise where anyone could see wasn't.

"We'll walk with you," Stephen offered.

She wouldn't mind his company a little longer, but she shook her head. "That's okay." By herself, she could set her own pace. If she wanted to stop and stare at the woods, she could. If she wanted to stroll aimlessly and listen to the birds in the trees, no one would be inconvenienced.

If she wanted to delay reaching the house and going inside as long as she could, no one would know.

The two males stood at the top of the steps as she made her way to the sidewalk, across the lawn and out the gate. She turned back for a smile and a wave, then headed south.

Her pace was steady, not the slow-and-go method Clary preferred. Her daughter could skip energetically for an entire block, then stop to examine everything from a crack in the sidewalk to a fallen leaf to an ant crawling over a blade of grass. Just the thought of her, squatting precariously to study some new discovery like a dandelion or a pinecone with such intensity, made Macy's heart ache with equal intensity. Today was Wednesday.

Clary, Brent and Anne would be here in time for dinner Friday. Only two and a half more days and she'd have her little girl at her side.

Only two and a half more days alone in the house looming ahead. She could already feel its weight—its memories of Mark—settling on her shoulders. Her steps were already slowing. But following the advice from all those months of treatment, she forced herself to keep moving, one step at a time.

Chapter 4

It was amazing how, on the north side of the brick arches, the pavement was smooth and the air was, well, simply air, but on the south side, Macy felt as if she were slogging through an invisible barrier, as if her feet were sinking into the concrete with each step. The dread trickling down her spine intensified when the hum of a well-tuned engine penetrated the buzzing in her ears.

Ahead a sleek white Mercedes glided to a stop at the end of her driveway. Though she didn't recognize the car, her stomach knotted, and with good reason: Louise Wetherby was sitting behind the wheel.

Macy groaned silently. Of all the people she'd wanted to avoid in Copper Lake, Louise headed the list. She was the biggest snob in town, with more money than anyone besides the Howard and the Calloway families and a stronger notion of her own self-worth than all of them.

She thinks highly of herself for a butcher's granddaughter, Mark's grandmother had often said disdainfully.

Had Willa Howard still thought so highly of herself after finding out her esteemed husband and her beloved grandson were murderers? Good breeding obviously didn't equal decent human being.

Neither did a boatload of money, she added as Louise climbed out of the car.

Her silver hair was simply styled, her suit summer-white, her nails icy pink, her gaze glacial. She would have been an attractive woman if she hadn't looked perpetually dissatisfied with the life she'd been dealt. "So you've finally come back."

Hello to you, too. I'm fine. How about you? Macy forced a deep breath and a polite smile that was as phony as Mark had been. "Hello, Louise."

"Are you planning to stay, and if not, are you putting the house on the market? It's not good for the neighbors to have an abandoned house next door."

Macy glanced at the house, then the neighbors'. There was absolutely nothing to suggest her house had been empty all those months. If anything, her house and the yard were in better condition than the others. But before she could respond, Louise went on.

"You've disconnected your home phone, and your cell phone isn't listed in the Woodhaven directory, so I was going to leave this in your mailbox if you weren't home." She held up a creamy-hued envelope but didn't offer it. "Let me just grab the paperwork and we'll go inside out of this terrible heat."

Macy automatically took a few steps up the driveway before good sense stopped her. She waited until Louise reappeared from the car's interior, a folder in hand, before asking, "Paperwork for what?"

Instead of answering, Louise gestured toward the house. "Inside. It's steaming out here."

She should have accepted Stephen's offer of a ride home. Then she would have already been inside when Louise arrived, she would have checked the peephole when the doorbell rang and she would have gone about her work, leaving Louise no choice but to drop off the letter and go home.

She should have stayed at Stephen's, so she really wouldn't have been home.

Louise set off for the door, and ingrained manners overtook Macy. Gritting her teeth, she followed in the woman's trail of Chanel, then unlocked the door. When she caught sight of the boxes stacked in the hallway, she wished she'd moved them to the garage instead, or that she had the backbone to tell Louise to come back at a more convenient time. As if there *were* a convenient time to deal with Louise Wetherby.

Since it was too late—and she didn't have that backbone—she stepped aside for the older woman to enter, then closed the door and went into the living room.

"So you *are* putting the place up for sale." Louise made no effort to hide her perusal of the handwriting on the boxes in the hallway, making Macy glad she'd settled on shorthand and a numbering system. There was a detailed itemized list of the cartons' contents in the kitchen, but nothing on them that would give much, if any, clue.

Of course she was putting it up for sale. The house was forbidding, dark, filled with memories of Mark and his lies. It seemed so obvious that she didn't bother to comment on it, but sat instead, fingers laced loosely together. "What kind of paperwork do you have?" Surely it was something to do with the homeowners' association. Louise had been president since it was formed, a position Mark had chosen her for. They had the same goals, he'd said, and she had the time to do the job properly.

What he'd really meant was that Louise had been so hungry for Howard family approval that she was fairly easy for him to manipulate, and he'd been too busy with his murders to worry about grass height, paint colors or parking.

Louise settled at the end of the sofa nearest Macy's chair and laid the folder in her lap. "Since you've been gone so long with no hint of whether you'd ever return, there's been some concern about your property here."

Macy blinked. Her so-called abandonment. The place had been cleaned regularly, the lawn watered and mowed, the house inspected routinely for any maintenance needs. Really, what more could the woman expect? "You can see the house is as well maintained as when I lived here." *Not that it's any of your business.* Of course, Louise liked to think that money and a sharp tongue made everything her business.

Diamonds flashed with Louise's dismissive wave. "Not this property. Fair Winds. Your daughter's ancestral home."

Another blink, followed immediately by a shudder. Fair Winds was a beautiful place, two centuries old, rising out of the middle of a lush expanse of lawn on the banks of the Gullah River. For generations there had been rumors the place was haunted. The discovery of more than forty bodies buried on the grounds made the rumors easy to believe.

"What interest could you possibly have in Fair Winds?"

Louise offered what passed for a smile. "I'm the president of the Fair Winds Preservation Society. You know the plantation holds an important part in Copper Lake history, along with the Howard family, and of course Willadene was one of my closest friends. It would break her heart to see the place falling into such disrepair, knowing that it's standing empty and all alone out there. We formed the society to come up with a plan for its future and—"

"'We' who?"

Louise listed a few names—ladies who lunched on the misfortunes of others, vipers every one—then opened the folder. "We're proposing that you sign the plantation, with its contents, over to the society for the purpose of preservation, education and promoting tourism for the community. Certainly you won't want to live there, and a donation such as this—"

Macy tuned out her voice and focused on her own thoughts. Georgia was filled with beautiful antebellum homes open to the public; the Calloway Plantation just north of town and River's Edge downtown were two prime examples. And as far as Louise being Miss Willa's closest friend…ha. Miss Willa hadn't had friends. Hadn't needed or wanted them. Had thought herself too good for everyone in Copper Lake besides Mark.

In eighteen months Macy had considered a lot of things—whether she could survive the loss of her baby, whether she could get past Mark's ugly secrets, whether she would ever be well enough to take care of Clary, where they might live, what she might do. But she'd never given a moment's thought to what she would do about Fair Winds. She certainly would never live there.

But sign it over to a preservation group she'd never

heard of until five minutes ago? With all its contents? And to a group headed by Louise Wetherby, no less?

What kind of gift would that be? She'd never asked what the place was valued at, and neither Mark nor Miss Willa had ever said. The furnishings alone were probably worth several million. Mark's ancestors had sailed the world and brought back the best goods each country had to offer, and they'd never parted with a single treasure. Add the house—in nowhere near a state of disrepair, no matter what Louise said—and the riverfront property...

A hell of a *gift*. And one that wasn't hers to give.

Realizing that silence had fallen, she looked at Louise to see her offering what appeared to be a contract. She took it but didn't so much as glance at it. "You realize I didn't inherit Fair Winds. Clary did."

Another dismissive gesture. "You're her mother. You control her inheritance. Until she's of age, you choose what's best for her. You certainly can't leave the house empty and forgotten for another fifteen years. How irresponsible is that?"

And yet giving it away free and clear *was* responsible?

"Of course, the Howard name would remain attached to the plantation, and it would remain a memorial to their history as well as their many, many contributions to Jackman County and Georgia. We would see that the house was restored to its former glory and would ensure its graceful arrival into its next century."

Macy swallowed a derisive snort. She'd been gone a year and a half, granted, but Miss Willa had never let a board go unpainted or a screw unloosened any longer than the time it took to make a phone call. The only restoration work it could possibly need was on the front lawn. The killing grounds.

Was that part of the history the preservation society wanted to memorialize? Macy shuddered. That really would break Miss Willa's heart. Four hundred years of spotless Howard reputation destroyed by the last two surviving Howard males. Thank God. If ever there was a name that deserved to die out…

"All you need to do is sign the papers and—"

"No." Swallowing hard, Macy set the papers on the coffee table.

She had the pleasure of leaving Louise Wetherby speechless, albeit temporarily. The woman gaped for a moment, like a fish trying to undo the hook in its mouth. Good heavens, she'd actually thought Macy would meekly acquiesce and sign away a seven-figure chunk of her daughter's inheritance at her command. Did she believe Macy was that malleable? That weak? Or that crazy?

Spending months in a psychiatric hospital tended to make people think that of a person.

Resolve smoothed Louise's features as she stood. "Of course you need time to think about it. That's understandable. Keep the papers. Read over them. Consider the welfare of the community along with that of your daughter. I'm sure, given time, you'll agree that this is the best solution to the problem. When you're ready to sign, you can let me know. You have my contact information, of course."

Macy supposed there was a homeowners' directory somewhere in Mark's office, but it would be a cold day in hell before she called Louise. *If* she decided to donate Fair Winds, it would be to the state, the local historical society—anyone besides Louise.

"I can show myself out." Louise made it to the hall before turning back. "Oh, and welcome back. Starting off new will be easier once you've cleaned up old business."

A moment later the door closed, and Macy sank down into the chair exactly like the spineless creature she was. Her gaze settled on the contract again, and she shook her head numbly. The nerve of the old hags, trying to manipulate her into such a decision on her second day back.

And *she* was considered the crazy one.

Stephen had had a productive afternoon, leaving his computer shortly after five with more than three thousand words added to his manuscript. It had taken him a while to get into the book after lunch. Hell, it'd taken him a good while to leave the porch after Macy had walked away. He'd watched until she was out of sight, and then a few minutes longer. Research, he'd told himself. A need to get all the descriptions right when he wrote about Ma'ahcee.

He was standing in the kitchen, bent to examine the contents of the refrigerator, with Scooter hanging hopefully at his side, when the cell phone rang. The only people who called him who merited their own ringtone were the ones at the clinic—yes, it was "Who Let the Dogs Out." He'd been too lazy to assign tunes, so everyone else had a regular old-fashioned *ring-ring*.

Flipping the phone open, he reached for the milk and a bag of deli turkey. "Hello."

"Hey. It's Macy."

Ah, speak of the Warrior Woman. He tossed a bite of turkey to Scooter and was rewarded with a snap of teeth and drool slung on his bare shin. "Hey, Macy. What's up?"

Hesitance, then... "I thought you probably wouldn't

answer the phone if you were working, but if I'm disturbing you…"

Only if distraction and curiosity count as disturbances. "No, I'm done for the day. Scooter and I were just debating what to do about supper. What do you need?"

"I've got to check on some property outside town, and I was wondering…I'd rather not go out there alone in the evening, and…it won't take very long. I can buy you guys dinner afterward."

"Sounds good."

"You're sure you don't mind?"

"I'm sure. We'd just be watching TV, and I get tired of watching Animal Planet."

Faint amusement entered her voice. "You do get other channels."

"Yeah, but Scooter doesn't like them."

This time she rewarded him with a chuckle. "You know he's spoiled."

"Dogs are like kids. What's the point of having them if you don't spoil them at least a little?"

"I agree. What time is good for you guys?"

He tossed Scooter another piece of turkey before sticking one in his mouth and talking around it. "Any time."

"Ten minutes?"

"That'll do. Do you really want Scooter to come?"

"Sure. See you."

He set the phone down then dragged his hand through his hair. "Hey, Scooter, Warrior Woman is taking us to dinner. Actually, I think she wants you for security, and I'm just part of the deal." He wouldn't hide behind her if anything was out of place at the property, but he wouldn't be charging heroically ahead, either. He was a writer. He observed, and he was great with speed-dialing a phone. He didn't derring-do.

The dog's attention was still on the turkey. Stephen gave him one last piece, took another for himself, then headed to the bedroom at the front of the house, stripping off his T-shirt on the way.

He'd known he was fashion-challenged since he was in middle school. Colors were just colors. As far as he could tell, they didn't particularly go together or clash. He did draw the line at ones like pink and light purple. Even he had always understood those were girly colors.

His mom had solved the problem for him in high school by stocking his closet with three items: jeans and shorts in either denim or khaki and T-shirts in black and white. Everything went together, and he didn't risk getting teased about anything other than the predictability of his clothes. He could live with that.

He pulled on a clean white shirt, brushed some dog hair from his khaki shorts and decided they were reasonably clean. After wiping his glasses on the discarded shirt, he was ready to go. With his cell in his pocket and keys in hand, he whistled for Scooter, still waiting hopefully by the refrigerator. The dog raced to the door, sliding into a sitting position an instant before hitting the wall, and Stephen attached his leash. "We're going for a ride, buddy. Be on your best behavior."

The mutt gave him a *whaddaya mean* sort of look, and Stephen laughed as he opened the door. By the time he got the house locked up and walked Scooter to the gate, Macy's fancy minivan was gliding to a stop in front of them.

"You sure you want to let him in there?" he asked through the open window. "I don't mind driving."

She glanced at the luxurious leather of the rear seat and wrinkled her nose. "I don't mind dog hair."

"Or scratches from his claws?"

"Don't worry about it. Get in."

Stephen slid the back door open and Scooter hopped inside, immediately going into sniffing-new-territory mode before settling on his haunches in the seat behind Macy. The front passenger seat sank under Stephen's weight, molding around him, reminding him that his car was old and well used and hadn't been this nice to start.

But it was reliable and paid for. That counted for a lot.

"Where are we going?"

Macy made a tight U-turn. "A few miles outside town. Mark— My husband's grandmother owned a house out there. She died a month after he did, so it's Clary's now."

"Are you going to keep it, sell it, live in it?" He caught himself before she could answer. "No, you're not planning to stay around here."

Her fingers tightened on the steering wheel as they passed through the gate into Villain country. "I've had a suggestion, but I don't know what I want. I figured I should start by at least looking at it and making sure everything's okay." She flashed a smile his way at the precise moment they passed her own house. "I appreciate your going with me."

He didn't say that he appreciated being asked. She'd lived in Copper Lake a long time before her absence, so she must have had other options—friends, neighbors, a lawyer. Hell, for someone who lived in Woodhaven, the sheriff's department probably would have been happy to provide her with an escort.

After they exited the subdivision at the other end, her grip on the steering wheel loosened and her shoulders relaxed. She clearly didn't like the place any more than he did. His reasons were simple enough: he was into reverse snobbery, and the residents had deemed him, the sisters and their families as unworthy to even drive on their precious streets.

But what was Macy's reason? Still mourning her husband? Not likely, considering her comment last night. *It would be tougher if I still loved him.*

Had she married up and been on the receiving end of the same scorn her fancy neighbors had shown him?

Had her husband abused her in that house?

He studied her while the idea rolled around in his head. After a moment, he let it go. He had a lot more experience with abused creatures than anyone should have, and she just didn't present that way. She had a lot of self-doubts, needed a boost in confidence and spooked easily, but she didn't act like a woman who'd been abused.

Maybe it was guilt because she didn't love her dead husband.

"You know, it's impolite to stare."

"Sorry. Didn't mean to." He blinked, realizing that she was glancing his way, that the van was slowing and the turn signal was clicking rhythmically. A look around showed that they were on River Road just north of the city limits, and a plaque set into a brick column on the left side of the road said they were turning into the private drive for Fair Winds.

He blinked again. "Fair Winds? The property your three-year-old daughter owns is Fair Winds? The plantation?"

Uneasiness fluttered through her. After a semi passed,

its blast rocking them, she turned onto the wide dirt road. "Yes. Her father was one of *those* Howards."

Didn't sound as if she thought much of her husband's family. The rich are different, someone had once said, so the super-rich were probably super-different.

"I have to admit, I don't know anything about the family, but I've seen the house from the river." Stephen wasn't much on fishing, but occasionally he borrowed Yancy's boat and spent an entire afternoon kicked back with a cooler of drinks and a life vest for a pillow.

"That's probably the best way to see it," she remarked as the road wound through stands of pines. Soon it paralleled a wrought-iron fence, then reached an elaborate gate. She stopped there, rolled down the window and pulled a slip of paper from the sun visor. Stephen watched her punch a code into the keypad, watch the gate swing open then draw a deep breath and drive inside.

If a person appreciated architecture, Fair Winds was probably a prime example. It stood three stories tall, glowing white in the lowering sun, its brick columns straight, its grass mown, its flower beds bordering the porch blooming brightly. It was the sort of place that made the Lessers of the World stare in awe, imagining how good life must be in such a mansion.

But Macy was right: seeing it from the river was better. With that stretch of yard, the wrought-iron fence and strips of riverbank and water adding distance. Up close, the place was…unsettling.

She stopped in the driveway underneath a live oak that showed the wounds from a not-too-distant lightning strike and shut off the engine. She dried her palms on her shorts, took out a key from the console, then opened the car door. Pausing in the act of getting out, she asked in an everyday-normal tone, "Do you believe in ghosts?"

"No, not really."

She smiled. "Good. Because they say this place is haunted. And I believe it."

Macy had been raised with a fine appreciation for Southern historic sites and elegant old houses, but she'd disliked Fair Winds from her first visit. At the time she'd written it off to nerves at meeting Miss Willa and Mr. Arthur for the first time. She'd already been woefully aware of the differences between her and Mark, and Fair Winds had been a flashing-neon reminder.

Later, she'd thought she'd just picked up on the less-than-warm vibes Mark's grandparents had put out. They hadn't been a particularly friendly couple. They'd oozed haughtiness, and affectionate hadn't been in their natures.

Now, as she stood beside the van and felt her gaze drawn, however reluctantly, to the front lawn, she wondered if the remnants of fear, anguish and loss permeating the place had been the cause for her dislike. So much ugliness had gone on within these grounds, from the slave labor that had built the place and multiplied the Howard fortunes to the sad people who'd lost their lives here.

Mark had lost his life here, somewhere in the field of green in front of the house. Suicide, everyone had said. He'd been so self-important; she'd never imagined he could even contemplate suicide.

She'd also never imagined he could lay a hand on another person in anger so, obviously, what did she know?

"Do you want to go inside or just walk around the outside?"

Stephen's voice startled her, and she took a deep breath to hide it. Rumor said there were ghosts inside, too, but as far as she knew, none of them had died violently. Better than she could say of the poor souls for whom the front lawn had been their graves.

"Just a quick walk-through." Pleased that her voice hadn't trembled, though it had come out a bit breathy, she started toward the front porch. The steps didn't creak, and though rarely used, the key turned smoothly and the door swung silently inward.

She flipped the switches beside the door, and lights came on down the broad corridor and up the stairs. Of course the electricity was still on, to provide climate control for the priceless antiques inside.

Her footsteps echoed on the wood floor until she reached the faded runner that ran the length of the hallway. Realizing that Stephen wasn't following, she turned back.

"I should leave Scooter outside. One swipe of his tail, and I'd be in debt for the rest of my life."

She spared a glance for the living room, then the corridor and smiled. "I always worried when I came here that I would break one of the prizes that Miss Willa treasured far more than any living being. Thankfully, I never did, or I would have been banished from the place like Clary was." She paused. "Bring him in."

"Was Clary really banished?" With Scooter's leash wrapped three or four times around his large hand, Stephen crossed the threshold, keeping the dog at his side.

"Not formally, but Miss Willa always made sure we understood that dinner invitations meant getting a babysitter. She wasn't a warm person. No embraces, no cuddling with babies, no tolerance for fussiness or sticky little fingers." Macy looked around the formal room to the left again and sniffed. "She didn't tolerate many adults, either. I believe she loved Mark the best she was able, but she was much better at showing disappointment and disapproval."

He stopped beside her, and a faint scent of something drifted into her space. Not dog or cologne or soap. No, he smelled like…turkey. Her stomach gave a quiet little growl, reminding her she hadn't had even a bite since lunch. For someone who snacked routinely, that was a long time to go without food.

"You said your husband had a cousin. Does she live around here?"

"No, she's in New Orleans." Disgustingly happy, working in Jones's historic garden restoration business and planning to start a family soon. Reece had worked hard to get where she was, but still Macy envied her. She didn't think she could ever be that blissfully happy.

Her stomach growled again, louder this time, and she moved on with the tour. Everything was clean and secure, and soon enough they were back outside.

It wasn't as much of a relief as it could have been, stepping through that door into the still evening, even though the damage done digging up unmarked graves had been repaired. Looking at the lawn, no one would guess it had suffered any disturbance greater than a mower. But she didn't have to guess.

With the sun on its downward slide, they walked quickly around the exterior of the house, circled the guesthouse out back, the former farm manager's office and the storage barns. Contrary to Louise Wetherby's claim, everything was in good shape, as Macy had known it would be.

She practically hustled Stephen and Scooter back to the van, sighing inwardly when the doors were closed and the locks automatically secured. "Where would you like to go for dinner?"

He fastened his seat belt, then she shifted into gear, backing up beneath the giant oak, heading toward the gate with relief.

"Any place but A Cut Above."

"You don't like steak?"

"I don't like Louise Wetherby." Abruptly he stiffened. "Sorry. I know she's one of your neighbors. Are you and she—"

A snort sputtered out despite her best efforts to stop it. "I can't stand the woman. She's smug and mean-spirited and tries to be the boss of everyone."

"But her restaurant sure makes an incredible steak." He said it regretfully, as if he were paying a real price for not supporting a business owner he disliked.

"So do I." Warmth spread through Macy as she drove through the gate, energizing her, making her feel damn near normal. "Come over tomorrow night and I'll show you."

Immediately upon hearing her invitation, she masked a wince. When had she decided she had first claim to all his free time? He could have plans for tomorrow night. He might want to watch Animal Planet with Scooter. He might just want a few hours away from her.

But he gave no sign of any of that. Instead he asked, "What should I bring?"

"Just yourself and Scooter." At the end of the dirt

road, she turned south onto the highway. "So where for dinner tonight?"

"Dogs are welcome at Ellie's Deli, at least outside. He behaves pretty well there."

"He behaves pretty well all the time." She liked his choice. Ellie Maricci was one of the nicer people in Copper Lake, and the food at her restaurant was outstanding. Following the example set by their boss, the employees were friendly and professional, and eating outside with the day's humidity literally hanging in the air, they weren't likely to rouse much attention.

She found a parking space across the square, on the next street over, and Scooter trotted toward the deli, head held high, compact body quivering. "He knows he's in for a treat, huh?"

"They always have cookies and water bowls, and I usually share with him," Stephen admitted.

"I hadn't noticed," she said drily.

"I'm careful about what I give him," he protested. "I am a vet, you know." He reined in the dog as they passed through the gate, then they turned to the left, where tables—all empty—were scattered across the small lawn. "Do you mind letting the hostess know we're here?"

Macy's smile faltered, but she quickly forced it back into place. She climbed the steps, crossed the porch and went inside, deliberately avoiding looking anywhere but the hostess station. The girl there was young, maybe sixteen, and didn't appear to know Macy from the man on the moon. She greeted her politely, grabbed menus and rolled napkins and followed her back out to the table Stephen had chosen.

"Hey Doc," the girl said. "Where've you been, sweetie?"

There was no doubt the endearment was directed to the animal as the girl dropped to her knees, scratched behind his ears, then sat back so Scooter, on cue, could roll to his back for a belly rub.

"Don't worry. I always wash my hands before I touch you," she crooned. "Humans are dirty, you know."

At the moment, Macy certainly understood her preference for four-legged creatures.

"Macy, this is Jacy, Scooter's favorite part-time vet assistant and restaurant hostess." Stephen left the introduction at that—no last names—and Macy appreciated it.

"Hello, Jacy."

The girl looked up at her. "Is your name really Macy? I broke up with a guy because his name was Casey. I couldn't bear the idea of going all the way through high school with a boyfriend whose name rhymed with mine."

Despite the studs piercing her nose and eyebrow and the electric-yellow shade of her hair, Macy liked Jacy. Shared pain, she figured. "My friends in college set me up with a blind date because he was named Tracy and they thought it would be cute if we hit it off."

Jacy shuddered. "Those people weren't friends. I'll tell your waitress you're out here. Nice to meet you, Macy. See you later, Doc. You, too, sweetie."

Stephen was smiling when Macy shifted her gaze from Jacy's retreating figure back to him. "Macy and Tracy? You could have named your first daughter Stacy."

"Or Lacy." She imitated Jacy's shudder. After spreading a linen napkin on her lap, she asked, "What did you think of Fair Winds?"

"Impressive place." He said the words with sincerity, but she thought he hadn't been impressed so much as taken by surprise. She appreciated that, too.

"Really impressive," he went on. "I was lucky to have my own bedroom all the time, and your three-year-old has her own mansion."

"Ridiculous, isn't it?"

"No," he said at first, then dragged his hand through his hair, leaving it on end. "Well, yeah. A little. So what was the suggestion you had about it?"

Did she want to discuss that now? Even want to think about it? Common sense said no, but when she opened her mouth, something else took control of her words. "I had a visit this afternoon from the president of the Fair Winds Preservation Society—an organization, mind you, that didn't even exist until just recently. She suggested I give the property, the house and all of its contents to them so they could turn it into a proper memorial."

Stephen's eyes widened behind the glasses and his jaw dropped. "You're making that up."

Macy shook her head.

"Just *give* it to them? Not sell, not lease, just 'here's the deed, and y'all have a nice day'?" His snort was both rude and comical. "Hell, why didn't they ask for a few million dollars to maintain it and keep it running?"

"They might have. I didn't read the contract they'd had drawn up."

"Contract?" Astonishment echoed in his voice. "Who in the world could possibly think that was even remotely—"

Something in her expression stopped him. She wasn't sure even exactly what was on her face. A bit of a smile. Sarcasm. Finally, some little hint of amusement to go along with the dismay.

"Louise Wetherby and her cronies. Wow. I didn't think even they were that outrageous. You told her no, didn't you?"

"I did, which she interpreted as I needed more time before I fall in with her plans. I may have to have the lawyer tell her. Compared to me, he's considered relatively s—"

She clamped her jaw shut so quickly that her teeth collided with an audible *click.* What had she been about to say? Sane? Stable? *She* was sane. *She* was stable. She'd had a problem with depression—granted, a serious couldn't-get-out-of-bed-in-the-morning, wouldn't-have-cared-if-she-lived-or-died-if-not-for-Clary problem—but she'd just undergone severe emotional trauma. She'd lost her baby, for God's sake.

She still had some trouble with depression. Anxiety. Uncertainty. But she took her medication, and she stayed busy, and she was perfectly fine. Functional. Able to be an independent adult and a mother.

Even though she *had* thought she'd seen someone in the guesthouse yesterday.

Even though she imagined the faint smell of Mark's cologne in the house.

Even though going to Fair Winds this evening had totally creeped her out. She couldn't have done it without Stephen.

"I believe the word you're looking for is *stubborn,*" he said, giving no sign he'd thought her behavior odd. "He *is* a lawyer, right? They're not generally known for being soft touches."

"Yes," she agreed with that breathiness in her voice again. "Stubborn. That's exactly what I was going to say."

Chapter 5

Darkness had fallen, their meals were pleasant memories and Scooter was snoring softly beside the table in the grass. With a cool breeze off the river and the faint sound of music from down the street, Stephen couldn't think of anything that could improve the evening.

Then his gaze settled on Macy, and he immediately amended that thought.

She was more relaxed tonight than he'd ever seen her. Not saying much since they'd met for the first time yesterday, but it seemed a lot longer. A long time, but nowhere near long enough. He knew a lot about her but wanted to know more. Everything. Including how she felt. How she tasted.

Slowly she stirred the straw in her tea, the few remaining ice cubes clinking against the sweaty glass. "Tell me again all the places you've lived."

"Why?"

"I'm looking for a place, remember?"

If she asked his opinion, he would put in his vote for staying in Copper Lake. He liked it. He'd come with the intention of spending four months and hadn't found any reason yet to leave.

Macy could be a damn good reason to stay if only she would, too.

Ignoring the thought, he began ticking off names on his fingers. "Los Angeles and El Cajon, California. Tucson and Flagstaff, Arizona. Los Alamos and Roswell, New Mexico. Baton Rouge and Slidell, Louisiana. Austin and Plano, Texas. I went to college in Albuquerque and vet school in Stillwater, Oklahoma, then worked in Cheyenne, Wyoming, before coming here."

"Wow, you ran out of fingers. I feel like a slacker." She held up her own slender, pink-tipped fingers. "Charleston, Columbia and Copper Lake."

"Did you ever want to live a lot of places?"

Lowering her fingers, she began twisting the glass on its sodden napkin. "No. I always wanted…stability." The way she said the word made it seem it wasn't exactly the one she wanted. "I told you, four generations of Irelands have lived in the same house. I like that sense of home."

"So why not find a place in Charleston?"

Her smile wavered as she sat back in the chair, hands folded in her lap. "Maybe I will. Not in Charleston itself, but Isle of Palms or Sullivan's Island."

"You're close to your family, so it's not exactly them you want to get away from, is it?"

"I love my family. I couldn't have survived the last year and a half without them. They've done so much for me. But now I just need…want a little space." Her head tilted to one side. "Does that sound awful?"

"Not at all. I love my mom and dad, but you don't see me settling in Alabama or California to be near them."

"But you did come to Copper Lake to be near your sister." She gestured. "I'm assuming she was here first."

"Yep. She got a job here six or eight years ago. She's a lab geek for the Copper Lake Police Department. Her name's Marnie Robinson."

"Different last name. Married?"

"Different fathers."

"What is she like?"

He laughed, and Scooter twitched at the sound. Stretching to the side, Stephen rubbed his spine until he settled in again, then rested both hands on the table. "Marnie is different. Best older sister I could ask for, but...she's got bachelor's degrees in chemistry and microbiology, a master's in forensic sciences and forensic toxicology, and she's getting a PhD in biochemistry and molecular biology. She's very logical, very rational, very unemotional."

Macy feigned surprise. "Your sister is Dr. Spock?"

The comparison made him laugh, not because it was original but because it wasn't. Marnie often put him in mind of *Star Trek* and Dr. Spock. "Yeah, that's her. She doesn't eat in restaurants because who knows what microscopic spores have been passed along in the handling of the food. She won't eat birthday cake where someone's blown out the candles because of all the germs in the human mouth. She handles body parts and fluids all day but doesn't like to touch people. I'm pretty sure when she kisses, she sanitizes her mouth afterward, and of course, it's got to be a minimal sharing of spit."

If she kissed. She hadn't had a serious relationship that he could remember. She was socially awkward and emotionally stunted and truly never seemed to need the simple warmth of human companionship. And yet she had a date for Saturday night's party. He really wasn't insulting his sister when he couldn't imagine the guy she would go out with and vice versa.

He had a date for that party, too. Remembering that was enough to take the edge off his pleasure in this night. Kiki Isaacs was about as far from his type as was possible while staying within the same species. Call him crazy, but he didn't date women who could break him in half, who carried a gun and who certainly had bigger balls than he did.

Too bad he hadn't somehow weaseled out of Marnie's request. He'd known Macy two days and had spent both evenings with her, and she'd invited him over for dinner tomorrow. Odds were pretty good that he could have spent Saturday evening with her, too, without a suit, a tie and worrying about his physical safety as well as his virtue.

Macy's voice distracted him from dire thoughts of the future. "I'd like to meet her sometime."

"Marnie? Yeah, she doesn't do well with the living."

"Neither do I sometimes. And truthfully, I wasn't wild about birthday cake that someone had just blown little bits of ick over, either, not until Clary was born. Kids kind of desensitize you to all that germ stuff."

He tried to imagine how mini-Macy looked. Blue eyes, brown hair, chubby cheeks, that toddler sense of wonder in everything? Or did she resemble her father more? When Macy looked at her, did she see the dead husband she didn't love?

Then the obvious occurred to him. "Do you have a picture of her?"

The smile that beamed across her face was practically enough to light the night. "Of course I do." Pulling out her cell, she scrolled to the photographs, then handed it over.

Yep, Clary Howard looked just like her mother, except for the chubby part. Macy didn't carry a pound of extra weight, but Clary was nicely rounded in that adorable-little-girl sort of way. Her hair was the same shade as Macy's, though finer, and she had the same serious air about her that Macy did.

The photo was taken on the beach, and Clary, crouching in the sand, wore a one-piece ruffled swimsuit that made her look like a pumpkin with legs. A floppy white hat framed her face, and her lower lip was poked out as she focused entirely on the seashell in her hand. She looked sweet as cotton candy and could undoubtedly be as hardheaded as granite.

"She's a cutie." Though he was tempted to see what other photos she kept, he handed the phone back without looking. "Three is a good age. Interested in everything, talking to everyone."

"Interested, yes. Talking…nonstop with people she knows but a little shy with strangers." Macy gazed at the photograph for a moment, tenderness easing across her features along with yearning. She was always pretty, but the combination made her stunning.

"It must be tough, being away from her even for a few days."

"Yeah, but she'll be here Friday."

With Macy's brother and sister-in-law, with whom she would do the things she'd done with him the past two days. So much for possibly spending Saturday evening with her. He might not see much of her after the family arrived.

Might not see her at all.

And though they hardly knew each other, he had no doubt that would be his loss.

"Well…"

Macy's sigh floated on the air. Dinner was gone, dessert just a few crumbs on the plates and she'd long since paid the bill. Time to go home. He unhooked Scooter's leash from the foot of his chair, stood and stretched, and the dog did the same.

"Thank you for going out to Fair Winds with me."

"Thanks for dinner." Their steps were muffled on the grass, then scuffed across concrete. "And for a look at how the other half live. Tell Clary she's got excellent taste in inheritances."

"You can tell her yourself." Macy glanced both ways, though traffic was allowed only one way, then stepped off the curb. After shooting him a glance, she added to that. "That is, if you're not ready to dump me and my needs into Brent's lap and run."

Warmth spread through him at the idea that he had a choice in the matter and, judging from Scooter's happy look, it had transmitted down the leash. "I'm not ready to dump anything."

Except the date with Kiki Isaacs, and he couldn't go back on that. But he could hope for her to find someone else.

As they stepped into the shadows of the live oaks in the square, he thought he heard Macy murmur a firm "Good."

"You're sure about this?" Macy turned into her own driveway but didn't shut off the engine. "I don't mind taking you home."

"Yeah, but then we'd just have to come back to make sure you get in okay. Besides, Scooter and I walk a lot, including at night. From here to our place is nothing."

With a soft sigh, she turned off the ignition and opened the door. The house was safe. Lights on timers shone in the living room, the kitchen and over the stairs. The alarm was armed. Nothing looked out of place. But it was a definite plus that she didn't have to walk inside by herself.

They went up the walkway, Scooter's nails clicking on the sidewalk behind them, and she opened the door and shut off the security system. The packed boxes were still in the hall. A pile of empty boxes and packing material were still visible in the kitchen. The lights in the backyard showed a tranquil, undisturbed scene.

"Nine o'clock and all's fine," she said, and the grandfather clock down the hall chimed a moment later. Good timing.

"The castle is secured. We'll leave and you can pull up the drawbridge."

She laughed. She tended to think of the house as a mausoleum instead, which made her… Well, she'd rather not think about what lived in mausoleums. But a princess in a castle…she hadn't felt like that since she and Mark first got engaged.

"Dinner about six? But you can come over whenever you're done for the day."

He nodded, hesitated, then leaned in and kissed her cheek. Before she could react, he flashed a grin, made coaxing sounds at the dog and left.

Having her feet knocked out from under her had been a fairly common occurrence since the day Mark died. Having it done in an unexpectedly good way was enough to make her lean against the door for support after she closed it. It had been so long since someone new and interesting had kissed her. So long since she'd been kissed so sweetly. Since she'd given serious thought to wanting more.

For a time she stood there, just feeling satisfied, until the green light on the alarm console caught her attention. She made sure she'd locked the door—for the first time in months, she couldn't remember—then reset the alarm. Then she headed down the hall to the kitchen. After the time away, with a cup of coffee, she would have the energy to pack at least a few more boxes tonight before going to bed.

The coffeemaker hummed as it brewed, and Macy found herself humming softly, too, a silly song about spiders and waterspouts. She'd already decided to leave packing the kitchen for her last job, but she could make a start on the family room. Hundreds of DVDs, even more books, small parts of Mark's vast collections…

She stacked the leather sofa with the smallest boxes she'd bought, recommended for books, and began packing without even glancing at titles. Some were old, bound in leather. A few had been published recently, but none of them were popular or fiction. Mark would have been the first to scoff at Stephen's fantasy novels. Her husband had been as snobbish in his reading materials as everything else, while *she* thought she'd like to know more about the mysterious man in the mysterious place on Stephen's cover.

About its creator, as well.

She took a break to fix her coffee the way she liked it, then, warming her hands on the hot mug, she strolled down the hall, turning right into the living room and

making her way to the big window. The street outside
was quiet, lights on in the houses across the street. There
was too much room between houses to hear televisions or
conversations. The Villains walked a fine line between
wanting privacy while also flaunting all they had. Louise was the worst.

But at least she came by her money honestly. Most of
the fortunes in these few square miles had been handed
down through generations, like Mark's, or married into.
Like Macy's.

Remembering Stephen's incredulity about Louise's
proposal made Macy smile. Had the women asked for
money, too, to fund their glorious memorial? All she
had to do was check the contract, right there on the coffee table—

Her hands trembled, and she barely managed to keep
the coffee from sloshing all over the ancient Turkish rug.
Her heart thudded so loudly she couldn't hear the sounds
of her own breathing, wasn't sure she even was breathing until her lungs suddenly choked and she forced out
a cough, then sucked in air audibly.

The only thing on the coffee table was an arrangement of roses. There was no contract.

"It has to be—" Carefully setting the coffee down,
she paced around the couch, went to the chair where
she'd sat during Louise's visit, checked the entire area.
Maybe she'd knocked it off when she'd left the room
earlier. Maybe she'd set it somewhere besides the coffee table. Maybe—

Squeezing her eyes shut, hugging herself tightly, she
replayed the visit in her memory. Louise handing her
the contract, herself holding it without looking at it, then
setting it on the table. Louise saying keep it, then show-

ing herself out. Macy thinking in the silence that they thought *she* was the crazy one. Walking out of the room to get back to her packing.

She had left it on the coffee table. She was certain of it.

Just as certain as she was that it wasn't there now.

Efforts to control the panic building inside her as she headed toward the kitchen failed. By the time she reached the island, she was frantic. She'd made a point of leaving all her papers there—inventories, notes, any records she came across that she wanted to keep.

There was no contract.

She'd packed in one of the guest rooms after Louise left. Taking the stairs at a run left her breathless, but that was nothing compared with the emptiness of her lungs when she found no contract there, either.

Not in the other guest room. Not in her bedroom. Not in her bathroom. Not in Clary's room. Not in the dining room. Not in the family room. Still not in the living room or kitchen.

There was only one room she hadn't checked: Mark's office. It was just down the hall, the doorway under the stairs. The sheriff's department had searched it after his death, along with his office in town, but they'd found nothing of interest. If he'd kept records or mementos of his killings, he'd hidden them well.

The contract couldn't be in there. She hadn't even looked at the closed door. Though she had to deal with the room eventually, she planned on doing it when Brent and Anne were here, maybe even letting them do it without her. She'd never planned on walking in there alone.

Her fingers curled around the doorknob as she forced deep breaths into her lungs. It was a room. Empty but for furniture, keepsakes, papers. The only thing in there that could hurt her were memories, and God knew she had enough of those. What were a few more?

She pushed the door and it silently swung inward. Mark had never been private about the office. Often she'd curled up in a chair to read while he worked at the mammoth desk one of his great-greats had had commissioned from one of Charleston's premiere cabinetmakers. Clary had napped on a quilt on the floor while he'd caught Macy up on his day. She'd always been welcomed inside.

Tonight she didn't feel welcome.

A flip of the switch lit the room brightly. Mark had teased his vision was receding, along with his hairline, so he'd liked good lighting. The room by its nature was dark: wood paneling and floors, marble fireplace surround, deep crimson paint on the walls, lots of gleaming mahogany pieces. It smelled of Mark and paper and disuse. If she listened hard enough, she was certain she could hear his voice, see his silhouette leaning back in the leather chair, feel the warmth of his presence.

She didn't listen. Instead, she stared at the desk. Rather, at the packet of white papers centered neatly on it.

"Oh, God, oh, God, oh—" Clamping her hand over her mouth, she realized she was trembling, her fingers unsteady, her legs shaking. "I didn't— God, I know I didn't—"

Her gulp of air did little to ease the strangling sensation in her chest. It fluttered, rose, overwhelmed her and sent her on a hasty dash to the bathroom just down the hall, where she emptied her stomach.

She was washing her mouth when she caught her reflection in the mirror. Eyes too wide, forehead wrinkled, face drained of color. She couldn't have looked more shocked if she *had* seen Mark sitting there in the chair.

"How could I go in there and forget?"

Her reflection didn't answer, but there was only one answer: she was losing control again. No, not losing. Had lost control. Had lost the memory of opening that door, walking inside, laying the contract—arranging it—on the desk.

It didn't make sense. It wasn't as if Mark would actually find the contract there to review it. She was keeping *her* papers on the island. She'd never kept *her* papers in his office, what few she had. She *wouldn't* have put it there. Couldn't have.

And yet there it was. Had it moved under its own power?

Do you believe in ghosts? she'd asked Stephen earlier. *Because they say this place is haunted. And I believe it.*

She really did believe Fair Winds was haunted. But not her own home. She wasn't living with ghosts. It just wasn't possible.

But her putting it there? Forgetting it? Sinking into the darkness again?

Dear God, that was entirely too possible.

After drying her mouth, she left the bathroom and made a circuit of the house, checking every door, every window, every item that came into sight. Could someone have gained access to the house? Had this been moved? Had that been touched?

The answer, she was forced to admit when she sank down on her bed after checking the entire place, was no. Access was secure. Nothing else was out of place. The only thing that had been moved was the contract, and there was nothing she could do about it.

Call the police? Oh, yeah, they'd take her seriously.

Tell Brent? He'd be on the phone with her psychiatrist as soon as he hung up.

Call Stephen? The little voice tempted and tantalized her. He was only a quarter of a mile away. He might think she was odd, but he liked her anyway. He didn't know anything about her past, her problems, her time in the psych facility.

Her fingers reached automatically for the cell in her pocket, but before she could dial, she pushed it away. She liked Stephen, too, and she wasn't calling him when he had to work tomorrow to tell him that she'd found the contract in a place she didn't remember being. She wouldn't give him reason to think she was any less stable than he already did.

Hugging herself tightly, she lay down on the bed, still trembling, too afraid to close her eyes, and held on.

The writing went extraordinarily well Thursday. Not having to go into the vet clinic helped. Thinking about Macy every other sentence didn't, until he finally managed to block her in a dark corner and concentrate on the other women in his life.

When he'd reached his daily goal and run out of words, Stephen took Scooter for a walk to Holigan Creek, then made it a quick shower. Now he stood in his boxers in front of his small closet while the dog lounged on the bed. "Not much to choose from, is there?"

Jeans and T-shirts, with shorts on the shelf above. Also, pushed into the very back, was a rarely worn suit, light gray, and a white dress shirt. He would have to wear that this weekend. And that was it on options.

When was the last time he'd cared how he looked? Probably the day he married Sloan, when her mother had forced him into a rented tux. His wife-to-be couldn't have cared less, but after paying for vet school, her mother had been determined to have the wedding of her dreams.

Too bad her dreams hadn't extended to the marriage.

"Last night I wore khaki, so tonight I guess I'll go with khaki." He pulled a black T-shirt and a pair of cargo shorts from the closet and yanked them on, gave his hair its usual finger comb, then put on his glasses. A spray of cologne, and he was ready to go—more than an hour early. But Macy had said come over when he was finished working, so he was taking her at her word. If she was busy with dinner, he could help. If she was still sorting and packing, he could help with that, too. Or he could just sit out of the way and watch her.

He was easy.

He and Scooter strolled the quarter mile to her house, burning time but still early. He kind of hoped his hair would dry on the way, but the humidity was so high that when he combed it one last time on the way up Macy's driveway, it was still damp. Oh, well. It wasn't as if this was a date, and even if it was, she wouldn't expect him polished and dressed up. She'd spent enough time with him to know better.

When she answered the door, her dress was sleeveless, her feet were bare and her hair was pulled back in a ponytail. With the soft, blurry pastels of her dress, she looked like a spring dream.

Until his gaze reached her face. There were shadows under her eyes, and her face was pale. She'd had a really bad day—or night. She was a different woman than the one he'd kissed right here last night.

He meant to be polite and not comment on her appearance, but when he spoke, it wasn't *hello* that came out. "Are you okay?"

Had she gotten bad news? Had something happened to Clary? No, of course not. If her daughter needed her, she would have moved heaven and earth to be with her. Maybe something had happened with her parents. They were in Europe, she'd said.

Or maybe packing up the house she'd shared with her dead husband was finally getting to her. Memories, good and bad. Reminders of what she'd lost, maybe what she'd escaped.

Her wan smile wasn't reassuring. "No sleep last night and a headache today. Come on in." Bending, she scratched Scooter as she unhooked his leash. "Hey, big boy, aren't you the prettiest baby."

Scooter gave her his biggest doggy grin. The instant the scratching stopped, though, his nose began quivering, and he followed it down the hall toward the kitchen, his tail slapping boxes on the way.

The family room looked as if a perversely neat tornado had blown through, with packed boxes stacked on the couch, chairs and tables, shelves mostly empty, even the throw pillows tossed into a large open box. "You've been busy."

"I'm getting rid of the easy stuff. The DVDs are going to the retirement center, the books to the library. I called Right Track today and offered them all the casual furniture, so they're sending a truck on Monday."

"Ellie Maricci's pet project." Right Track was a residential training program for young women who were booted from the juvenile system at eighteen with no help and little hope for their futures. They got job training and counseling, learned to cook, clean and do laundry, helped pay expenses with part-time jobs and took on the responsibilities of their homes. He'd found a few dogs and cats to be pets at the center and donated the food and care necessary for them and a few strays who'd joined them.

Ellie didn't believe in turning any strays away, two- or four-footed. Neither did he.

"They're getting the televisions, too, and the stereo and Mark's computers. I'm taking them in tomorrow or Saturday to have copies made of whatever I need and get the hard drives erased."

"No wonder you have a headache. You've done a lot."

She smiled that faint smile again and muttered as she turned to the kitchen. He thought it sounded like *I wish*.

He followed her to the island. Scooter sat on the other side, staring up at the counter. A pan of gooey brownies sat there, far back out of his reach, but that didn't stop him from drooling over the incredible aroma.

"Since we're grilling, I thought we'd eat outside. I could use a little fresh air. Could you grab that pan?"

He picked up the large tray and followed her to the rear door. Scooter darted between them, second one out, and immediately tore across the yard. "Aw, man, I forgot you have a pool. Scooter loves water. About half the time he escapes, he goes for a swim in the creek, and he likes to wallow in puddles after it rains."

"Creeks, puddles, my daylilies. He wallows a lot, doesn't he? It seems a veterinarian would have a better-trained pet."

Tilting his head, he put on a perplexed look. "It's

funny how many people think that. But remember, I'm only a part-time vet, and Scooter's a full-time character. Besides, what's a little wallowing between friends?"

She laughed. "I've got plenty of towels. Wallow away, Scooter."

Stephen had been in the backyard before, but that was the first night, when she thought she'd seen someone in the guesthouse. He hadn't paid a lot of attention to the area. Now he took the time to really look around. The flagstone patio extended into lush green grass, with outdoor furniture better than his indoor stuff, a fire pit for chilly nights and a grill and sink set in a massive brick outcropping to the right.

The rest of the large space was filled with guesthouse, pool, swathes of grass and extensive flower beds, the kind that took hours of planning even before the first spade or shovel was turned. "My mom would love this garden."

Macy set down the items she'd carried on the stone counter next to the giant grill. "*I* love this garden. It's the only thing I'll miss about the house."

"But you can have a garden anywhere, right? That was Mom's theory. She said she was beautifying the Southwest one home at a time."

He put the tray next to her, then stepped back as she unfolded foil to expose thick slabs of steak, aluminum-wrapped potatoes and a wire basket filled with sliced vegetables. She seasoned the meat with salt and pepper before setting the potatoes on the grill and closing the lid.

"Would you like something to drink? I have water, pop and iced tea."

"House wine—" He caught himself. "I bet you've heard that hundreds of times."

Her smile confirmed it. "Actually, the house wine for Mark's Southern family was a Chateau Lafite something or other."

"I can only guess that's as expensive as it sounds. I'll get the drinks." He returned to the kitchen, filled two glasses with ice and grabbed both tea and pop. When he returned to the patio, she was standing at the beginning of a stone path that led to the yard, hands on her hips, watching Scooter. The dog jumped into the pool at one end, swam to the other, jumped out and gave a great shake, spraying water fifteen feet, then raced to the other end to do it again.

"His needs aren't many." Stephen handed her a glass and a can of pop, then filled his glass with tea. "You work in the yard yourself?"

"I drew up the plans, found the plants and dug every bed. I even did about half the fountain." She gestured toward the back corner opposite the guesthouse and, with a silent prompt from him, started walking that way. He let her lead, just by a little, just enough that he could watch the dreamy fabric of her dress sway and shift with each step and the lean muscles in her calves contract and release.

It was a lovely sight.

The fountain was the part of the garden Macy had worked hardest on. It sat beneath a maple tree, with lush shade plants on all sides giving it an air of privacy. Though Mark had hired the nursery in town to build the rocky grotto, she'd been a full partner in the work. She'd gotten filthy, sore and bruised, and paid the men a bonus not to tell anyone. It had been her spineless way of going against Mark's will, even if he'd never known it. And he definitely had never known. He'd never been one to let little rebellions pass unnoticed.

The same rocks that formed the fountain made a small patio in front, just big enough to hold two comfortable wooden chairs, painted dusky lavender to play off all the green. The paint was flaking, exactly the effect she'd wanted when she'd painted the wood, but Mark had declared it tacky and she'd redone it, giving it a glossy, perfect surface.

But surfaces were just illusion. They always cracked after a time.

"Wow. I'd stretch an extension cord out here and write on the laptop all day." Stephen settled in one of the chairs and propped his feet on the low rim of rock encircling the pool that constantly refueled the fountain. If he noticed the spray that dotted the toes of his sneakers, he didn't care.

"No extension cord necessary." Settling herself in the second chair, she lifted a leaf of a giant elephant ear plant to reveal the electrical access hidden underneath.

"Very cool. My favorite place here."

"Mine, too." She sipped her pop and alternated between watching the water tumble and sneaking looks at him. Head bent back, long legs stretched out, he looked easy, loose. Comfortable. She liked the fact that his wardrobe was unimaginative, that his hair always stood on end, that his glasses made his eyes look a tiny bit bigger, a tiny bit more intense. That he wouldn't fit into the Howards's world. That he wouldn't want to.

She especially liked that he'd noticed she'd had a rough time. She just wished she could tell him about it.

But then he would look at her the way Brent, Anne and her parents did, as if she weren't quite sane. She could barely tolerate it from them. She didn't think she could stand it from Stephen. After all, her family loved her anyway. They hadn't walked away yet and never would.

Stephen, on the other hand, would be perfectly able to do so.

And maybe she really wasn't quite sane.

"Did you entertain a lot when you lived here?" He glanced at her, catching her sneaking a look, but didn't seem to mind.

Her cheeks heated a little anyway. "I could get a job as an event planner. Twelve for dinner, fifty for dessert, a hundred for cocktails... And note I said planner. Not much of a doer. Mark always insisted on catering meals. But I am the best at sending out invitations, picking menus, ordering flowers, hiring musicians, dressing up and looking pretty."

His solemn gaze didn't shift away. "Did you enjoy it?"

Her first-impulse answer was no, but she gave it a moment's thought. "I did." The acknowledgment rather surprised her. "My family was solidly working-class, and it took a long time for Mark's lifestyle to become normal for me. It was like taking a very long, very luxurious vacation. Shopping, being pampered, showing off, without ever having to even think about money..."

Did he think she was shallow for admitting that she'd liked it? She didn't know much about his own finances, though he had mentioned that at times he'd been lucky to have a room of his own. His house was nowhere near as lavish as this one, but it was cozy. It was a home, and he seemed happy with it.

She would trade all of Mark's and Miss Willa's money and both their mansions to be happy.

She felt obliged to go on. "When I met Mark, I didn't know exactly who he was. Howard is such a common name. It was obvious he had some money, but I didn't care. I fell in love with a college student, not the heir to a few fortunes. It wasn't until we went shopping for my wedding gown that I began to really understand how different life was going to be. Weekly flights to New York with his mother, meetings with advisers, back for fittings... You know that old tradition that the bride's family pays for most of the wedding? Mark bought my gown. It cost more than my dad made in a year."

She shook her head. Outrageous for a dress that was meant to be worn only once. She'd stored it with thoughts that maybe someday she'd have a daughter who would wear it for her own wedding, but given the way Macy's marriage had ended, she'd rather see Clary wed in a T-shirt and shorts.

"But you looked beautiful in it," Stephen said. When she raised her brows, he shrugged. "I saw the portrait in the living room."

"Oh. Thank you." He'd thought she looked beautiful. Of course, she'd been younger, foolishly in love and hadn't had a clue about the true nature of the man she'd married. Still...

"It was a good thing my ex's parents could pay for our wedding, because between us, all Sloan and I had was two veterinary degrees and a whole boatload of debt."

"Did you always want to be a vet?"

"Nah. I wanted to be Han Solo and fly the Millennium Falcon. Or Batman. I'd've looked good behind the wheel of the Batmobile."

He said it so naturally that she burst out laughing.

Grinning, he took a swig of tea. "Hey, I believe in superheroes. Don't you?"

"Uh...sure. Why not?" After all, if supervillains existed, then by deduction so should superheroes.

"Sure, why not," he repeated, then snorted. "You had a sense of wonder and magic at some time. Kids are born with it—well, except Marnie. She came out of the womb wanting just the facts. When did you lose yours?" It was a simple teasing question, and she would have tried to answer it in the same way, but a frown crossed his face and he sobered. "Was it the way your husband died?"

"No. It was the way he lived." Tension streaked through her, and she gripped the chair arms tightly enough as she stood to take away lavender flakes on her palms. "I think it's probably time to put the meat on the grill."

She crossed the lawn with long strides, Scooter joining her halfway. He was dripping, tongue lolling out of his mouth, and just the sight of him eased the tightness in her shoulders a little. Hearing Stephen not far behind, she said, "Scooter really likes the pool, and I'm sure Clary will really like him. Any chance he could just stay here until we're gone?"

"I wouldn't know what to do without him. However, anytime you want to make a visit to the animal shelter to pick out one of your own, let me know. I'd be happy to go with you."

"All right. It was worth a try, wasn't it, sweetie?" She moved the potatoes to one side of the grill, cranked up the heat, then closed the lid again. "I need a few things from the kitchen. You want towels for the baby?"

"I can get them if you tell me where."

She hesitated only a moment. She could run upstairs and get the oversize chocolate-brown bamboo towels, each one pricey enough to cover the cost of tonight's steak dinner and then some. She *could* go, but she didn't have to, and by the time he got back, she would be too busy at the grill for him to follow up on her latest episode of telling too much. "Top of the stairs, closet down the hall to the left."

He held the door for her, and she turned into the kitchen while he continued down the hall. As she gathered marinade, steak sauce and butter, she listened to the tromp of his footsteps on the stairs and overhead. It was a nice feeling, not being alone in the house. If it was haunted, for this evening, at least, she had someone to be scared with her. If she'd gone crazy instead, there was someone to make the call to lock her up again.

Her hands trembled as she balanced the items on a tray holding dishes, silverware and napkins. *Dear God, I know I don't pray for much besides Clary, but please don't let me be crazy.*

Chapter 6

At the top of the stairs, Stephen paused to study a photograph of Macy and Mark. She looked so very young and innocent and happy. And Mark…he was good-looking, self-assured, reeking—even in a one-dimensional photograph—of superiority. His arm was around Macy's shoulders—possessive, Stephen first thought, then reluctantly amended it. They were engaged, with a honker of a diamond ring that looked too heavy for her delicate hand. If Stephen were engaged to her, he'd be holding her, too, with the intention of never letting go.

What had Mark done to steal his wife's sense of wonder and magic? Infidelity was the first thing that came to mind. Stephen had been lucky. Sex had never been a problem with him and Sloan. Even when they couldn't bear to be in the same room with each other at the end, they'd had no problem being in the same bed. But he could imagine how it must feel to find out the husband you loved was unfaithful to you. That could put a damper on the way you viewed life.

Turning away, he went left past what was obviously Clary's room, all bright colors and activity. Across the hall and down a few feet was a closed door. Assuming he'd reached the closet, he opened the door and froze in place.

The room was painted pale green with nursery scenes in soft colors forming a band around the middle. Poufy curtains on the windows, white crib, dresser, rocker, a couple of piles of outfits and stuffed toys with the price tags still on them. It was a nursery.

Had Macy had another child, one she'd lost along with her husband? Had she been expecting one? Or merely planning ahead for the time she would get pregnant again?

Intensely aware that he didn't know nearly enough about Macy, he gently closed the door. He'd avoided doing a Google search on either her or Mark so far; he just felt friends and maybe more should get to know each other the old-fashioned way. But when he got home tonight, Google, here he came.

Behind the next closed door, he grabbed an armload of thick towels and headed back downstairs and onto the patio.

The vegetables were roasting and the steaks sizzled on the grill, filling the air with aromas that made both him and Scooter stand taller and drool. Macy glanced briefly at him as he knelt beside the dog, then turned back to the food.

"I thought you might have some old worn-out towels up there for dog drying, but you didn't."

"No," she agreed. She didn't need to say it; he understood. *Not in Mark's mansion.*

The only thing Scooter loved more than getting wet, possibly, was getting dried off. He stood still, lifting each foot when Stephen touched it, tilting his head back, then to each side. He gave Stephen a long-suffering look when he felt the towel around his tail, but waited patiently.

"So tell me about your brother," Stephen said as he continued to rub, turning the drying into a massage.

"Brent? He's seven years older than me. Best older brother I could ask for."

He recognized his own words describing Marnie the night before. He'd bet she didn't have a *but*...following hers.

"He started his own lawn service when he was fifteen. By the time he graduated from high school, he had so many customers that he didn't have time to go to college. Now he has about sixty employees, but he leaves the administrative stuff to others and still goes out four or five days a week to mow grass."

"Smart man. Where's the success in owning a business when you have to manage instead of doing the work that attracted you in the first place?"

She moved the wire basket filled with vegetables to the cooler side of the grill, next to the potatoes, asked how he liked his steak, then added another question. "Is that why you've chosen not to open your own practice?"

"I'd rather be an employee than the owner. Whole different realm of responsibilities. And there's the writing gig, too. Need time for that."

After placing another foil packet on the grill, she faced him, leaning against the brick, hands next to her hips. "Brent's happy doing what he does. He gets off when he wants and has all the work he can handle the rest of the time. His wife, Anne, works for him when he needs extra help. They've been married about eight or nine months. They've talked about having kids soon—Anne's nearly thirty-eight—but…" Shadows darkened her eyes. "The time hasn't been right."

Were they having trouble conceiving? Was their brother-in-law's death enough stress for the family to deal with for the present? Or did that nursery upstairs have something to do with it, too?

He wished he knew, but even Marnie would recognize there was no polite way to ask such questions.

He finished with Scooter and draped the damp towels over nearby chairs before finding a post to lean his shoulder against. "You like Anne?"

"I do."

"That counts for a lot. Sloan had three brothers, all married. Their wives were the worst nags, gossips and whiners I'd ever known. Remember, my only sister is the female Spock, so I had no clue how to deal with such drama queens. One of the best things about the divorce, other than avoiding another Wyoming winter, was never having to listen to those women again."

"Anne's not like that at all." She pressed the steaks with a practiced fingertip, then used the tongs to place them on plates. "She's smart, warm, unflappable and compassionate. She's good for Brent. She's good for all of us."

Within a few minutes, with an ease that belied her earlier planner-not-doer statement, dinner was on a teak table at the other end of the patio. He took the seat she indicated, his mouth watering thanks to the aromas wafting off the plate. "This smells incredible."

"My dad is a grill master. He insisted Brent and I learn a few tricks before we left home."

The first bite of steak was more than incredible—just the right amount of char, spice and cool center. The potatoes had creamy interiors, the vegetables a sweet smoky flavor and the bread—the last item she'd put on the grill—was nicely garlicky.

"You are definitely a doer, Macy," he said when he'd eaten all he could. "All your friends who came here to eat other people's food don't have a clue what they were missing."

Her only response was a faint smile and to slip another piece of steak under the table to Scooter. Though she'd been subtle, Stephen had known the first time she'd done it and that she'd continued to do it by the way the dog abandoned him about two minutes into the meal.

She was pretty, nice, had a sense of humor and sneaked treats to his dog. What more could a man want in a woman?

Maybe a clearer, more hopeful look in her eyes. Those shadows didn't belong. Whatever had put them there—Mark's death, his life, the empty nursery—still held powerful influence over her. He'd like to see the smile on her lips chase those shadows away permanently. He'd like to see her really, truly happy.

Because he was a nice guy. He thought everyone—more or less—deserved to be happy. Though maybe not Mark Howard or his baby-snubbing grandmother.

"Did you stay in touch with your friends here when you left?" It wasn't too nosy a question, was it? She could ask him the same. She could ask him anything. His life was pretty much an open book.

She slid a last piece of steak to Scooter then folded

her napkin on the table, creasing it with one finger. "No. It was a tough time. I didn't have the energy to spare for keeping up with anyone but my family."

She didn't seem to have much energy tonight, either. It was funny how emotions could smack you down harder than the toughest physical labor ever could. Packing up the house, closing out a part of her life that had started so well and ended so badly, along with the uncertainty of the future, had drained a lot out of her.

Stephen watched her worry the napkin a moment before tugging it from her grasp and laying it aside. She looked startled, as if she hadn't realized what she was doing, then linked her fingers loosely.

"Can I ask you…"

She tensed, and he almost switched to something unimportant. But he really wanted to know more—about her, about the important things in her life—and she could always refuse to answer.

"How did Mark die?" He'd been a young man—late twenties, early thirties. Had it been a car wreck, cancer, a heart attack? A jealous husband, random bad luck, a simple case of being in the wrong place at the wrong time?

Abruptly she pushed back her chair and stood, gathering dishes. When she reached for his plate, he caught her hands, small and soft, the muscles clenched. "You can always say 'I don't want to talk about it.'"

She stared at their hands, stress radiating off her strongly enough to compete against the humidity in the night air. "I don't want to talk about it," she said. He'd bet his next publishing contract that she was trying to sound normal, but anxiety overlaid the casual effort.

Then her fingers went limp in his, and a sigh shuddered through her. "Can we—" Her gesture took in the entire yard, an invitation to move.

He slid back his chair with a scrape of wood on stone, and she used the opportunity to tug her hands free. She moved onto the path then hesitated before turning toward the pool. Scooter, his yen for swimming fulfilled and his belly just plain full, decided to let them wander, settling instead into the plush cushions of a chaise on the patio.

Macy stopped beside the pool. The water was a glossy surface, lit from below, undisturbed by wind or creature. Peaceful and calm, it seemed to be what she needed at the moment. Stephen thought he would have preferred the bubbles and splashes of the fountain.

Hugging her arms across her middle, she stared at the water a moment before meeting his gaze head-on. "He killed himself."

That was an option that hadn't occurred to Stephen. It stunned him into glancing at the elegant house, the lush gardens, the guesthouse, then Macy again. Mark Howard had had a beautiful family, all this, more money than most people even dreamed of. What could possibly have been so bad in his life that ending it was the best solution?

"God, Macy, I'm sorry." Then, before he could control his tongue… *"Why?"*

The more times you tell it, the easier it is to tell.

So claimed Macy's psychiatrists during her inpatient stay. She wasn't convinced they were right. In fact, she was pretty sure they weren't. She was totally sure she would rather never discuss Mark's death with anyone ever again in her life.

Though someday Clary would have to know.

Please, God, not for another twenty-five or thirty years.

You can always say, "I don't want to talk about it." Those eleven words meant a lot to her. The doctors had always made her talk about it eventually. Her parents and Brent put less pressure on her, but they'd needed to discuss it, too.

But she could tell Stephen and he would drop the subject. He very well might go home and search the internet or ask someone at his clinic tomorrow, but he wouldn't make her give the details.

And she wasn't yet able to give the important ones. The real *why*. Mark and his grandfather's ugly secret.

But she wanted to tell Stephen something. Amazing, since she'd never thought she would want to tell anyone anything.

"He had some…issues. I didn't know until…" Backing a few feet away from the water, she sank into one of the lounge chairs. "Did you know it's possible for love to vanish instantly? To just go away?"

The cushions in the next chair gave a soft whoosh as he sat, too. "Yeah, I've heard."

Her hair swung against her cheek as she grimly shook her head. "I didn't know. I thought people fell out of love, they grew out of it or it just died a slow death from lack of attention. I didn't know that you could love someone totally, completely, one moment and not love him the next. But that's what happened."

His gaze shifted from her to the house, then back again. "He didn't—"

"Do it here? God, no. At Fair Winds. On the front lawn. He shot himself." She watched Stephen shudder, presumably at the thought that they'd been there just last night. Did he think it odd that she'd said nothing then, reacted to nothing then? Or was he too shaken by the story now to think about her behavior last night? Would that occur to him later?

"His grandmother didn't—?"

"No. Miss Willa wasn't home. In fact, she was with me. We'd had lunch with Mark at the country club, then she and I went to a meeting of the local historical society. But his cousin was at the house, and her husband. They saw him do it." She left out the fact that he'd been trying to kill Reece and Jones at the time. Had it been desperation that made him turn the gun on himself? The certainty he was caught? That all the money and influence in the world couldn't buy his way out of the nightmare he and Arthur had created?

Maybe it had been the shame he'd brought on the Howard name. That damn name had always meant so much to him and Miss Willa. He would have killed to protect it.

Though, apparently, finding a reason to kill hadn't been difficult for Mark.

And truth was, she didn't care why he'd done it. She was just glad he had. The evil residing within her husband's heart and soul hadn't deserved to live.

"I'm so sorry you had to go through that," Stephen said quietly. "I'm sorry I asked you about it."

She drew a deep breath and smelled flowers, the lingering aroma of steak and, fainter, the scent that was Stephen. It was nothing special. It didn't smell as if he'd bathed in money. But it was comforting. It didn't make her stomach churn. Even the slightest memory of Mark's cologne inside the house could do that.

"It was a huge shock," she admitted. "But that part of

my life is almost over. Once I leave this place and settle down somewhere with Clary, it *will* be over. Done. Until Clary's grown, all she'll know is that her father is dead."

"What about his mother? Won't she want her son's memory kept alive for her granddaughter?"

Macy listened to the song of a whippoorwill in the trees beyond the yard as an image of Lorna Howard formed. Average height, sturdy, the sort of woman who could have taught General Patton a few lessons about being in charge.

At least, that was Lorna before Mark's death.

"Lorna rarely sees Clary." Not since Miss Willa's funeral, in fact. Lorna had visited Macy a time or two in the Columbia hospital, but she'd had little to say. Loss and grief had overwhelmed her. She'd insisted Mark was guilty of nothing. He'd been a good man, a loving son, husband and father. She'd sworn he wasn't capable of hurting anyone. After all, she was his mother, and a mother knew these things.

She'd never believed the manner of his death, either. She'd accused Reece, Jones, some unseen stranger passing through. As far as Macy knew, nothing had changed her mind. Lorna had become reclusive, hiding away at her Raleigh estate, convinced her son had been murdered and falsely accused. Though Macy had contacted her several times, offering to take Clary to visit for a few days, the answer had always been no.

Secretly relieved by the flat refusal, and guiltily ashamed of the relief, Macy had quit offering. Lorna knew how to reach her if she changed her mind.

"It's a good thing Clary has your family," Stephen said quietly. "Sounds like the Howards aren't worth much besides money."

"Yeah. But Reece is different. So is Clary. She'll be the complete opposite of them all."

"I have no doubt."

On the patio, Scooter stirred, stretched, then trotted out to them. Standing between them, he scented the air and a sound started low in his throat as the hair on his spine straightened. The growl sent a chill straight through to Macy's bones.

It didn't seem to concern Stephen at all. He gave the dog a reassuring pat. "What do you smell, buddy? Neighbors have a cat?" He chuckled. "He's friendly to every animal around except cats. There are feral ones in the woods, and they drive him nuts when they come out."

Macy stared in the direction Scooter was looking, the back side of the property, and told herself sure, it was just feral cats. The fence was tall and solid on all three sides of the yard. The only gates were on the house sides, and they were locked. The motion detector lights that lined the fence remained off.

The growl stopped, the dog's hair returned to its normal position and the air of vigilance faded. Scooter sat down, backing up to his master for a scratch.

Just feral cats. Not a person. Not a ghost. Not a figment of a fragile imagination.

Stephen sighed lazily. "I guess we'd better get home. Tomorrow's a clinic day."

The anxiety Macy had just calmed flared again. She wished she could ask him to stay longer. Better yet, could she go home with him? She'd be happy to sleep on the sofa.

But instead, she took a breath to level her voice. "Sounds like fun."

"Not always fun, but usually different." He stood,

then offered his hand. She took it without hesitation, letting him pull her to her feet, almost pulling her into his arms. When he realized how close they were, he stood motionless, and so did she. Her fingers were warm in his grip, and the heat spread up her arm and through her body. With her next breath, she caught another whiff of his scent and closed her eyes for a moment to savor it.

When she opened them again, the distance between them had diminished by half. Had he moved, or had she? In the next instant, it didn't matter because he was bending his head to hers, brushing his mouth to hers. Her eyes fluttered shut again, and her free hand touched his chest, resting there on warm fabric.

Sweet kiss, but not really so sweet, not with its promise of hunger, of need and heat and being alone way too long. Her heart thudded louder, her breath turned liquid in her lungs and her body trembled in that incredibly nice yearning way that it hadn't in far too long.

She moved closer, and their noses bumped, knocking his glasses askew. Ending the kiss, he pushed them back into place and gave her a slow, warm smile. "I'm awfully glad Scooter ran away the other day."

Her smile felt smaller, shakier. "Me, too."

Curling his fingers around her hand, he lifted it to his chest, then caught hold of the other one, too. "Can I see you tomorrow?"

"I'll be here all day." Breathless words, little more than a whisper.

Still holding her hands, he made a smooching sound for the dog, then led the way to the patio. There he let go and filled his hands with dishes instead. It took them a few moments to carry everything inside: dishes in the sink, towels in the laundry room, leftovers in the refrigerator.

"I get off around noon," he said at the door. "Is that too early?"

"No. I'll fix lunch."

He fastened the leash on Scooter's collar, then kissed her again. "I'll see you then."

Her lips tingling—her entire body tingling—she locked the door, set the alarm, then sighed. It was a precious feeling, this sense of normalcy. At least, almost normal. More or less. If she discounted her jumpiness and the contract she'd moved without knowing it.

Then she lifted her gaze to the wedding portrait above the living room fireplace and her features settled stubbornly. *No.* She *was* normal. The jumpiness was normal. As for the contract… If she wasn't entitled to a little forgetfulness, then who was?

She was three months shy of her thirtieth birthday, a widow, a single mom and having a bit of a hard time closing out this chapter of her life. No one had expected it to be easy. Brent, Anne, her psychiatrist—they'd all told her it would be tough. She'd known it without their warnings.

But she would get through it. Mark had cost her so much already. Tying up the loose ends of their life together wouldn't steal her self-confidence, and it damn well wouldn't steal her sanity. Not again.

Stephen woke Friday morning to the eau du doggy, thanks to his bed partner sprawled in a limp, doggy-breath-emanating heap, pinning him to the mattress.

The fragrance drifting on the air when Macy woke was exotic with notes of sandalwood and orange and cost $200 an ounce. It came in an elegantly curved black bottle that sat on the counter in Mark's dressing room and had a faintly off scent, as if something had turned with age.

Stephen hardly noticed the doggy breath or the chlorine lingering from last night's swim or the fine grit four massive paws had spread over the bed after their walk home. Smells and dirt were par for the course with a dog in the house. He started the coffee, jumped in the shower, then checked his email while scarfing down protein bars with the java.

Macy lay paralyzed in bed, hating that cologne as intensely as she hated the man it represented, until finally she couldn't stand it anymore. She jumped from bed, marched into her bathroom for a can of germ killer, then stalked across the room to Mark's bathroom, filling both it and the closet with a fine mist of medicinal-smelling lemon. Try to overpower *that,* sandalwood, she thought as she grabbed the black bottle and tossed it in a box in the hallway holding trash.

The Howard house looked quiet and imposing as Stephen drove past. A lot of curtained windows, a lot of impenetrable brick. He wondered if Macy felt like a prisoner locked away in its unwelcoming interior.

"It's a house," he said aloud to rein in his imagination. "A beautiful house that someone will eventually pay a cool million or two for."

After living like a Howard for so many years, her idea of prison would probably be the little house he lived in. Clary's bedroom was three times the size of his office. The linen closet was nicer and bigger than his bedroom.

But he could afford more. He didn't make a lot of money, but other than expenses such as the computer, the internet, research groups and the professional dues he paid in both jobs, he didn't spend much money, either. It wasn't as if he was poor. He worked part-time at two jobs, neither of which paid a lot, because he loved them, not because it was all he could do.

When he reached the clinic, he parked out back, then let himself in the rear door. Lights were already on, and music filtered down the hall from the reception counter. It didn't matter how early he got in, Zia Cruz always beat him. He didn't know where she found the energy. She was five years older than him, worked here six days a week and spent evenings caring for her five nieces and nephews while her brothers worked their night jobs.

"Hi, Zia," he called as he stopped in his office to set down the fast-food breakfast he'd brought along, then he followed the smell of coffee to the break room. She sat at a table, feet propped up, reading the newspaper.

"Hey Doc." She didn't look up from the paper. For a small city, the *Clarion* was a decent paper, published six days a week as well as online. They had the benefit of extremely generous support from the Calloway and Kennedy families, which made their battle to survive more of a skirmish.

"Anything interesting in there today?"

"Interesting, sad, depressing." She finished the front section and laid it aside in trade for the next.

Stephen filled his coffee mug, stirred in sugar and creamer, then leaned against the counter. The position immediately reminded him of Macy. "How long have you lived here, Zia?"

She looked at him over the paper, one brow raised. Her skin was olive-toned, her hair black, her eyes almost black. "Despite my name and my appearance, I was born and raised here. All of us kids were, except Jimmy." She wrinkled her nose as if in distaste. "He was born in New York."

Stephen ducked his head. "Pardon my jumping to conclusions. I just haven't met many people born here."

She rolled the newspaper and swatted his leg with it. "You don't do hangdog well. Do you wanna know something about this burg, or are you just trying to make polite conversation?"

He put off answering by sipping his steaming coffee. He hadn't gone straight to the computer when he and Scooter got home the night before. He'd felt too... hopeful. Whatever the internet could tell him could wait. He'd rather hear it from Macy anyway.

But would it hurt to ask just a question or two?

"Do you know a family named Howard?"

Zia's white smile flashed. "In Copper Lake, there are plenty of families named Howard, but there's only one Howard family. Money, tragedy and scandal—the kind of stuff people do one-hour TV shows about."

Stephen went back to drinking coffee hot enough to scald and impossible to taste with the thoughts rattling in his head. Zia's pronouncement didn't sound good. He knew the Howard money went back generations. How about the tragedy and scandal? In Southern families, the age of the scandal didn't always matter; some people talked about ancient history as if it were just a year or two ago.

And which was Mark's suicide? Scandal? Or tragedy?

"You know, they own that big beautiful place on the river," Zia added.

"Fair Winds. I've seen it."

Zia drummed her fingers on the table. "Wonder what

the daughter-in-law will do with it. It's been empty since the old woman died." She shuddered exaggeratedly. "Hateful old woman. Never had patience for anyone but her own family, and not even all of them. Her only grand-daughter wouldn't have anything to do with her. Miss Willa was the biggest snob you ever met. Compared to her, Louise Wetherby is super friendly, all-welcoming and oozes compassion."

"That's a scary thought."

"Not that I'm gossiping or anything," Zia said with a smirk as the back door opened and multiple voices filtered down the hall.

Stephen took his coffee back to his office, passing a couple of the vet techs on the way. He greeted them, joked for a minute, then slipped through the door into the tiny windowless room that contained his desk, computer, a couple of file cabinets and a chair held together with duct tape.

Ah, the gracious life he lived. It was a miracle a woman like Macy bothered to spend time with him, much less let him kiss her.

Immediately he regretted the thought. Macy hadn't been born into all that money. She hadn't been raised with a silver spoon and an inflated sense of entitlement. She was an average person, just like him, just like Zia, who'd fallen in love with a very wealthy person. It had changed her life forever—marriage always should—but not in a good way.

And even if she had stopped loving Mark back when he died, she still had some things to deal with. Trusting someone new with her whole story was one of them.

So he'd stick around until he wasn't new anymore. Until she had no choice but to trust him. Until even a fly on her wall could see that he was nothing if not trustworthy.

Worthy, period.

He'd just finished breakfast when his first patient arrived. He did routine exams and vaccinations, checked out an eleven-year-old hound whose appetite was off, put a few stitches in a Jack Russell terrier who thought he ruled the jungle, or at least the woods around his house, and barely escaped with his fingers intact after treating a cat for gingivitis.

He loved animals, he reminded himself as he cleaned the cat scratch on his left arm. He really did. He just loved cats a little less than the dogs, guinea pigs, snakes, birds, ferrets, rabbits and hedgehogs that made up the pet population at the clinic.

After finishing his reports, he went to the reception counter. "Zia, I'm heading out."

She didn't look up from the computer. "You're on in the morning. Don't forget."

"I won't."

Then she sneaked a sly glance at him. "I hear you're on tomorrow night, too. Are all your shots up-to-date?"

The idea of spending an entire evening with Kiki made him groan. "How do you hear these things?"

She shook a finger at him. "Your sister may not gossip, but everyone else in town does. You keep your wits about you. I hear the Kiki Monster bites, and her toxin might be fatal."

"Thank you," he said with a scowl, "for making me anticipate the evening even more than I already was."

Her laughter followed him down the hall. "See you tomorrow, Doc."

Chapter 7

Lunch was sandwiches of leftover steak and vegetables warmed and topped with gooey melted cheese, plus homemade chips Macy had picked up at Ellie's Deli. By two o'clock, it was a dim memory. After eating, she'd begun packing in the living room while Stephen moved the stacks of boxes from the hallway to the garage. Without prompting, he'd organized them: keep, donate, get rid of, with *donate* meaning something of historical or collectible value, *get rid of* referring to things that could be donated anywhere.

She liked a man who could organize things on his own.

Hands on hips, she looked around the room before her gaze settled on the wedding portrait again. She'd felt foolish having an actual portrait painted; it was so outside the realm of Ireland experience, where even professional photographs were a rarity. Snapshots were good enough for her family.

But Mark had insisted—as had Miss Willa—and the artist had been more than happy to work from a photo. They'd had a big party when it had arrived, coinciding with their first anniversary and their move into the house, and people with their own portraits looming over them at home had admired it.

For the first few months, it had disconcerted her, confronting a six-by-eight-foot image of herself and Mark every time she'd walked into or past the room. Eventually she'd stopped noticing it, but now it disconcerted her again. It was a huge lie done in oils.

Dragging a chair to the fireplace, she climbed onto it and was gripping the bottom of the elaborate gilt frame when Stephen spoke from the doorway.

"What are you doing?"

"Taking it down." Not as easily said as done. The sucker was heavy and attached to the brick far above her head. Holding on tighter, she leaned forward and shoved upward. The frame moved wildly, and so did she, losing her balance on the chair. Letting go, she flailed her arms then found herself steady with both hands on Stephen's shoulders. He held her a moment before lifting her to the floor.

"Wait till we get a ladder," he said reasonably.

"I don't want to wait. I don't want to look at it anymore." But it was hard to be pouty when his hands were still cradling her waist and the heat radiating from his body was a match for her own. "Can we cover it with a sheet?"

"When we get a ladder." He studied her a moment, then said, "How about this? I'll get the marker and draw mustaches and glasses with fuzzy eyebrows on both of you. You won't recognize yourself."

"Sounds good." She hesitated then rested her forehead against his shoulder. "Thank you for coming over. I know you've got better things to do."

"Other things," he agreed. "Not better." His hand slid up her spine in the same sort of deep-tissue, muscle-relaxing massage he'd given Scooter the night before. She thought she might react the same way the dog had—a few guttural moans, then going limp and sinking to the floor with her tongue hanging out.

Before that could happen, though, he pressed a kiss to the top of her head and stepped away. "What are you going to do about all the furniture? The antique stuff."

It took a moment for strength to replace the laziness he'd created in her body, then she glanced around. Every single piece in the room, including the chair she'd just climbed on, fit in that category. As far as she could remember, the newest piece was somewhere around one hundred fifty years old. "Sell what I can and donate the rest, I guess."

"You have anyone in mind to handle the deal?"

"If I had ever needed an antiques dealer, I would have asked Miss Willa or Lorna. Now…" She shook her head.

"Lydia Kennedy is a client of mine. You know her?"

This time her head bobbed. The Kennedy family had been in Copper Lake for six generations or more and, like the Howards and the Calloways, were blessed with riches. "Her husband is a distant cousin of Miss Willa's."

"She likes to buy and sell antiques. Why don't I call her and see who she recommends?"

"I'd appreciate that." Macy hadn't wanted to think about the furniture beyond getting rid of it, so sources of referrals hadn't even made it to the back of her mind. There was no doubt Lydia dealt with only the best—she and Miss Willa had had that in common, though little else. Lydia was a kind woman who actually cared about people.

He pulled his cell phone from his pocket and started toward the hallway. Turning back, he asked, "What were you going to do with the painting if you'd gotten it down?"

She didn't hesitate. "Taken it out in the backyard, chopped it up and burned it in the fire pit."

His head shake was regretful. "The artist put a lot of work into it."

"He was well paid."

"Still…"

"The painting—however many thousands of dollars. Not having to see it again—priceless." She smirked as he rolled his eyes. When he walked out of the room and began speaking to someone about getting Lydia's number, she gave another serious look around her. All the smaller pieces were packed. Even the Tiffany lamps were solidly cuddled in Bubble Wrap, the boxes labeled *Fragile* and *Handle with Care* in big red letters. There was nothing left in the room that she could deal with on her own.

Hearing the murmur of Stephen's voice from the kitchen, where he was probably making notes at the island, she went into the library across the hall. Mark hadn't been an avid reader, but of course they had an entire room to house books. These were the really old ones, the rare ones, handed down through the family. It wasn't likely that ungloved hands had touched them in her lifetime. No one read them for pleasure or even out of obligation. They simply sat on their shelves, looking old and tome-ish and neglected except for regular dustings.

"Lydia said she'll get in touch with her two favorite dealers and set up an appointment." Stephen stood beside Macy a moment before walking farther into the room. He stopped in the middle, right in the center medallion of the hand-woven Tunisian rug, and turned slowly.

What did he see? She saw a pretty, dark, lavishly decorated room with plush chairs, more Tiffany lamps, cherrywood and mahogany and oak tables that gleamed with age. She saw the library ladder, propped against one wall like a praying mantis, and the eight-foot-high shelves filled with row after row of books bearing uninspired covers and often script nearly impossible to decipher.

But he was an author. Words and books were his passion. Did his fingers itch to sit down with an armful of these? Could he spend a few hours or days in here, browsing and appreciating?

From the oak library table, he picked up a piece of jade, turning it gently in his large hands. Three dozen carvings were spread across the surface, none bigger than an egg, ranging in color from typical green to white and in between.

"Those belonged to Mark's father. They were his passion. He made countless trips to Asia, selecting each one himself. When he died, they passed to Mark, though without the passion. He displayed them because that's what you do with valuable old things. They used to be in the living room, but Clary could reach them there, and she was in that putting-everything-in-her-mouth stage, so he moved them in here." She hugged her middle. "Clary didn't like this room. All her crawling, walking and wandering, she wouldn't come in here."

Stephen carefully replaced the jade. "I don't much like it, either. It's not exactly a welcoming place. Libraries should be about comfort and books, not about hands-off displays. Though I bet some collector would pay a fortune for the whole set of books."

"These books are going to the library, too. They never have enough money to do what they need. They can be the proud owner of all these rare books, or they can sell them and supplement their budget for a while. As for the jade…I'll offer it to Lorna or maybe keep it for Clary." Her smile was on the bitter side. "I don't hate her grandfather."

Distantly there came the sound of a thudding car door. Macy's gaze jerked to the clock on the library wall. It wasn't even three—early for Brent and Clary. If it was Louise Wetherby wanting an answer on the disposition of Fair Winds, Macy would give it to her: *No. Not in this lifetime.*

Brushing her hair back, she went to the door as the bell pealed, that awful funereal tone that Mark had picked. She opened it to find no one there, and for one instant a terrible fear started to form in her chest. Then a giggle came from around the corner, and from opposite sides of the steps, Brent, holding Clary, and Anne stepped out from where they'd pressed themselves flat against the wall. "Surprise!"

Breathe deeply. Don't let them see they frightened you. She took a breath, then forced an animated exaggerated fright onto her features. "Oh, my gosh! You scared me!"

"Don't be scared, Mama. It's just me an' Uncle Brent

an' AnAnne." Clary leaped from Brent's arms into hers, making her stumble back a step or two. Her little girl felt so solid and warm and smelled so sweet, and she'd missed her, God, more than she'd been willing to admit. She held her tightly for an instant, enough to make Clary squirm, then pressed loud smooches to the girl's cheeks, throat, stomach, sending her into another fit of giggles.

"I know we're early, but we can take Clary to the park for a few hours if you want," Brent offered as he followed Anne through the door.

She swatted his shoulder before hugging him, too, then her sister-in-law. "You could never be too early. Not with my baby."

There was a soft shuffle behind her, and everyone's attention shifted that way. Macy saw surprise and curiosity on Brent's and Anne's faces before she shifted Clary to one hip and turned. An odd sense of nerves and pleasure went through her. It had been so long since she'd introduced a man to her family, and look how that had turned out.

But Stephen wasn't Mark. He was so much more.

"Stephen, this is my brother, Brent, and his wife, Anne—"

"Uncle Brent and AnAnne," Clary clarified.

Anne ruffled Clary's silky brown hair. "She doesn't quite get that there's a *t* on *aunt.*"

"And my daughter, Clary," Macy continued. "Guys, this is Stephen Noble." She thought about clarifying him, too—*my neighbor, my friend, the man who kissed me last night and made my whole body go weak.* She didn't add anything, though. Stephen was enough.

He and Brent shook hands; he and Anne exchanged greetings. His expression when he turned to Clary was serious, gentle, not overly friendly like so many adults. "Hey, Clary."

Clary curled a strand of hair around one finger. "Why you wear those?" She pointed to his glasses with her other hand.

"Because I don't see very well without them."

"Can I try?"

Macy was about to tell her no when he removed the glasses and handed them over, apparently uncaring whether she got prints on them. Of course, they were way too big for her, but she held them with one hand over the bridge and half of each lens, then looked at each adult. "I see silly."

"You are silly, Jilly. Now give them back carefully."

Her daughter obeyed, and Stephen cleaned the glasses on his T-shirt—black today—before putting them on again.

Macy tuned out the conversation. She was here with the people she loved best and the man she liked best in the whole world. Finally, this house didn't seem so cold.

After giving them all a tour of the house—it was Anne's first visit and Stephen's first time to see everything— Macy suggested they go outside to catch up. It was a warm afternoon, but with the shade and the ceiling fans over-head, it was comfortable.

Macy and Anne stopped in the kitchen to get drinks while Stephen, Brent and Clary went ahead. She ran in the yard from one flower bed to another with the un-failing energy of a three-year-old, and they more or less drifted to the teak love seat and chairs nearby. Stephen, who never found himself at a loss for words, wasn't en-tirely sure what to say to Macy's protective older brother.

He'd caught Brent's first wary look when he'd come out of the library. He figured none of the Irelands would be happy to see her getting involved with another man unless it was someone they knew and approved of.

"So…Macy says you're a vet."

Stephen nodded. "I work part-time at a clinic in town."

Brent's own nod was kind of measuring. Wondering what else he did with his time? If he was part vet, part lazy bum? If part-time work was the best he could get?

Stephen sat in one of the chairs, facing the love seat, its cushions sighing under him, and Brent took a seat across from him.

"How long have you been in town?"

"A little under a year."

Another measuring nod. "Has she told—" Brent broke off, then substituted another question. "What brought you to Copper Lake?"

"My sister lives here. When the vet job came open, I decided to take it."

"Is she younger or older?"

Stephen suppressed a smile. "Older. She works for the Copper Lake Police Department."

As he'd expected, that took a little of Brent's edge off. He was worried about his sister. Mark's suicide had been tough for her. Stephen had no doubt that was what Brent had started to ask: *Has she told you how her husband died?* He didn't want her hurt again.

They were on the same side there.

"Do you do anything besides be a vet part-time?"

Before Stephen could answer, Clary ran up, skidding to a stop right beside his chair. "What's a vet?"

She looked like her mother. He'd seen it in the photograph, but gazing into her face, flesh and blood and dimension, it was so much more obvious. If there was a hint of her father in her, he couldn't see it. Or maybe didn't want to see it.

"A vet is a doctor for animals."

"I go to a doctor for kids. His name is Dr. Chris. Do you give the animals shots?"

"When they need them."

Her little face screwed up. "I don't like shots, but I don't cry, and I get a Band-Aid with a *puppy* on it."

"That's pretty cool. Do you like puppies?"

Her hair bounced with her emphatic nod. "Do you have any?"

"I have a dog. His name is Scooter."

"Where is he?"

"At home."

She pointed to the house. "In there?"

Of course she didn't remember that this was *her* home, where she'd lived half her life. Granted, it had been a very short life. "No, my house is down the road that way."

She looked to the north, gaze narrowed as if she could see through the fence and trees all the way to his little place, then turned that calculating look back on him. "Is it very far?"

"No."

"Can we go see Scooter?"

Brent's snort indicated he'd seen that request coming. Stephen didn't mind introducing her to the dog. If he was going to help Macy pick out a puppy for her, it would be good to see how she interacted with him. "We'll have to ask your mom about that."

The kitchen door opened at that moment and Clary

skipped over to meet Macy and Anne, each carrying a tray with drinks and plates of cookies. "Mama, *he* has a dog and we want to go see him. Can we, please?"

Macy's expression as she smiled down at her daughter was enough to make Stephen's chest hurt. Mothers loved daughters—no surprise there. But this look was so sweet, so intense, so...hell, *so* loving that he had to swallow hard to clear the lump from his throat.

When she shifted her gaze to him, the lump was right back. "You want to bring Scooter over? He can go for another swim."

"Sure." Stephen would have agreed to anything for that look. Go get the dog? No big deal. Flap his arms and fly the quarter mile? Easy. Slay a few monsters along the way? You bet.

With an excess of energy, he surged to his feet, pulling his keys from his pocket at the same time. Clary, cheering and swirling wildly, bumped into his legs and glanced up to give him a similar look. "Thank you, Dr. Stephen."

He brushed his palm against her hair. "You're welcome. We'll be right back."

"Thank you, Dr. Stephen," Macy murmured when he passed her.

"You can repeat that later," he whispered before stepping through the door.

He'd gone home after work to change clothes and walked back for lunch. His return walk was more of a jog. It took him maybe half a minute to wake Scooter and get his leash attached, then they headed for Macy's.

"Home really is close," Anne commented when the two of them came back onto the patio. She was sitting on the love seat next to Brent, a sweating glass of tea in hand. With straight black hair and a narrow face, she reminded him of an editor he'd once worked with, though Anne's ready smile diminished the resemblance. That editor had had no sense of humor or compassion for brand-new authors.

"It's just down the road," he replied.

"Hey, Scooter," Macy said, scratching between his ears. "We've got someone who wants to meet you, sweetie. Clary?"

The girl popped up from the carpetlike grass between two large beds of flowers, and her eyes widened to saucer size. "A puppy!" Scrambling to her feet, she ran across the lawn. At the last instant before collision, she stopped beside Stephen and Scooter and beamed at each of them. Excitement vibrated through her.

Stephen commanded Scooter to sit, then knelt beside them. "Clary, this is Scooter. He's three years old, like you, and he likes to run and get tickled."

"Like me!" she exclaimed. "Can I pet him?"

The dog had had plenty of exposure to kids, but Stephen stayed close anyway, holding her hand so Scooter could sniff her, showing her how to pet and where to tickle, explaining the importance of not startling or hurting him. When he was sure Clary understood as well as Scooter did, he stood and stepped back, letting them interact together.

"Have a seat," Macy said, bumping his leg with her elbow.

He watched Clary a moment longer, then took the armchair next to Macy's. A glass of tea had been placed on the coffee table in front of the chair, on top of a napkin that was soaked and dripping. After taking a long drink, he picked up a cookie, too, oatmeal with walnuts, and bit in.

"How's it going with the packing?" Brent asked.

Macy's slim shoulders lifted in a shrug. "I delivered a few boxes to the retirement center this morning. A group that helps young women is picking up the family room and some of the guest room furniture Monday, plus one antique dealer is coming then, the other one Tuesday morning. If you guys see anything you want, please take it or let me know." She turned to include Stephen. "You, too."

He pushed his glasses back up his nose to disguise his grimace. He didn't want anything of Mark Howard's... except his widow. And his little girl.

"We tried to get Macy to just turn the whole place over to an estate sale place," Brent said. "She could have packed what she wanted in a couple hours and been done with this already."

Anne rested her hand on his knee. "*You* tried. I agreed with her that she should do it the way she needed to."

Stephen could understand needing to oversee the packing and sorting. Though she didn't seem interested in any of the stuff for herself, there were surely items she wanted Clary to have and others, like those jade carvings, she intended to give to someone else. There must be a few things inside that belonged to her, that didn't hold bad memories of her marriage.

None too subtly, Macy changed the subject. "I planned to put you two in one of the guest rooms, but since I've already started clearing them, I'm putting you in the guesthouse. It'll give you a little privacy, which I know you haven't had much of since the wedding. It'll be a bit of a break until we get you sent on a proper honeymoon."

Anne's smile brightened her face. "Ooh, privacy. Hmm. Tell me again what we do with that?" After a half groan, half growl from her husband, she gestured toward the pool. "I know it's only April, but how's the water?"

"Scooter loved it last night," Macy replied. "I haven't been in."

"Anyone mind if I dip my toes in? Otherwise, after my next three cookies, I'm gonna need a nap." Anne looked around the group, then stood. "Hand me the keys, babe, and I'll get our bags."

"I'll get our bags. You can get baby girl's." Brent polished off the last of his own cookie, then followed Anne inside.

After the door closed, silence settled, comfortable, familiar. "They seem like nice people," Stephen said.

"Very nice."

"They seem like they've been together for years."

Macy kicked off her sandals and turned sideways in the chair to face him, her knees drawn up. "Actually, they've only known each other about fourteen, fifteen months. I guess it's just one of those things. You know what you've found the minute you've found it. Not love at first sight but...more."

Stephen had experienced a few of those *things:* people he'd known he would be friends with, people he'd known would be important to him long after their meeting. Not Sloan, though. His first impression of her wasn't flattering. Smug, self-absorbed, aggressive.

It hadn't been wrong, either.

He didn't regret the marriage, though, or the divorce. He didn't regret anything. Everything he'd done or had done to him had brought him to this place and made him who he was. He liked this place. He liked who he was.

He liked whom he was with.

"I should get the key for the guesthouse," Macy said. "Can you keep an eye on Clary?"

"Sure. It's not often I get to see someone wrap Scooter around her little finger. He's usually the one who does the wrapping."

She looked at her daughter, talking earnestly to the dog on a nearby patch of grass, and Scooter, listening just as earnestly, and that incredible smile returned. "My daughter is a charmer."

He waited until the kitchen door closed behind her to quietly add, "She gets it from her mother."

The clock in the hallway struck ten, only distantly audible through the glass door. Brent and Anne had said good-night and retired to the guesthouse a half hour before. Macy and Stephen remained on the teak love seat, Clary sprawled across her lap, snoring softly. Scooter, on the chair Brent had abandoned, was doing the same.

Ten or fifteen minutes had passed since either she or Stephen had spoken, but it didn't bother her. Being able to talk with someone was important, of course, but being able to stay quiet with them was even more so. Mark hadn't been much of a believer in silence, not just with her but with everyone. He'd liked to talk. Miss Willa had understood the value of silence, but she'd used it as a weapon. Quiet equaled disapproval in her life.

Macy definitely approved of her life at the moment. Clary in her arms, Stephen at her side, Brent and Anne only a shout away. If her parents were there, the moment would be perfect.

"How often do you see your parents?" she asked.

If Stephen wondered where the question had come

from, it didn't show. "Mom comes to Copper Lake three or four times a year, and Marnie and I go to Alabama for Mother's Day, her birthday, Thanksgiving and Christmas."

"What about your father?"

"We see each other in June—his birthday, Father's Day, my birthday—then we shoot for a visit in the fall. We rely on the phone more than Mom and I do." He shifted, a whisper of sound, a creak, a pop, and propped both feet on the coffee table. Basketball player-sized feet, big enough to dwarf hers when she rested them beside his. "You see your parents a lot."

She laughed. "I've lived with them for the better part of the last eighteen months. When my dad gave me away at the wedding, he thought I'd stay away. The joke was on him." And on her. When Mark had promised to love and honor her, she hadn't known he would be killing people in his spare time.

A shudder ran through her, and she clutched Clary a little tighter, enough to make the girl stir.

Deliberately she changed the subject. "Do you have to work tomorrow?"

"Yeah, until one."

"Brent mentioned going to out to dinner to that great little barbecue place near the interstate." She hesitated, because she had claimed an awful lot of his time off this week, then took a breath and went on. "Would you like to join us?"

"Yeah. But I can't." He combed his fingers through his hair then pushed his glasses up before facing her in the dim light. "I have…an obligation tomorrow night."

Something in her stomach looped and tightened. "That sounds serious." Another hesitation. "It's okay if you have a date. I mean, I've only known you a few days, and you don't owe me an explanation. It's really none of my—"

Reaching over, he laid his fingers across her mouth. "It's not a date. The police chief is retiring, and they're having a big party at River's Edge, and Marnie asked if I'd take one of the female cops she works with. Believe me, I wouldn't have said yes for anyone but Marnie because this detective scares me spitless. She makes my ex look spineless, and Sloan wasn't intimated by anything."

But Macy was. She was vulnerable, unsure of herself. Was that a point for or against her in Stephen's estimation? Did he enjoy being able to take care of a woman for a change, or was she too needy for his tastes? Would the novelty wear off soon?

"River's Edge is beautiful." The antebellum mansion sat in downtown Copper Lake, a gleaming Greek Revival of a house overlooking the square and the river. Though built about the same time as Fair Winds, it was a far more inviting place where people had lived, loved and laughed—where they still did now that it was used for weddings, parties and other events. "You'll have a good time."

"Right," he said morosely. "I have to wear a suit. And a tie."

"I wouldn't have guessed you owned long pants or a shirt with buttons, much less a tie."

That made him grin. "I prefer an uncomplicated wardrobe."

"I've noticed." She thought of the dozen custom-tailored suits in Mark's closet, the tuxes, the dress shirts hung in rows that cost enough per shirt to feed a family of four for a week. And his hand-painted silk ties, the Italian leather shoes… "'Uncomplicated' is nice."

Nice. It was a greatly underrated word. She could be deliriously happy with *nice* for the rest of her life.

"And maybe you could tuck a muzzle into your pocket for Detective Scary Pants," she added.

"Not a bad idea." Slowly he straightened. "I'll be brave. I've treated a lot of angry animals over the years. I've had my hand—hell, my whole arm—in places those animals didn't want it, and I've survived. Maybe I can survive Kiki Isaacs."

The name was familiar to Macy. Naturally, the Howards hadn't socialized with mere police officers, but she'd read the newspaper regularly, and she'd seen the woman's name and photograph a few times. Her vague recollection was curly hair and round face. No horns, no fangs, no six-inch claws.

"If I do survive and it's not too late, can I stop by when it's over?"

Warmth curled through her and she smiled. "I'd like that."

He stood, causing Scooter to slowly rise, too, then gestured. "Do you need help getting her upstairs?"

"No, thank you. I don't think I'm going to let go of her tonight." Though she had to shift Clary to take his hand since getting out of the deep cushion without help wasn't likely. He opened the kitchen door, then closed and locked it behind them and switched off the lights she pointed out as they made their way to the front door.

There he brushed Clary's hair gently back from her face. "She's beautiful. Though how could she not be, with you for a mother? You sure you don't need help?"

"Sure."

He fastened the leash to Scooter's collar, then bent to kiss her. It wasn't the kind of kiss they'd shared last night that had made her remember things in her very cells that she'd never felt before, not with Clary's limp body between them, but maybe an even better kind of kiss.

A normal one. A routine one that was quickly becoming one of the best parts of her life.

"Good night," he murmured, then opened the door and followed the newly energetic Scooter out.

"G'night," Clary murmured unexpectedly before snuggling deeper against Macy.

Macy locked up and armed the alarm, balanced her daughter precariously while snagging the strap of the pink-and-purple backpack Anne had left hanging on the newel post, then headed up the stairs. She intended to have a good night. Her baby in her arms, Brent and Anne out back and sweet dreams of Stephen.

When she reached the landing, she ignored Clary's room to the left and carried her into the master bedroom, laying her gently on the bed. She'd still been sleeping in a crib when she'd left a year and a half ago, a situation that certainly wouldn't please her now. Only babies slept in cribs, and she was no baby. She was a big girl.

The backpack that carried her clothes was as big as she was, Macy noticed with a smile as she dumped it on the bed. Anne had covered every possibility: shorts, T-shirts, jeans, skirts, a dress and appropriate shoes, plus pajamas, swimsuits and hats. Macy stacked the clothes on a nearby chair, stripped her daughter and easily maneuvered her limp body into a pink nightgown with a picture of a smiling cat on the front.

After settling her baby, smelling distinctly of sweat and dog, on Mark's side of the bed, she propped pillows along the edge as a barrier, tucked the covers around her, then carried her dirty clothes into the dressing room. They went into the laundry hamper along with Macy's own clothes, and she changed into her own pajamas.

Pleasantly tired, face washed, teeth brushed, Macy returned to the bedroom and stopped so suddenly she stubbed her toe. She hadn't heard anything out of place, didn't see anything, but the hairs on her nape were rising as goose bumps popped up along her arms. She held her breath and listened but heard nothing. She breathed deeply to fill her starving lungs, and the difference registered so quickly that she choked on the air.

Mark's cologne was drifting faintly on the air.

It was nothing unusual, she told herself. He'd lived in this room with that cologne for six years. It had probably permeated into the very structure of his dressing room, where he'd sprayed it at least twice a day. Tiny particles had drifted onto the carpet, absorbed into the walls and the furniture. And, look, the curtains were swaying slightly. The central air had come on, and the outrush of air was spreading the scent.

Shoulders relaxing, she crossed the room to the door. She might have an open-door policy during the day, but at night she wanted the security of closed doors, especially with Clary here. She didn't want her little girl wandering around a strange house at night.

Her gaze skimmed across the box just outside the door that held bits of trash: crumpled paper, packing tape that had stuck to itself, other detritus. The box she'd thrown Mark's cologne into just that morning.

There was no sign of it. She rifled through the contents, thinking the heavy glass must have sunk to the bottom, but no, it wasn't there.

Arms hugged to her middle, Macy backed into the bedroom. Maybe Stephen, Brent or Anne had seen it there and thought it was in the trash by mistake. Maybe one of them had set it aside to ask her about and had forgotten. Maybe...

She closed the door, locked it, then dragged a heavy chair in front of it. Hands clenched to keep them from trembling too much, she went to Mark's dressing room, slowly turned the knob, even more slowly turned on the light and stepped inside.

The elegant black bottle sat on the dressing table.

Oh, God.

Chapter 8

Saturday was the longest day of Stephen's life, or so it seemed. Time, thankfully, had taken the edges off some of the other longest days. Everything seemed easier in retrospect.

But he wasn't interested in retrospect. He just wanted this evening—at least, this part of it—to be over so he could say good-night to Kiki, go home, change clothes and see Macy. Kiki wouldn't even mind if she knew what was going through his head. So far, she'd spent the entire time doing some sort of weird stalking dance around Ty Gadney, one of her fellow detectives. From what Stephen could tell, she and Gadney had dated for a while, breaking up, getting back together and breaking up again. Apparently, the last breakup had been final, at least in Gadney's mind. Not so in Kiki's.

Stephen was pretty sure her mind was a very strange place.

They'd been at the party thirty minutes without so much as a glimpse of Marnie and her date. Had his sister lied about coming to the party to get him to bring Kiki? Had she been stood up, or had there never been a date in the first place? And who in Copper Lake could Marnie possibly consider—

"There's your sister." Kiki gestured with her wineglass, nearly sloshing the liquid over the rim, and gave a high wave with her free scarlet-tipped fingers. "Robinson! Over here!"

Stephen turned to see Marnie just inside the double doors. He blinked, did a double-take. She wore a dress. When had he last seen her in a dress? High school graduation? Bigger surprise: it was red. She was about as color-friendly as he was. If his closet was white, khaki and black, hers was brown, black and gray. Even bigger surprise: her shoes weren't the score-one-for-comfort-zero-for-style clunkers he'd thought was all she owned but sandals. They were high heels. With thin straps. And also red.

And the biggest surprise of all: he recognized the man holding her hand. The great-grandson or -nephew of the elderly sisters who lived down the road from him. The long-haul trucker. How the hell had they even met? Marnie knew only police officers, lawyers and the occasional medical personnel who got involved in cases. Outside of that bunch, she didn't know anyone alive and breathing besides Stephen.

"You clean up well, Robinson," Kiki said when Marnie and her date joined them. She thrust out her hand to the man. "I'm Katherine Isaacs."

"John Gutierrez." He shook hands with her, then

turned to Stephen. "I've seen you down the road. My aunts talk about you a lot."

Stephen was still having trouble comprehending that Marnie was dating a truck driver. He really wasn't a snob. She'd just *never* shown any interest in a man who didn't have a string of letters after his name.

Marnie narrowed her gaze at him, and Kiki slapped him on the arm. "Jeez, say hello to the guy, Noble."

Great. Kiki, queen of the bold, brash and insensitive, had to correct his behavior. That was just wrong.

"Sorry. I'm Stephen." He shook hands then shoved both of his in his pants pockets. "I like that color, Marnie."

Her gaze flickered to the trucker. "John suggested it. It's…" She ran her fingers over a bit of fabric. "Red."

Stephen grinned. He knew what she'd wanted to say: around 640 nanometers. She had always preferred to identify colors by their wavelength or spectrum. "It looks good on you."

She glanced down at herself. "Yes, it does."

"Hey, Noble, I'll be back." Kiki moved into the crowd with no stealth or, as far as that went, grace. She'd spotted Ty Gadney alone for a moment, and he was in her sights.

"Does she call everyone by their last name?" John asked.

"Only those not in her social circle." Marnie immediately lost interest in her friend-of-a-friend. "I understand you're spending time with Mark Howard's widow."

Stephen blinked. "And how did you hear that?"

"Never discount the effectiveness of gossip."

"I work with real live people and I haven't heard any gossip."

Marnie shrugged. "The people you work with like you. They're not going to gossip where you can hear."

With little-brother sympathy, he wondered if the people she worked with didn't like her. More likely, they didn't know what to make of her.

"Mark Howard." John frowned. "Isn't he the guy—"

"I'd like a drink, John. Bottled water."

Marnie never meant to be rude. She just saw no point in continuing with a conversation that had lost interest for her. Apparently, John knew her well enough to understand that because he grinned as if the interruption didn't faze him. "With the cap still sealed. You want anything, Stephen?"

"No, thanks."

They both watched until John disappeared into the crowd, then Stephen turned his gaze on Marnie and waited until she looked at him. He could ask what John had been about to say but figured he already knew: *Isn't he the guy who shot himself at the fancy plantation house?* And though there were details Stephen didn't know, he'd resisted Google and asking Marnie so far. He could wait for Macy to tell him herself.

"So…how long have you been seeing this guy?"

Marnie's cheeks turned pink. "I assume by 'seeing,' you mean dating. This is actually our first date, though he spends most of his nights in town at my house."

It was an evening for surprised blinks. He would probably need eyedrops before it was over. "He's a truck driver."

She didn't take that the wrong way. He'd known she wouldn't. "With degrees from Yale, Stanford and Princeton."

"Wow. And most guys just take the commercial truck driver's course."

"He wasn't happy with the confining nature of his life. He likes being on the road."

"And he likes you."

Her smile was faint and stilted. Thirty-seven years of practice had never succeeded at making it look natural. "What's not to like? I'm intelligent and conversant on numerous subjects. I hold an interesting position in the lab. And I look good in red."

"You do." He gazed across the room and spotted Kiki cozy in a corner with Ty. "It's not fair, you know. You're here with someone you like and he likes you back, and I've got Detective Scary Pants."

Macy's nickname for Kiki actually made Marnie laugh. "I dare you to call her that when she's within striking range. She considers Kiki a bad enough burden to bear."

"I don't accept life-threatening dares." Stephen nodded to a couple of Calloways and their wives who said hello on their way by, saw his boss, Yancy, across the room and Zia with one of her brothers and Sophy March—and strolling through open doors onto the veranda. "I have been spending a lot of time with Macy Howard," he said without thinking.

"How is she?"

"She's a little uneasy being back here."

"Who wouldn't be?"

An interesting comment from a woman who dealt with death and violence on a regular basis, one who found it difficult to relate to people on an emotional level. Again he resisted asking her to spill everything she knew about Macy and Mark.

"Gossip says she's donating Fair Winds to be a museum and leaving town. Where is she going?"

That confirmed the identity of at least one of the gossips, not that he'd needed confirmation. If there was a story to be told, it was a sure bet Louise Wetherby would be telling it. Even if it wasn't true. Maybe especially if it wasn't true. "She hasn't decided yet. And that applies to donating the home, too."

"I feel sorry for her," Marnie said, though the matching emotion was absent from her voice. "It wasn't her fault her husband was the way he was, but people still included her in the talk. 'She must have known, she must have suspected.'" She scoffed. "As if living with someone means you know what's going on in his head."

Stephen's jaw clenched. It was getting harder not to ask. Hell, River's Edge was filled with cops, lawyers and city officials. Probably every single person in the room knew way more about Macy's life than he did.

But he was the only one who'd kissed her. Who knew how she tasted. How she felt. He was sure of that in his soul.

John returned with two bottles of water, one wrapped in a paper napkin for Marnie. He was good-looking, about forty, with glints of silver in his brown hair. He wore his suit better than Stephen did, and the calluses on his hands, as well. A long-haul trucker with degrees from three of the top universities in the country and obvious affection for Marnie. Stephen didn't need to know anything else to like the man.

"Are you gone most of the time?" Stephen asked. "I was just thinking the other day that I hardly ever see you."

"I'm here three or four days each month, but I spend most of that time with Marnie."

"I had no clue."

"We aren't exactly hiding it. We have limited time. We prefer not to share it with anyone else."

Marnie spoke up. "Just as you would rather be spending your evening alone with Macy than here with all these people." She gestured around, then her faint smile returned. "Here comes Detective Scary Pants." She finished with a soft snort of amusement.

Kiki was on her way back, making a beeline for him, and she didn't look happy. He looked behind him. Ten feet to the hallway, another ten to the front door. He could claim an emergency call from the clinic.

Nah, she probably had her service revolver in her purse and would suggest putting the poor critter out of its misery.

"Come on, Noble, we're outta here." Ignoring Marnie and John, she dozed her way to the door, where she shot him a look that could kill over her shoulder.

"You're getting lucky, man," John said.

Stephen stared at him, both dismayed and turned off by the mere idea.

"She's getting you out of here early," John explained. "Another guy's got her panties in a wad, and she's not going to be asking you to help her out of them. You get to go home without her."

"Noble!"

Stephen glanced at her, arms crossed, gaze narrowed, then at John—three prestigious university degrees? *Panties in a wad?*—then touched Marnie's shoulder. "See you. Nice to meet you, John."

By the time he caught up with Kiki, she was striding

through the wrought-iron gate onto the sidewalk. He'd parked two blocks to the north after dropping her off at the entrance so she wouldn't have to walk that far in her killer heels. Now she waited as if she expected him to pick her up.

"I'll get the car," he said, pausing beside her.

To his surprise, she turned. "I'll walk with you."

They'd covered a block in silence before he hesitantly asked, "What's up with you and Ty?"

"Ty's an idiot. He thinks we need a break."

"I'm sorry."

She scowled at him. "*You're* an idiot if you think he's getting it. Like I told him, it was a mutual decision to start dating. It has to be a mutual decision to stop. I don't acknowledge his breakup."

"I didn't know you could refuse to acknowledge a breakup."

"Of course you can." Though she didn't add an insult, her tone made clear there was another *idiot* implied. "There are two people in every relationship. Each one has equal say in what happens. You can't start a relationship with someone who doesn't want to be in it, and you can't walk away from someone who doesn't want to end it."

Stephen grimaced, grateful she wasn't looking at him. He was pretty sure she didn't tolerate people who grimaced at her logic. "Substitute 'marriage' for 'relationship,' and you're talking about divorce. And I'm pretty sure 'breakup' is the relationship equivalent of divorce."

She stopped beside his car and gave him a scornful look from head to toe. "No wonder you're single. Let me explain it in terms you can understand. Ty has commitment issues. We date. We have sex. We get intimate.

He backs off, breaks up, wants to play the field. He gets over his fears, we get back together, we repeat. It's our routine. But this time I'm going to get a different outcome. We're going to deal with his issues, and I'm going to get a commitment."

When she waited pointedly for a response, he said, "Oh." It was the best he could manage.

But thirty minutes later, sitting at the island in Macy's kitchen, he said what he really thought. "If Ty has any sense, the only commitment she'll get is an involuntary one into a high-security loony bin for stalking him. She's not only scary, she's nuts."

The spoon Macy was holding clattered to the floor, and she ducked to pick it up. It clattered again when she dropped it into the sink. When she turned, her smile was wan, her eyes shadowed. "From what I've heard, Ty Gadney is a smart man and a good detective. It probably *is* their routine to break up, get back together, break up again. My college roommate and her boyfriend were like that. We actually kept a chart on the refrigerator door. It had a green magnet for On and a red one for Off. I swear, sometimes it was the only way *she* could keep track. They got married after graduation."

"And let me guess—they lived happily ever after?"

"Nope. Divorced at least three times in six years. They can't live together, can't live apart. I'm glad I'm not her."

He slid off the stool and circled the island to slide his arms around her. "So am I, because I don't believe in messing with a married woman, but I sure do like messing with you." After brushing his mouth across hers, he quietly added, "I missed you."

She didn't say anything, but the squeeze of her fingers on his arms was comment enough.

Commitment. High-security loony bin. Nuts.

The words had made it almost impossible for Macy to breathe. Her first commitment had been voluntary and, for all its apparent openness, the hospital had definitely been high-security. It was the place where wealthy people went to rehab, recuperate and regain their sanity.

But she had not been nuts.

"You're tense. Have a bad day?" His hands kneaded slowly along her spine, making her groan when they reached her shoulders.

"The day wasn't so bad. I had trouble sleeping last night." She'd tried to read, to sing herself to sleep with Clary's favorite tunes. She'd paced the bedroom until her legs ached. She'd even moved the chair from the door, lifted Clary into her arms and searched the entire house for anything out of place. She'd wound up both physically and emotionally exhausted and had found nothing. Just that damn cologne bottle.

She was not nuts.

"Have you tried a sleeping pill?" Stephen asked, still rubbing knots from stiff muscles.

"I've taken them before. After Mark died. They knocked me out. I couldn't wake up for a few hours, and when I did wake, I was groggy and tired. I also found out I was getting out of bed in the middle of the night and doing things—making coffee, calling people, carrying on entire conversations, even falling—and I couldn't remember any of it. I couldn't take care of Clary like that." Not that she'd been taking care of Clary at the time.

"Clary could spend the night in the guesthouse."

Adamantly she shook her head.

"I could spend the night here and make sure nothing happened."

The offer sent sudden heat through her that eased her muscles even more. She raised her head and smiled at him. "Why would I want to be unconscious if you were spending the night?"

For a long time he looked at her with such intensity, such need. She recognized it because it was in her, too, sharp and edgy and restless. She hadn't felt such complicated need in so long. For months all she'd worried about was gaining and maintaining control over the depression and anxiety that had crippled her, about being home again, being normal again, being a mom again. She hadn't given much thought to being a woman again.

Timing was everything, and her family's was exquisite. Just as he started to lean toward her, just as she stretched onto her toes to reach him, the back door flew open to the accompaniment of giggles.

"We're not looking," Clary and Anne chanted as they came into the room, though of course they were peeking through the spaces between the fingers covering their eyes.

"We just came for ice cream stuff," Clary said, pretending to stumble around blindly before crashing into their legs. "Hey, Mama. Hey, Dr. Stephen."

"Don't mind us," Anne instructed. "We're just borrowing scoops and hot fudge sauce and...did I forget something, Clary?"

"AnAnne! We can't have ice cream sundaes without ice cream!"

Smiling, Macy put a few steps between her and Stephen. "When you called, we'd just decided we needed ice cream to top off all that barbecue. Okay, ladies, you can open your eyes now." She gestured to the tray she'd been fixing when Stephen dropped the *nuts* bomb. "I've got scoops, hot fudge, caramel, whipped cream and pecans."

Both Clary and Anne danced around the kitchen, arms over their heads. "I scream, you scream, we both scream for ice cream. Yay!"

Stephen was laughing at their antics, and Macy couldn't help but do the same. She adored her daughter's silliness and her sister-in-law's ability and willingness to dance and sing along with her. Anne had been such a blessing for their entire family.

As Stephen picked up the tray, Macy took two cartons from the freezer, then they headed for the guesthouse. Clary claimed Stephen's attention, leaving Macy with Anne, who leaned close. "Do you wish we'd waited five minutes?"

"Nah. Well, maybe."

Anne's snort was soft. "If we'd been even two minutes slower, I'd be explaining to your daughter why Dr. Stephen's tongue was down Mama's throat and his hands were inside her clothes."

As they passed the pool, serene and still in the cool night, Macy sighed. "Hmm. I wish you had waited."

Impulsively Anne reached across and hugged her. "I like this one, Macy. He's so much better for you than Mark."

Macy totally agreed, but something perverse—a sense of fairness?—forced her to point out, "You didn't even know Mark."

"Hello? Serial killer? Suicide? Scandal? Months at the resort?" That was how Anne always referred to the hospital. It sounded so much better, she said, especially when telling people where her sister was. Her voice lowered even more. "The baby. That bastard cost you so much, Macy. He wasn't worth any of it."

Macy's heart twinged at the mention of the baby, but she breathed it away and said, "He was worth Clary."

Anne watched Clary skip up the steps and open the guesthouse door for Stephen, and she nodded. "He was definitely worth Clary. But the cute little nerd vet is so much better in every other way. And think of the cute little nerd kids he can give you."

Cute little nerd. Not at all the way Macy would describe Stephen. Oh, he was certainly cute, if "cute" also meant "gorgeous." Little, nah. He was tall enough and broad enough of shoulder to make any woman feel secure. Nerd? Well, maybe. Those glasses, the perennially uncombed hair and the limited wardrobe did tend to push him toward that classification.

But he was so much more. Sweet. Sincere. Real. There were no horrifying secrets hiding in *his* past.

Inside Brent scooped ice cream into dishes while Anne set up a topping bar. Declining the extra calories, Macy made herself comfortable on one of the couches, kicking off her shoes and tucking her feet beneath her. Clary had climbed onto a chair dragged to the counter and was giving Stephen directions for the perfect hot fudge sundae *covered* with whipped cream.

For only the second time all day, Macy was relaxed. She could breathe without struggle. The common denominator: Stephen. She was falling hard for him, and it wasn't fair. While he might not have any nasty secrets in his past, she had plenty in hers. He was fine with having a fling with the needy widow down the street, but didn't he deserve to know before he had one with a serial killer's widow? A woman who'd spent months in a loony bin? A woman who'd been so mentally fragile over her husband's crimes and the loss of her baby that she couldn't even deal with her baby who still lived?

Didn't he have a right to decide whether to commit, even for one night, to a woman who might not be sane?

So much for relaxation and struggle-free breathing.

Stephen settled on the sofa next to her and placed Clary's bowl on the coffee table. When he leaned back, he offered Macy his bowl. "Sure I can't tempt you?"

She glanced at the chocolate chip ice cream nearly covered by caramel sauce and pecans and shook her head. "Not with that, you can't." In the past few minutes, her stomach had knotted enough that nothing more substantial than water could possibly get through.

Kiki Isaacs came up in the conversation, with Brent agreeing that she was stalker-crazy. Anne delicately licked a dollop of hot fudge from her spoon, then gestured with it. "Of course you can refuse to accept a breakup. It happens all the time. People fight, one of them says it's over, the other one goes on with life as usual and before long it's all forgotten. If this man keeps getting back together with her after he breaks up with her, what is she supposed to think? You know, it's like the boy who cried wolf. Sooner or later, she stops believing he means what he says."

"The boy who cried wolf was fibbing, and then there was a real wolf," Clary announced. "That's why I don't fib. I don't like wolves."

Macy brushed her hand across Clary's baby-soft hair.

"Maybe the guy's afraid of her," Brent said. "She's nuts, and she carries a gun."

"So does he," Anne pointed out.

"Yeah, but being sane, he doesn't want to use it against his wacko girlfriend."

Macy's nerves tightened before she realized that thought of her was nowhere in Brent's mind. He wasn't censoring himself or stumbling around trying to avoid words like *nuts* and *wacko* because he didn't think of her that way. Affection flooded through her, then immediately dissipated. How quickly would his opinion change if he knew about the incidents this past week?

"Maybe she does come on a little strong," Anne conceded, then she smiled a slow, warm, teasing smile. "Just for the record, sweetheart, I don't accept breakups, either. When I said till death do us part, I meant it."

"So did I." Brent leaned over to kiss her, making Clary drop her spoon and clamp her hands over her eyes.

Mark apparently had meant his vows to last until death, as well. Heavens, so had Macy. She wondered if he'd ever imagined that would be only seven years. Had he known he would stop taking other people's lives by taking his own? Had he worried how it would affect her? Had he cared?

The doctors had said he'd been capable of normal emotions. That he could have loved her and Clary as much as he'd claimed and still have the compulsion to kill. They hadn't been able to say with as much certainty what had driven him to kill. Surely there was more to it than *a memorable way to spend visits with Grandfather.* There must have been something wrong in his brain, some damaged area that made murder acceptable for more reasons than the fact that his grandfather had done it.

When the leftover ice cream had melted in their bowls and Clary was running in hyper circles around the room,

Macy and Stephen said good-night, and he gave Clary a piggyback ride to the house.

"Let's go see Scooter," she suggested as she ducked her head to get through the door.

"It's too late. Scooter's in bed asleep. That's where you're going to be in fifteen minutes." Macy's estimate was hopeful. Sometimes bath and bedtime ran closer to an hour, and she really didn't want this to be one of those times.

"I'm not tired, Mama. Dr. Stephen, let's watch TV. Do you like cartoons?"

"I do, but not at bedtime." He grasped her by the waist and swung her to the floor.

Propping both hands on her hips, she scowled at him. "Quit saying it's bedtime. I'm not sleepy!"

"Do dogs ever get this cranky when you try to send them to bed?" Macy whispered as she passed him.

"Are you kidding? They happily sleep twenty hours a day if you let them."

Twenty hours of sleep sounded good to her at the moment. Maybe tonight would be more restful than the past few. "Tell Dr. Stephen good-night, then we have to get you into the bath."

Clary's eyes filled with tears, and her lower lip trembled. "I don't wanna! I want to watch cartoons and play with Scooter! I don't want a stupid bath and I don't wanna go to stupid—"

"Clara." Macy didn't know if it was the look on her face, her tone or the use of her daughter's given name, but that one word, said exactly like that, was usually enough to make Clary go silent. "Tell Dr. Stephen good-night."

She scowled up at him again and automatically repeated, "Good night, Dr. Stephen."

"Good night, Clary."

"And tell Scooter good-night since I didn't get to see him *at all* today."

Stephen hid a smile. "I will."

She started down the hall toward the stairs. "I didn't get to watch cartoons, either, or go swimming or do anything fun at all, and now I have to go to bed when I'm not even tired."

"Go in my bathroom and brush your teeth," Macy called after her. "I'll be there in just a minute."

For a little girl, Clary made a remarkable amount of noise on the carpeted stairs. When the sound faded, Macy looked at Stephen, who'd given in to his amusement. "She's a funny kid."

It was a simple comment, but it warmed her heart. She'd known a lot of people during her marriage who weren't as taken with children, neither their own nor anyone else's. None had carried it to the extreme of Miss Willa, but there'd been definite boundaries—including nannies and boarding schools—to keep kids at a distance.

"I know you've had a long day, but..."

When she trailed off, he grinned. "I'm not tired, and I don't want to watch cartoons or play with Scooter."

She smiled back. "Can you hang around while I get her bathed and tucked? I'll do it as quick as I can."

"Sure. I'll be—" He glanced around. The family room sofa was still filled with boxes, and the living room was so obviously not comfortable. "Out back. By the fountain. Is that okay?"

The thought of having that privacy with him, with

the accompaniment of the bubbling and splashing of the fountain, was lovely. She'd hoped when she'd installed it that it would prove to be an intimate, romantic space to share, but Mark hadn't cared for it. Still, it was all the way across the yard. Distance and the fountain could obscure any sound Clary might make. Any sound an intruder might make.

She gazed up the stairs, and Stephen must have caught it. "On the patio. Right by the door. Okay?"

Her smile came automatically, filled with gratitude for his understanding. "I'll meet you there."

Chapter 9

Bedtime was running twenty-one minutes and counting. Yes, Stephen was timing it. Though normally patience was one of his virtues, he didn't have much of it at the moment, but not in a bad way. It was anticipation, really, rather than impatience. He wanted to see Macy. Wanted to spend more time alone with her. Wanted to touch her.

He really wanted to kiss her.

He thought back to his first kiss ever. Seventeen years old, high school graduation. He'd been what his mother called a late bloomer. Totally clueless about style and most everything else, thick black-framed glasses, more interested in books than people, all his friends high IQs and low human-interaction skills.

The girl had been home from college for the summer, partying with the local kids, and in the instant before her mouth touched his, he couldn't have cared less whether she kissed him. Ten seconds later, he'd discovered a new aspect of life, and he liked it.

Kissing Macy was like that, only a whole lot better.

Vaguely wondering if he should be worried about just how much better it was, he heard the back door click. Macy came out, wearing something fluttery and white, and seemed to float above the flagstone, ethereal, graceful. When she joined him on the sofa, he caught a couple of sweet fragrances. Baby lotion and...bubble gum?

She handed him a bottle of water, then sat down and uncapped hers. "Do you know how many times a three-year-old can repeat, 'I don't wanna go to bed'?"

"I would imagine endlessly."

"She usually goes to bed much more easily. Tonight we let her stay up past her bedtime and loaded her up with ice cream. She was overtired and overexcited."

"Everyone should get overexcited at least once a week."

The words made Macy laugh, a sweet soft sound. Stephen thought she should laugh every day, not the restrained sort just now, but an all-out, bring-tears-to-her-eyes laugh. He blamed the fact that she didn't on Mark. Dead eighteen months, and still affecting every moment of her life.

And, now, his.

"How much longer do you think it'll take to finish up here?" he asked somewhat hesitantly. How much longer could he walk down the street and see her? How many days to feel this attraction, this sense of *something?* How many days to find out whether anything could come from it?

She was hesitant, as well. "I don't know. Maybe a week. Once I've sorted through everything, the lawyer can take care of the pickups by the antiques dealers. I'll put the stuff I'm keeping in storage, plus the family stuff for Clary, and then she and I will…"

Will leave. Will move on. Will start over. Without you. Stephen gave her a sidelong look. "You and Clary will…?"

She breathed deeply. "Find a place to live."

"And you've definitely ruled out Copper Lake." He tried not to sound disappointed. She'd told him from the start that she wasn't staying here. Hell, there was no guarantee that *he* would stay here.

Though when he imagined his perfect life, the practice looked a lot like Dr. Yates's, the town looked a lot like Copper Lake and the people in the background looked a lot like his friends here.

This time her breath was more a sigh. "There are bad memories."

Setting his water on the sofa arm, he took her hand, her skin warm and dry against the cool dampness of his. "So replace them with good memories."

"Like it's that simple?"

He stroked his thumb over her palm. "I've never had any really bad memories. Yeah, it was upsetting when Mom and Dad divorced, and the first couple of moves threw things out of balance for a while. By the time Sloan and I realized we were headed for divorce, we were already out of love, so the disappointment that our marriage had failed was overshadowed by the fact that we were glad it was over. So I'm not one to give advice."

"But you're going to do it anyway." Her tone was level, even mildly amused.

"As I understand it, you don't dislike the town. You were happy here right up until the end. You had friends.

You were involved in activities. Your brother visited, and you saw your parents regularly. You were pretty content with your life." He paused for her to respond, and she nodded. "It's not the town, Macy. It's this house. Fair Winds. The Howard family legacy. So you move out of this house. You sell it, you tear it down and you find another one, one that's perfect for you and Clary. You sell or donate Fair Winds.

"As for the legacy, you and Clary are the only Howards left around here. You don't have to be concerned about it anymore. You don't have to be a part of it. You can even get rid of the name for both of you."

She tilted her head to one side, studying him. "You think calling ourselves Macy and Clary Ireland would make people forget that we used to be Macy and Clary Howard?"

Macy Ireland. It did have a much sweeter sound to it.

"Eventually. Sooner rather than later if you marry again, make a new family." Macy Noble…that sounded even better. Not that he was actually thinking about marriage. He just liked to consider all the possibilities. What was the point of a serious relationship if there wasn't at least a chance it would last? That she would stick around long enough for them to decide what was between them?

Though he was already past that point. He didn't even know how it had happened, how someone he'd met less than a week ago had become so much a part of his life. But she had. It would be a loss if she left before giving them a chance.

"Marry again." The words didn't even qualify as a whisper. "I'd have to love someone, like him, *trust* him an awful lot to consider getting married. I don't know if I have that kind of trust to give."

"You trust your brother. Your sister-in-law. To some extent you trust me or you wouldn't let me near Clary." He willed her to look at him, and she did, and he willed her to acknowledge that, yes, she did trust him. Hadn't she turned to him for help a couple of times? Hadn't she chosen him to accompany her to Fair Winds? Hadn't she let him kiss her in the night by the pool?

Or had he merely been the only guy handy for all those things?

But her expression gave away nothing on her version of trust versus his.

Defeat like a cold brush over his shoulders, he said, "You'll get married again. You're too young, beautiful, perfectly suited to motherhood, to stay single the rest of your life. You'll trust someone, you'll get married and you'll have more babies—"

"I lost my daughter after Mark died."

Puzzled, Stephen glanced to the faintly illuminated window upstairs that showed where Clary slept. "You lost custody—"

She shook her head, her face as pale as her dress. If her hair had been blond, she could have easily passed for something from the other side, a heartbroken angel or a weary spirit. And like a runaway train that suddenly crashed to a halt, his heart stopped beating, his lungs stopped pumping air, as he realized what she was saying. "You were pregnant...."

She nodded.

"Oh, Macy." He released her hand and wrapped his arms around her, drawing her close. "God, I'm sorry. I had no idea...."

For a time she remained stiff, but then she relaxed, sinking against him, warm and delicate and trembling.

He wished he'd dropped the subject before marriage had come into it, but since he hadn't, he wished he knew what to say to ease her loss. A baby, another Clary but younger, tinier, needier... As if anything could ease that.

"I lost the baby two weeks after Mark died. My doctor thought it was because of the stress." Her small hand reached out, curled itself into the fabric of his T-shirt. "I was pretty logical growing up. I always believed that when it was your time to die, you would die, no matter what precautions you took, no matter what heroic measures were taken to save you. When horrible things happened, I thought God had a plan. When people died too young, I believed God wanted them back in heaven."

Glancing up, her face only a few inches from him, her eyes damp with tears, she said, "It's damn hard to apply logic to your own baby's death. I blamed Mark with a hatred that surprised even me. I do have friends here—not many, but good ones. That's one reason why I stay so close to home. I don't want to see them. They know everything, and there's just this...pity."

"Sympathy," he corrected her. "There's a big difference." Though hadn't Marnie said just tonight that she felt sorry for Macy? Did the difference really matter?

"Maybe." She rested her head on his shoulder and felt so right. "You were right, though. I don't hate Copper Lake. I hate Mark. I hate what he did. I hate how he destroyed so many lives."

Hers, her daughter's, her unborn child's, his mother's, his grandmother's. The selfish bastard. Gently Stephen stroked her hair from her face. "Your life isn't destroyed, Macy. Clary's isn't. You've got to deal with the memories, but she's a happy, funny, smart, cheerful, ever-hopeful little girl who's going to have a wonderful life.

You'll make sure of that. You need to make sure of it for yourself, too. Don't let Mark win by running away from your family and all the people who care about you."

She looked up again, and in the dim light he could barely make out the emotions on her face. Curiosity. Doubt. Need. "Does that include you?"

For an instant he felt like the inexperienced kid comfortable only with other nerds, who'd known he and girls weren't a good match. He'd gained some confidence since then, but not enough to keep his voice from going all froggy on him. "Yeah, it does."

"There's so much you don't know about me."

"There's plenty of time to learn if you don't leave town." Maybe even if she did.

"And what if you don't like what you learn?"

"Let's see…are you computer-phobic?" He waited for her to shake her head. "Are you kind to small animals and elderly people?"

"Of course."

"Do you like chocolate?"

A nod.

"French fries or onion rings?"

"Fries."

"Coffee?"

"Every morning."

"Do you run for fun?"

She laughed. "Dear heavens, no."

"Do you mind the smell of doggy breath in the morning?"

"Not as long as it's coming from a dog."

"Okay, that covers all the big stuff."

She stared at him, her smile slowly fading. "You like things simple, don't you?"

"Life *is* simple. You find a job you like and a person you love, you do good when you can, you work hard and play hard, you take care of those you bring into the world and you always remember to be kind to others." He bent close to her. "No matter what Mark taught you, it doesn't have to be any harder than that. Trust me."

And then he kissed her, wondering if his *trust me* had sounded normal enough or if she'd heard the faint plea underlying it.

When Macy awakened Sunday morning, before she even opened her eyes, a familiar feeling settled in her chest, right above her cleavage. It was insubstantial, fluttering, the way she imagined a butterfly's delicate wings might beat.

It was nothing, but it made her lungs constrict, and perspiration popped out across her forehead. Eyes still closed, she groped across the bed until she found Clary and scooted close to her daughter, nuzzling her soft brown hair, letting the scents of baby shampoo and bubble gum bath gel filter through the buzzing in her brain.

She was *not* having a panic attack. She was taking her medication regularly, and she'd been staying physically active, not just since she got here but since before her release from the hospital. Exercise was a great help in keeping the flutters and trembles and buzzes at bay. One day soon, her doctor said, she could probably come off the medication completely.

But not today.

A small hand touched her face, then fingers pried her eye open. "I know you're awake, Mama. I see your eyes movin' in there."

Macy opened both eyes to find her baby grinning at

her, wide-awake and as cheery this morning as she'd been cranky the night before. "Good morning."

"Mornin.' What're we gonna do today? I wanna see Scooter."

"I think we can arrange that."

"I *don't* wanna do any more packing. It's *bor*-ing."

"Well, maybe AnAnne can do something else with you while Uncle Brent and I pack."

Then came a hint of last night's crankiness. "I don't wanna do it with AnAnne. I wanna do it with you."

Macy's heart tugged as she squeezed Clary closer. Her child had spent so much of her time in someone else's care, and she'd been far too young to understand why. Her visits to the hospital, first with Brent and their parents, later with Anne, too, had been infrequent. The place had scared her, and she'd always cried when she had to leave without Macy.

"All right, sweetie. We'll find something fun to do." Brent and Anne, bless their hearts, wouldn't mind working while she took Clary to the park or out for a treat.

Or maybe walked down to Stephen's house for playtime with Scooter.

When this was all taken care of and she and Clary had settled—well, wherever—she was sending her brother and sister-in-law on the best honeymoon ever as thanks.

The sweat had gone away and the fluttering stopped, though the knot in her gut was slower to unwind. Not a panic attack. Not even a precursor to one, even if it was identical to all the other precursors she'd ever suffered.

Throwing back the covers, she gathered clothing for both of them and headed for the bathroom. "Come on, sweetie, up, up. Time's a-wasting."

Clary giggled as she rolled across the mattress, then slid to her feet. "That's what Grandpa always says."

"Well, Grandpa's always right." He was a role model for his children and grandchild.

Mark's grandfather had been a role model, too, damn him.

They brushed their teeth and dressed, Macy in denim shorts and a purple tank top, Clary in a watermelon-print sundress with green-and-red polka-dotted flip-flops. With a white sunhat, she looked adorable. She skipped downstairs ahead of Macy and turned toward the kitchen.

The aromas of coffee and bacon drifted down the hall. Brent and Anne were early risers and, always thought-ful, Anne had fixed breakfast for them. They sat at the kitchen table, interrupting their talk to greet Clary.

"Guess what?" Clary helped herself to a piece of bacon from Anne's plate. "Me and Mama are gonna do something special this morning. Aren't we, Mama?"

Nothing like easing into a subject. Macy poured her-self a cup of coffee before facing them. "If it's okay with you guys. She's bored with packing."

"So are you, I bet," Brent said.

Macy responded with the raise of her brows.

"Go ahead," Anne added. "We'll work in the library. All the books are going to the local library, right?" She made a shooing gesture. "Go on, take your coffee and get out of this house."

"Thanks, guys." Macy hugged each of them, then went to the island. She slung her purse strap over her shoulder, then hesitated. Her keys were supposed to be right there next to her bag. Maybe she'd left them inside...but why would she have put them inside after letting them into the house last night after dinner? "Have you guys seen my keys?"

Brent cut into the over-easy egg on his plate. "You had them in your hand when we came in the door."

She glanced at Anne, who shook her head. "I was helping Clary carry the ice cream. I didn't pay attention. Maybe you put them in the freezer?"

Macy checked. No keys. She rummaged through the papers on the island. Nothing. Brent and Anne left the table to help her look, and even Clary helped, though the first time she looked in a box and saw books, she lost interest.

"Here they are," Anne called from down the hall.

Macy followed her voice into the living room, where her sister-in-law dangled the keys from her finger. "Where were they?"

Anne looked at Brent, then shrugged. "On the fireplace mantel."

Under their wedding portrait. Macy chilled. Not once in the six years she'd lived there had she ever left her keys on the mantel. And not once last night after dinner had she set foot in the living room. She *knew* it.

"Th-thanks." She took the keys from Anne, avoided making eye contact with either her or Brent and called for Clary. "Let's go, pretty baby."

"Have fun," Brent said with a noticeable lack of enthusiasm.

As she buckled Clary into her car seat, she considered how the keys had wound up on the mantel. 1) Brent had put them there. 2) Anne had. 3) Stephen had. 4) A ghost had. Or 5) she'd had another episode and done it herself. The only thing she could say beyond a doubt was that Clary hadn't done it because she couldn't reach the mantel, and there wasn't a single piece of furniture in the room the girl could have moved by herself.

But why would Brent or Anne or Stephen move her keys? The idea was ludicrous. When had any of them had the chance? Brent and Anne had come in from dinner and gone straight to the guesthouse. When Stephen arrived, he'd been in the kitchen with Macy before they'd gone to the guesthouse. When he left, she'd walked him to the door, where he'd given her a couple of toe-curling good-night kisses. He'd never had the chance to go into the living…

Except the twenty minutes or so he was alone on the patio while she bathed Clary and put her to bed.

She shifted the van into Reverse and automatically checked the back-up camera but didn't move her foot from the brake. What reason could Stephen possibly have for moving her keys? And why last night, when he was the only one whose time in the house was unaccounted for? If he'd wanted to play mind games with her, he'd had plenty of other opportunities.

But if it hadn't been him, that left her. Why would she misplace her own keys? Because this whole trip to Copper Lake had her a little unhinged. Because she'd imagined an intruder in the guesthouse and misplaced the Fair Winds contract and the cologne bottle. Because she had a history of mental illness related to Mark and his passing. Because she was one of those people all her friends and acquaintances said things like *Poor thing* and *Bless her heart* about.

Because that fluttering and sweating and shaking this morning *had* been the precursor of a panic attack, even if she was taking her medicine and staying active.

Because she was losing control again.

Blowing out a heavy breath, she checked the camera once more, then backed out of the driveway. Even driving slowly, it took only a minute or two to reach Stephen's house, where she parked on the side of the road next to the gate.

"Is this were Dr. Stephen lives?"

She checked her smile in the rearview—steady enough for a little girl—then faced her. "Yep."

Clary unbuckled her harness in the time it took Macy to unhook her seatbelt and open the door. Clary scrambled over the console and the driver's seat, then jumped to the ground, raising little puffs of dust in the soft dirt. They'd reached Stephen's door and Clary had banged on the wooden frame of the screen before Macy had time to second-guess coming here. He might be writing. Sunday could be his day to sleep in until noon, or he could be getting ready for church or have plans with someone else.

A welcoming bark sounded inside, then the door opened. It was a toss-up whose greeting was more excited—Clary's or Scooter's. Though Stephen's was much quieter, just a smile that sent warmth all the way to her toes, it persuaded Macy of two things. She wasn't interrupting his morning, and he hadn't played some weird mind game with her keys last night. Granted, Mark had fooled her, but she'd learned to be cautious as a result. If Stephen knew about her inpatient care, if he'd moved the keys to screw with her, she was ten times the fool Mark had made her. Something deep inside, something primal and instinctive, said she wasn't *that* big a fool. She could trust this man.

Which meant there'd been an intruder—not likely with the alarm always armed—or a ghost or she couldn't trust herself.

"What brings you two pretty girls to our place this morning?" Stephen asked.

"We wanna do something fun," Clary replied.

He unlatched the screen door and held it open for them to enter. Scooter hesitated a moment as if he couldn't quite resist the lure of freedom, but in the end the lure of playing with Clary won out. "I can think of a lot of fun things to do," Stephen murmured as Macy followed her daughter inside. "We'd have to ditch the little one for some of them."

This time the intensity on his face ignited the heat. She resisted the urge to fan herself because common sense told her the temperature rise was all internal. With the windows open and the ceiling fan whirring, the small living room was perfectly comfortable.

"No ditching," she said just as quietly. "My baby said, 'But I wanna do something fun with *yooouu*, Mama.' I was thinking we'd start with breakfast."

"Hmm. I have protein bars and coffee. I'm not sure I want to see Little Bit on caffeine."

"It's not a pretty sight. I thought maybe the four of us could go to Ellie's, then do…something."

His laughter was genuine. "Have you forgotten what constitutes fun, Macy?"

"Back in Charleston, we'd go to the beach or to the Battery downtown or visit one of the historic sites."

"Here we go to the lake or the parks or to the square downtown or visit one of the historic sites. We have an active historical society, the botanical society's gardens are in full bloom and we even have a couple of museums. Oh, wait, I bet you worked on all of those, didn't you?"

Because he was standing so close and it had been her standard response to Brent's teasing, and because he was right, she smacked him on the shoulder. "We could just take Scooter and leave you here, you know."

"Yeah, but you wouldn't have near as much fun." He grinned and turned toward the bedroom off the living room. "Just let me change."

"Into what? Another white T-shirt?"

His only response was a childish tongue stuck out.

He was back in a couple of minutes in a clean white T-shirt and denim shorts that still bore the creases from being folded.

Clary chatted all the way to the restaurant and was thrilled to help hold Scooter's leash on the walk from the car. They were seated at a wrought-iron table and chairs, patterns mismatched, in the shade of a crape myrtle. It would be a beautiful setting when the tree was in bloom, though the dropped blossoms would make regular cleanup a necessity.

It was Ellie Maricci herself who took their order, greeting Stephen affectionately, making a big deal over Clary and Scooter and hugging Macy. "I'm glad to see you back here. It's been way too long."

A strange sensation swept through Macy, both pleasant and alien. She'd gotten dozens of hugs at Mark's funeral, but since then, physical contact was pretty much limited to her immediate family—and, now, Stephen. Like Anamaria's embrace at the park her first day back, Ellie's hug felt nice and genuine.

"Are you here to stay?"

Aware of Stephen's gaze on her, Macy shrugged. "I don't really... There's so much to do before I think about..."

At least it wasn't a flat, certain refusal. Stephen would probably find optimism in that.

"I can imagine. But it would be a shame to deprive the young boys of Copper Lake the pleasure of knowing Clary. She's going to be a heartbreaker someday." Ellie grinned and winked at Clary, who did her best to wink back, then switched from friend to server mode. "What can I get you folks today?"

Copper Lake on a pretty spring Sunday was at its best. With little to no touch-up, it could more than do justice to the cover of a glossy tourist brochure. Flowers were blooming, the square was neatly manicured, the war memorials gleamed and the river lazily flowed. Cars filled church parking lots, and delicious aromas drifted on the air as restaurants geared up for the after-church crowds. It was welcoming. Peaceful.

It was home, Stephen realized. Because of his mom's regular moves, he'd never developed a connection to the places they lived. What was the point when he knew they would be moving on before long? But this town... It had been luck that brought him here, and now he wanted to stay. He belonged.

If only Macy felt the same.

They'd done nothing special—a leisurely breakfast, play on the toys at the riverfront park, a walk around downtown showing Clary her hometown. They didn't call it that to her, of course. She regarded this visit as a vacation, a trip to a strange place to do boring stuff before returning to the only home she remembered.

How would she feel when Macy took her away from that home? She was three. She would miss her grandparents and Brent and Anne, but she would adapt. He was proof that the ability to adapt was a good thing.

As they approached the square, Clary pointed to River's Edge across the street. "Is that a church?"

"No, sweetie. It used to be a house. Now people have parties there."

"It's a big house," she said dubiously.

"Yes, it is," Macy agreed. She didn't mention that Clary owned such a house herself. It would be one more of those things she didn't understand.

Clary turned her head and sniffed the air, like a hound on a hunt. "I smell cookies."

Stephen sniffed, too. "I smell fresh-ground Topeca."

"Can we have a cookie, Mama? And some whatever he said?"

Macy gave them both reproving looks, then faced A Cuppa Joe, and her own nose delicately twitched. "Coffee." Though she'd had a cup with her when they picked up him and Scooter, plus another cup with breakfast, she practically sighed the word. "Okay," she said sternly. "One cup, one cookie. And something besides coffee for you, Clary."

They turned the corner, where a couple of tables and chairs flanked the coffee-shop door. Stephen looped Scooter's leash over an iron hook set into the wall, then held the door for his girls.

His girls. He liked the sound of that.

There was never anything simple about a coffee run in Copper Lake. Both Joe Saldana and his wife, Liz, were working, and their dogs were patients of Stephen's. They knew Macy, too, and talked warmly with her while Clary narrowed her choice of treat from the entire refrigerated case to a row of brightly decorated cookies. With Liz's help, she settled on a sugar cookie as big as her head decorated like a watermelon. As Stephen picked up the tray, Joe tossed on a couple of dog biscuits for Scooter.

"You gotta love a place that takes care of their four-footed customers," Stephen said as he maneuvered the tray onto one of the outdoor tables.

"You gotta love a place whose coffee smells this good." Macy cupped both hands to the ceramic mug—A Cuppa Joe was big into recycling, reducing and reusing—but all she'd done so far was sniff the steam rising. Could he put a similar supremely content look on her face, given the chance?

He'd like to think so, but Joe's coffee was hard to compete with.

"Did you sleep well last night?" he asked after dragging a chair to the two-person table for Clary. The kid didn't bother sitting in it but crouched next to it, feeding Scooter his cookies one half at a time—and slipping a few bites of her own in, too, if the green frosting on Scooter's beard was anything to judge by.

He looked back at Macy in time to see her shoulders stiffen slightly. If he hadn't spent much of the past six days with her, he might have missed it entirely. But her hands didn't tremble as she took a sip of Topeca's Manzano blend, then set the mug on the table, and her face didn't show any emotion beyond pure appreciation for a cup of El Salvador's best coffee.

"I did. It was nice having Clary to cuddle with." She gazed across the street as a couple of teenage boys jogged through to River Road, then met his eyes again. "But when I got up this morning, I couldn't find my keys. I leave them on the kitchen island. I always have. But we finally found them on the mantel underneath the wedding portrait."

He faked an accusing look. "Were you planning to scratch out your faces with the keys? 'Cause I've got to tell you, car keys weren't made for destroying canvas and oil. Now that your brother's here, we'll get a ladder and have that bonfire you were talking about."

Her smile was unsteady. "I don't remember putting them there."

He wasn't sure why that was so important to her, but he shrugged. "You forgot. You were preoccupied. It happens all the time. My mom once found hers in the medicine cabinet, and Dr. Yates left his once in a cat's crate. The cat and his owner were halfway to California by the time she found them."

"I'm not normally forgetful."

He curled his fingers around hers. "But this isn't a normal time for you, is it?"

"No," she agreed with another weak smile.

Stephen couldn't help but wonder why the incident troubled her more than he understood. But if there was a subtle way to ask, he couldn't think of it, so he just went with straightforward. "Tell me why it bothers you so much."

Her gaze drifted away—not an obvious shift, as if she didn't want him to see her eyes, just sort of moving off toward the square, but he would bet his first-ever book tour, if it ever materialized, hiding was exactly the reason.

"You'll think I'm crazy. The hell of it is, I might be."

His natural snort faded away. She wasn't laughing, wasn't teasing. The smile was just barely there, wobbling, and even with her head turned away, he could see the heat in her cheeks and the glistening in her eyes. He tightened his grip on her hand, not too tight, just letting her know he was there. No matter what.

A long time passed before she looked at him again. "You had a front-row seat for the intruder-in-the-guest-house show. The night we went to Fair Winds, when I got home, I couldn't find the contract I'd left in the living room. It finally turned up in Mark's office. A day or two later, I threw a bottle of his cologne into the trash, and it reappeared in his closet, where he'd always kept it. Then my keys…"

So that was all it was. Worry over incidents that probably wouldn't mean anything if they'd happened anywhere else. But to happen in the house she'd shared with her suicidal husband, while trying to deal with closing that part of her life and opening a new one…

"A couple of incidents don't make you unbalanced, Macy. Stress manifests itself in strange ways. You probably just forgot because you need to forget. That's part of what this trip is about for you." He snorted self-deprecatingly. "I'm not a people doctor, but I'm happy to diagnose and give advice."

"I'd be happy to accept your diagnosis and advice, except…" She glanced at Clary leaning against the wall, Scooter's head in her lap, and the tears glistened again. "This is a really bad time to have this conversation."

"Want to drop her off at home?" Because he really didn't want to put it off. These kinds of confidences didn't come easy, and he didn't want to give her a chance to reassess and decide she didn't trust him enough to share. He wanted her trust. He needed it.

His mother hadn't raised him and Marnie in church, but he believed in God, miracles, divine intervention. At that moment it came in the form of Anamaria Calloway and her two children, waving from across the street. "Hey Doc! Hey Doc!" Will called while his younger sister vacillated. "Scooter! Doc!"

Despite the seriousness of the conversation a few seconds ago, Stephen couldn't have stopped the smile crossing his face if he wanted to. Will and Gloriana, and their mother and father, were among his favorite people in town, and their yellow Labs, Lucky and Ducky, yes, named by the kids, were two of the biggest characters in his practice.

"Will thinks my name is Hey Doc," he said quietly to Macy as the Calloways started across the street, "and Gloriana couldn't care less what it is as long as Scooter's around." His smile broadened as they stepped onto the curb, released their mother's hands and rushed over for a hug. "Hey, guys, how are you?"

Gloriana returned his hug, then immediately turned to Scooter and Clary. "I know you. You're *her* little girl." She pointed at Macy.

"Who are you?" Clary asked.

"I'm *her* little girl." Now her finger turned to Anamaria.

Fidgeting in front of Stephen, Will claimed his attention. "Hey Doc, guess what? Mama let us skip the boring part of church. She made Daddy stay, though. Said he needed it more."

From what Stephen had heard about Robbie Calloway's life pre-Anamaria, that was probably true.

"We're not being total heathens," Anamaria said. "We're having Robbie's birthday dinner this afternoon, so we're down here to pick up the cake from Ellie's. Just the very immediate family, and I think it's going to be twenty-some people."

"Sounds like fun. Tell Robbie happy birthday."

"I will." Anamaria rested her hand on Macy's shoulder, studying her intently. People said the woman was a psychic, and Stephen figured it wasn't his place to say yes or no. There were more mysteries in the world, blah blah. After a moment, she bent to hug Macy. "We have a few minutes before the cake's ready. Can we borrow Clary and Scooter for a little play in the square?"

Psychic, intuitive or just an insightful woman— Stephen didn't care. At that moment he adored her.

Macy hesitated until the kids, including her own, started clamoring. Finally she nodded. He thought her reluctance might have as much to do with the conversation that awaited them as it did with letting Clary go off.

Linking hands, the kids headed off with Anamaria, Scooter trotting alongside with his leash in both girls' hands. Stephen watched until they were in the square proper then turned his gaze to Macy. "You can see her and make sure she's safe, and she can't overhear a thing. You believe in fate?"

"I guess I do." She shifted in the chair then folded her hands together. It took her a long time to start, but he didn't push. Skittish creatures tended to push back or flee entirely.

"I told you last night that I—I lost the baby I was carrying when Mark died."

He didn't need to be particularly insightful to know she'd said those words to very few people. They were still difficult for her. They still tore at the raw place in her heart.

"I also, in a sense, lost Clary. I was hugely depressed. I couldn't get out of bed in the morning, not even to feed or dress my daughter. I couldn't think. I couldn't feel. I didn't care if I lived or died. The only times I wasn't depressed, I was in a constant panic, almost manic in my behavior. I would get up at two in the morning and scrub the bricks in the fireplace because if I didn't keep busy, I felt like I would explode out of my skin." She gazed at her hands as if searching for telltale signs of that frantic scrubbing, grimaced, then went on.

"I couldn't sit still. I couldn't stop imagining horrible things happening to Clary, to my family. I tried to anticipate every disaster, every tiny little mistake. I couldn't bear to let her out of my sight. Then the anxiety would fade—though it never went away—and the depression would come back. I wouldn't bathe, wouldn't eat. It was too much effort to even open my eyes most of the time, but even then, there was a little voice in my head, warning me of all the ways I could lose Clary. I didn't have the ability to act on it, but it wouldn't leave me alone." Her voice trembled, her breath catching. Across the street, Clary called to her, and she looked up, smiling tightly, waving to her daughter.

"Finally, in a rare lucid moment, I asked my parents to hospitalize me, so they did. They committed me to a psychiatric hospital in Columbia."

Stephen wanted to look away, to close his eyes, to take some time to process her bleak words, but he kept his gaze on hers. The shadows in her eyes were haunted, sad enough to make him need to gather her into his arms and never let go. He settled for tightening his fingers around hers.

"You'd been through a lot, Macy. Your husband's suicide, losing your baby, Miss Willa's death, all in a month. It's no wonder your brain shut down for a while. You needed time to deal with it."

"I wanted so badly to just go back a few months, a year. To wake up and find myself back in Copper Lake, still happily married to the man I knew in college, because he was definitely not that man at the end. But instead the doctors forced me to move forward—and Clary. She was a powerful incentive. I got out of bed for her. I took medications for her. I sat through hundreds of hours of therapy for her. I knew by then that she might not need me, but I damn well needed her."

He wanted to argue the statement that Clary didn't need her. She was her mother; she adored her; of course Clary needed her. But the girl had been barely one and a half when her father died, when Macy was hospitalized. She would have adapted to being raised by her grandparents, or to being Brent and Anne's daughter.

Watching Macy stare into her coffee cup, he tried the whole scenario on in his mind. Macy, suffering such cripplingly severe depression and anxiety. On the one hand, it wasn't such a surprise. Millions of people relied on antidepressants to get through the day. He could rattle off a dozen names of family or people he worked with in a dozen seconds.

On the other hand, the profound depression and anxiety she described… He looked at her and couldn't quite imagine it. She struck him as gentle, yes. A little insecure. Maybe even a bit fragile. But he also thought she seemed strong, capable, on an even keel most of the time. Wasn't that the best any of them could claim? That they were okay most of the time?

He glanced up as a couple of his clients, dressed for church in summer-weight suits, said hello, then went inside the coffee shop, and he wondered if they, like Will Calloway, had skipped out on the boring part of the sermon. When the door swung shut behind them, he said, "I'm really sorry for everything that happened, Macy. The words don't do justice to the way I feel. I am overwhelmed and so very sorry you had to go through this, and I think the way you've come out of it is amazing. But just for the record, you're not losing it again. You're not crazy. Being back in that house, doing what you're doing, is enough to give the most analytical person in the world the creeps."

Her fingers squeezed his just slightly, and her wan smile reappeared for a moment. "Thank you for the vote of confidence, Stephen, but you've haven't heard the rest of the story."

Chapter 10

Most people had a *rest of the story*. Macy's was a *worst of the story*. What she'd said already had been hard enough. She didn't know if she had the courage to tell the worst. But the emotions on Stephen's handsome face were in her favor: sympathy, sadness, sorrow. No sign of dismay that she had been, at one time, mentally defective. No revulsion. No horror. No hint of *She was broken once; what if she breaks again?*

But that was why the rest of her story was the worst.

She sighed. It was a beautiful sunny day. Foot traffic was picking up a little, along with the cars. Church bells tolled nearby, and she imagined the big broad doors opening, kids spilling out first, followed by mothers who had pot roasts in the slow cooker or hungry folks wanting to reach the restaurants before everybody else.

She and Mark had always been slow to reach the parking lot. He'd greeted everyone he'd felt worthy, exchanging small talk, and she'd said hello to friends and acquaintances and people like Louise Wetherby. It had been part of their routine: Clary dressed like a little angel, Mark in his custom-tailored suits, Macy in dresses or skirts. No pants in church for her *ever*. They hadn't had to hurry to dinner because Mark had a standing reservation at the country club—the best table, the best server and tips well worth the inconvenience of holding the table.

She sighed again. It was a beautiful sunny day, and if she couldn't tell Stephen the worst of the story now, when could she? No one was close enough to listen. Her daughter was in Anamaria's perfectly responsible care, playing with kids her age and loving it. And Stephen was waiting patiently, not pressing her. She could say, *I can't talk about it,* and he would accept it.

She really didn't know if she *could* talk about it. Outside of therapy, she'd never tried. But there was a first time for everything.

"Mark's suicide was a huge shock to everyone. He was happy. He had a very strong sense of entitlement, of ego. He was quite convinced that he truly was one of the reasons all this existed—for his satisfaction, his pleasure." She indicated the town with a wave of her hand. "But for all that, he was a decent man. People liked him. They were happy to call him their friend. Clary and I adored him."

Stephen's expression was open, nonjudgmental, though there was a flash of something at her last sentence that looked like envy. By the time she was done with this story, he would know beyond a doubt that her one-time feelings for Mark were no threat to him.

"His cousin Reece had come to town that October. I

never got to meet her until…after. She and Mark were never close. The one summer they'd spent together, he'd tormented her regularly." Long story that Stephen could learn later, if he was interested. If he was still around. "That day, he took Miss Willa and me to lunch at the country club, then she went to a meeting with me. He was supposed to be playing golf, but instead he went out to Fair Winds, and he—he—"

A customer went into the coffee shop. Two came out. Two more passed on their way down the block. When the sidewalk was clear in every direction, she blurted it out. "He tried to kill Reece and her boyfriend."

That knocked the calm, studied look right off Stephen's face. How many people outside law enforcement ever knew a murderer? How many lived next door to one, went to church with him, played golf with him?

How many had babies with him and slept in his bed every night without even the faintest hint of a clue?

"Oh, my God, Macy." He barely breathed the words.

Her smile trembled, and her vision got blurry. Allergies, with all the newly bloomed flowers around. "You haven't heard the worst of the story yet." She checked their surroundings once again, noted Clary and Gloriana seated primly on the gazebo steps with Anamaria while Will and Scooter performed tricks in front of them.

"You see, the reason Reece and Mark were never close was because he'd tried to kill her once before when they were kids. The last time, she and Jones had dug up a bone from a grave on the front lawn at Fair Winds, and Mark had no intention of letting them call the authorities because either Mark or his grandfather had murdered the man. He couldn't be sure which, since there were more than forty graves on that front lawn. It had been their hobby, the pastime that bonded them. No one knows exactly when Arthur started killing, but Mark was fourteen. He killed one of the two boys who saved Reece from him. The other boy was Jones, now Reece's husband."

Now the horror was in Stephen's eyes. She made her fingers go slack around his so he could pull away if he wanted. She breathed out a sigh because the day was still beautiful and sunny, and she *could* talk outside of therapy about the evil she'd lived with and slept with and gotten pregnant with.

What would Stephen do now? Flee? Suddenly find excuses to avoid seeing her? Immerse himself in work and his real life and push her into a dark corner of his mind where, thank God, he didn't often have to go?

She waited, feeling oddly calm. She'd told the worst of the story, and she'd survived the telling. Her palms were sweaty. Her chest was tight. But she hadn't cried. She hadn't shattered into a million pieces. She hadn't lost control. And she felt…

Freer. Cleaner. Less tainted.

Seconds ticked past. Ten, fifteen, twenty. He was shell-shocked. Apparently, he didn't know what to say or what to do, and so he said nothing, did nothing. Somewhere after thirty seconds, he released her hand, and her gut tightened. Disappointment tasted raw and sour in her stomach, rising up her throat.

Then he stood, pulled her from the chair, wrapped his arms around her and held her tightly. His cheek rested against her hair and his soft words hovered over her ear. "You're an amazing woman, Macy."

It was the same day as thirty minutes, thirty seconds, ago, but somehow it seemed more beautiful, the sun brighter and warmer and full of healing light. For the first time since finding out she'd married a psychopathic killer, surely for the first time since she'd lost the baby she carried, she knew she was a lucky woman.

Because everything was going to be all right.

Stephen had been speechless plenty of times in his life—practically any interaction involving nongeeks when he was a teenager—but usually he recovered his ability of speech quickly enough. Beyond those five words, though, he had trouble settling his mind on any single aspect of Macy's tale.

She'd been married to a serial killer.

Spent months in a hospital to treat severe vegetative depression.

Had a daughter with and been pregnant again by a man who killed to let off steam.

A serial killer who, along with his partner, had killed more than forty victims.

And Macy and baby Clary had had no clue.

God, no wonder she didn't want to move back to Copper Lake.

No wonder being in the house freaked her out.

No wonder she had difficulty trusting.

But she'd trusted *him*. She'd trusted him enough to tell him everything. To tell him nightmares she'd never shared outside of her family and the hospital where she'd been committed.

Committed.

God, he still couldn't completely grasp it. These sorts of things just didn't happen to normal people, and those were the only kind of people he knew. Everyday normal, worked for a living, loved their families, worried about jobs and crime and keeping their kids out of trouble. *Those* were the kind of people he dealt with.

But he was falling in love with a woman who was as different as they came.

Not true, he immediately denied. Macy loved her family. She worried about her daughter. So she had money, didn't need a job, had no concerns on that angle. She'd been married to a serial killer so crime had struck closer to home for her than most.

She was as everyday normal as anyone could be.

And she felt so damned good in his arms.

Barely audible over the mingled sounds of their breathing, she whispered, "If you want to walk away and forget you ever met me, I'll understand."

She would regret it, the quick tightening of her hands against his back suggested, but she would understand.

"Hey," he said gently. "I'm a geek. I'm fashion-challenged. I'm a vet. I'm a midlist fantasy author. Obviously, I'm not easily deterred."

Her hands tightened again, and she rested her cheek against his chest. After a moment of simply breathing, she finally lifted her head. "I suppose we should reclaim my child from Anamaria before she begs to go home with them. She's a sucker for birthday cake."

"So am I." Releasing her, he took the coffee mugs and cloth napkins inside, then came back. She automatically tucked her hand inside his, and they crossed the street to the square.

"Mama, guess what?" Clary jumped up to meet them. "It's Gloriana and Will's daddy's birthday. Isn't that cool?" Without pause, she scrunched up her face. "I don't have a daddy. But that's okay. I got a grandpa and an Uncle Brent and Dr. Stephen."

The kid knew how to wrap her little fingers around a man's heart. He felt as if he'd been bestowed a great honor.

Macy reached for Anamaria's hand and squeezed it. "Thank you."

Anamaria might be psychic, but she hadn't expected the touch. The surprise showed in her dark eyes and the deep relief of her smile. "You're welcome. We'd love to have Clary over for a playdate this week. When my two get tired of playing with each other, it becomes more like combat. 'Oops, I didn't mean to hit you with the bat.' 'Sorry I tore your doll's head off, and oh, gosh, there goes her leg.' They would be thrilled with the distraction of Clary."

"That sounds wonderful. She's been here less than two days and already she's *booored*."

"I'll call you tomorrow," Anamaria said. She rose gracefully from the steps, the very essence of beauty and serenity, and called to her kids. Before walking away, though, she faced Macy head-on. "Remember what I told you your first day back?"

Macy nodded.

"That hasn't changed." Moving away from her, Anamaria patted Stephen's arm reassuringly. "It's good to see you."

After Anamaria and her children crossed the street, Stephen glanced at Macy, who was watching them. "What did she tell you?"

She looked at him and smiled. "Just something that I really needed to hear. And now something that I really need to say—it's time to head home. We've left Brent and Anne to work long enough."

"Mama!" Clary stomped one foot and somehow managed to collapse in on herself while remaining standing, then huffed and straightened. "Oh, all right. I wish Grandma and Grandpa weren't off on that stupid trip. I bet Grandpa would take me to the beach, and then to a movie, and he'd buy me a giant popcorn and pop and would read me stories when we got home. He wouldn't just put stupid things in stupid boxes…"

Tuning out the rest, Stephen met Macy's gaze and at the same time they rolled their eyes.

When they returned to the big house that, knowing what he now knew, kind of freaked out Stephen, too, Brent and Anne were working in the library. About a third of the shelves had been emptied, and a small mountain of book-packing cartons were stacked in the hallway. They were both pink-cheeked and looked in need of a break.

Stephen picked up a leather-bound volume and turned it carefully. "You do have an inventory of all these titles, don't you?"

Anne's eyes doubled in size. "We were supposed to be inventorying them?" With a pointed look at the boxes already sealed, she sank into a chair.

"I'm sure there's one…somewhere." Macy didn't say more, but Stephen figured they all understood where: in Mark's office. "Besides, I don't need an inventory to give them away."

"What about the tax deduction?" Brent asked.

"Don't care." Dismissively she assembled a box on one of the tables and taped the bottom seam with a loud rip of the dispenser.

Exchanging shrugs, Brent and Anne went back to work, and Stephen did what he did best: began moving the boxes from the hallway to the garage. Any library

in the country would be thrilled to receive this donation, but particularly one in the South, given the number of Southern histories and biographies he'd seen on
his first time in the room. The collection was probably
worth a not-so-small fortune, but Macy couldn't wait to
see the last of it.

Now he understood why.

Clary was fussy by the time he finished moving the
boxes, so he led her to the table holding the jade figu-
rines. "Would you like to help me wrap these in a box
so your mom can send them to your…"

"To Grandmother Lorna," Macy supplied from her
position on a ladder handing books down to Brent.

"Are we gonna wrap them like presents?" Clary's eyes
lit up. "Like birthday presents?"

"Well, sort of, but in plain paper."

"Okay."

He gave her two of the carvings to carry, cautioning
her to be careful, then filled his hands, and they went
into the kitchen. After two more trips, he lifted Clary
onto a stool at the island, assembled a box and got a new
package of paper from the garage.

"Are these toys, Dr. Stephen?" she asked, clutching
one in her pudgy fingers and looking at it from all angles.

"No, honey. They're just carvings for people to look
at." He laid out a few sheets of paper, showed her where
to place the piece in one corner, then rolled it into a
chunky package.

"I'd rather have toys. Who are they a present for?"

"Your mother's sending them to your grandmother.
They used to belong to your grandfather."

"I don't know them," she said casually. "Do you have
a daddy?"

"You bet. His name is Dave, and he lives in California."

"Are you divorced from him? We learned about divorce in preschool. That's why some kids don't have daddies. Grandma says my daddy is just gone, and Grandpa says good riddance, and Mama says he's dead."

Stephen watched as she picked up a piece of jade that might have been a dragon or a tree with flowing branches. It was hard to say. "Do you know what *dead* means, Clary?"

She shrugged, a strand of brown hair sticking to her cheek. "Uncle Brent says it means he's not here, and AnAnne says that's okay."

It wasn't his place to try to explain an inexplicable concept like death to a three-year-old, so he changed the subject instead. "My dad lives near Disneyland."

"Wow. Really? That's cool." Eyes wide with awe, she asked, "What's that?"

Stephen laughed. His skills with little girls needed brushing up, but she still counted him among the important men in her life. Did that say something good about him? Or sad about her?

After lunch—sandwiches delivered from the Sammie Shop—Stephen had to beg off on moving boxes for the afternoon. He'd missed his word count for the week and needed a few hours to add to it. He let Clary talk him into leaving Scooter behind and lured Macy out into the driveway with him, sliding his arms around her middle. "You realize as long as my dog is here, I *will* be back."

"Aw, and here I thought it was the complete uncomplicatedness of me that was bringing you back."

He liked that she could tease with him. That she seemed more at ease now, not just with him but with everything. Sometimes she'd hidden her anxiety well, other times not so much, but right now she looked like a woman with nothing more important on her mind than the job she had to do and the people she got to do it with.

"That, too. Sometimes us simple guys are just naturally drawn to you complicated girls." He leaned closer, kissed her and was just starting to feel the effects of oxygen deprivation when a car door slammed a few yards away. He took a step back and forced a smile while whispering, "It's your lucky day. The great white land shark is circling."

"Quick, can we run back inside and pretend we're not home?"

In a white suit with killer heels, stalking up the driveway, Louise Wetherby had a predatory look about her. Stephen gave Macy's hand a squeeze. "Sorry to abandon you, but I've got dragons of my own to slay. I'll call you."

Halfway down the slope, he grinned broadly. "Hey, Miz Wetherby."

Despite being inches shorter, she gave him a look down her pointed nose. "Dr. Noble, can you not manage to comb your hair just once in your life?"

He dragged his fingers through it, well aware it would spring back at odd angles. "I was born this way. Sorry."

She made a *hmph* sound, and he picked up his pace. Macy might be having a tough time, but she could handle Louise. That was more than he could say for himself.

Louise looked past Macy to the neatly stacked boxes in the garage, now filling more than half of the three-car bay, and for a moment greed shone in her eyes. The only family treasures decorating her mansion a few blocks over were purchased from other families that had died out or were more in need of cash than sentimental objects. On her rare visits to the house for meetings with Mark, she'd coveted more than a few paintings, art pieces and dishes. Macy was somewhat surprised that she didn't try to buy some of them cheap. *To save you the hassle of appraisals, packing and such.*

"I've come to discuss the papers with you. Let's take this inside. A glass of tea will be nice, to say nothing of air-conditioning."

Louise was halfway to the utility room door when Macy spoke. "I'd rather not go inside. My family is working, and I don't want to disturb them."

So used to getting what she wanted, Louise seemed to hover there for a minute, her mind clearly intending to go into the house, her feet seemingly stuck to the concrete. She looked as if she might issue a command anyway, but apparently remembered that she wanted something from Macy. A lot.

On her ridiculously high heels, she came back to stand in front of Macy. "So. You've had a chance to go over the contract and showed it to that Calloway boy. The sooner we get your signature, the sooner we can get to work on saving Fair Winds—"

"I went out there last week. There's nothing to save it from. Everything is in excellent shape."

Only the glint in Louise's eyes showed her surprise. "On the surface, perhaps, but a house of that age—"

Macy could probably count on one hand the number of times she'd interrupted one of Mark's friends or associates. She did it again. "Louise, I'm not giving the house to you."

Splotches of pink appeared in the older woman's cheeks. "Not to me, of course, but—"

"Not to you, not to your preservation group, not to anyone at this point. I realize something must be done with it, but it's not in the top ten of my list of things to deal with right now. Robbie Calloway has made sure that the house has been protected and maintained for the past eighteen months. He'll continue doing so until I'm ready to deal with it. I'm sure you're disappointed, but you have to understand that this is Clary's inheritance. Her legacy. As her mother, I've got to consider what's in her best interests. Now I appreciate your coming out on such a hot afternoon, but I have to get back to work."

Without waiting for a response, Macy walked past the woman and into the utility room, closing the door and leaning against it. She wouldn't put it past Louise to barge in, trying to use sheer will to force Macy into the decision she wanted.

But there was no shove on the door, no imperious knock. Faintly she heard the thud of the car door, followed by the sound of the engine. Louise was retreating. For the moment.

"That was one scary woman." Anne came around the corner with a box cradled against her, and Macy obligingly moved aside and opened the door. While Anne placed it with the other books, Macy closed the garage door. If Louise did come back, or anyone else, for that matter, she could pretend she wasn't home.

Macy told her what Louise had wanted.

"Ballsy woman," Anne said with a grunt. She stretched her arms over her head. "I'm gonna need a massage before long."

"I'll send you to the best resort in the world when we're done."

"You come, too?"

Macy opened her mouth to answer, sure, of course, but nothing came out.

"Aw, you're gonna be here cuddling up to Dr. Stephen, letting him work out all those kinks."

Heat spread from her cheeks all the way down through her body. "Stephen and I—"

"That has a nice sound to it, doesn't it? 'Stephen and I.' That's how I knew I was falling in love with Brent, when saying 'Brent and I' gave me warm shivers. You know it's not just you anymore. You're part of a couple. There's someone who will notice when you're sad or happy or late. Someone who will always be there for you, who puts you first. It's the coolest feeling in the world."

Macy didn't know Anne's life story, but she did know her sister-in-law's family wasn't warm and fuzzy like the Irelands. Parents out of the picture, a brother who died in the war, a sister with more psychiatric diagnoses than an entire team could treat successfully. When she and Brent had met at the resort, she'd been hungry for affection, looking for somewhere to belong. Anne's family's loss was Macy's family's gain.

Focusing on Anne's comment, Macy primly said, "Stephen and I aren't in love." Though the words gave her a pang.

Anne snorted. "News flash, darlin'—you're well on your way, and I think he's already there. He adores you, adores your child, likes your family and couldn't care less about your money. And he's not Mark. This one's a keeper."

And he had Anamaria's thumbs-up, too.

Smiling as broadly as a child at Christmas, Macy made a sweeping gesture toward the door. "Let's get back to work so you can get to that spa sooner. Be thinking what region you want to go to. France, the Bahamas, the South Pacific."

"You know we're doing this because we love you. We don't need bribes."

"That's why it's not a bribe. It's a thank-you. For everything." Most especially for loving her. Hell, she'd been a dysfunctional mother locked up in a psych hospital when Anne met her. No one would have blamed her if she'd gone screaming the other way.

Or Stephen.

Back in the library, they ran out of small boxes long before they ran out of books. Hands on her hips, Macy surveyed the room. "The rooms are starting to sound empty." The high ceilings gave a faint echo back at her.

"Besides the furniture, the lamps and art and the rest of these books, what's left downstairs?" Brent asked.

"The kitchen. That'll take an afternoon. The china cabinets in the dining room. A few things in the powder room and laundry room." She swallowed. "Mark's office."

"Have you been in there yet?"

"Once. For a minute."

Sympathy flashed through her brother's brown eyes. "Why don't you let me start that room? You girls can go shopping or cook dinner or jump in the pool."

"Well…" Part of her wanted to say sure, jump right in. But part of her felt as if she should do the work. Next to Mark's closet, the office was his most personal space in the house. He'd kept photographs there, souvenirs, all his important papers. The room smelled of him; his presence remained strong.

"I'll just sort through things, pack it in boxes. Then

when you and Clary settle, when you've got plenty of time and space, you can go through it yourself."

"Okay." She hoped she hadn't given in too easily, but truth was, she would be clearing out Mark's other most personal space: his closet. The clothes he wore. The jewelry that had passed down from his father and grandfathers. The suits he'd worn to church, the tuxedo he'd married her in. Wasn't that up close and personal enough? "I'll start in our bedroom."

"If you're both going to keep working," Anne said, "tell me what you want for dinner. I want to cook in that kitchen at least once."

Macy left them to figure that out and began carrying wardrobe boxes upstairs. She planned to donate most of her clothing to Right Track. Some of the more formal clothes wouldn't be of much use, though maybe they could sell them online. She would offer them first dibs on Mark's clothes, as well.

"Clary," she called when she returned downstairs for a second load of boxes.

"We're in here." She and Scooter were sprawled on one of Miss Willa's treasures, a petit-point sofa that predated the Great War, looking at a book Clary had brought with her from Charleston.

"AnAnne's going to the store, so why don't you and Scooter come upstairs with me while she's gone?" There was no telling what they could get into given free run of the house with only two adults inside.

"Okay, Mama." A smile wreathing her face as if it were the best idea in ages, Clary closed the book and tucked it in the crook of her arm, then spoke to Scooter as if he'd always been hers to command. "Come, Scooter. Upstairs."

In the master bedroom she sat on the bed and chattered, mostly to the dog, while Macy taped together a half dozen tall cartons and inserted the metal rods for hanging clothes. She didn't really tune in until Clary spoke her name. "What, sweetie?" she asked absently.

"Whose house is this?"

"It's ours."

"But we don't live here."

"No."

"And you're taking everything out. Why?"

"Because we're going to find a new house."

"Why don't we just stay at Grandma's and Grandpa's like we been?"

Macy checked the pockets of a suit coat on the rack, then transferred it to the carton. "Because grown-up mamas don't usually live with their own mamas and daddies."

"Can we get a house by Scooter's?"

Five days ago, two days ago, it had been easier to give an unconditional *no* to that question. Now… Was Stephen right? Was it only the Howard family that she hated about Copper Lake? It wasn't a bad town. She knew and respected a lot of people here. Of course, there were plenty she didn't like—Louise and her cronies came to mind—but that would be true anywhere. She liked the idea of Clary going to school with kids whose families she knew. The weather couldn't be better nine months out of the year, and she was a Southern girl. She knew how to stay cool those other three months.

The downside to Copper Lake: people knew *everything* about her.

The upside, Stephen would say, was that people knew *everything*. There'd be no worrying about when or how to tell her secrets. And she knew small towns: another scandal would come along, another sensational story that would push her and Clary's return to the back burner, and before long people would forget that they'd ever left.

And the big upside to Copper Lake: Stephen.

"I don't know exactly where we'll get a house, babe."

Clary stroked Scooter's fuzzy head. "Well, if I can't live with Grandma and Grandpa, I wanna get a house by Scooter." A tiny pause. "Did I live in this house, too?"

"Yes, when you were little."

"Where did I sleep?"

Macy placed another garment in the carton, then faced her daughter. "You want to see your old room?"

Clary bounded off the bed. "Yes!" Scooter looked a little miffed at losing his pillow but stretched out and closed his eyes again.

Macy took her hand and led her down the hall to the first door on the right. She turned on the lights and stepped back to let her daughter enter first. It was painted in primary colors, red, yellow, blue, with an alphabet theme. Macy had thought it busy and overstimulating, but Mark had sided with the designer he'd hired.

Clary stood in the center of the room and turned a slow circle, as if she'd found herself in the spotlight of a circus arena. When she faced Macy again, she giggled. "It's a baby room, Mama! Look, it's got a baby bed!"

"Well, you were still pretty much a baby then." The crib, with each side a different color, was designed to convert into a single bed, but they hadn't made the change yet. At eighteen months, Clary had been a climber.

"Stuffed bears. Diapers! Binkies!" She shook her head with good-natured dismay. "Wow. I'm glad I don't have to sleep in here now. It's like all the colors in the world spilled."

Macy felt some small satisfaction that her daughter shared her opinion. So much for Mark's high-dollar designer.

Clary poked around in the toy box, looked at the clothes in the closet and shook her head over the board books, then wandered back into the hall. "What's that room?" she asked. "And that one?"

"Guest rooms. For when we had company."

"And that one?"

"Bathroom." Though the two guest rooms had their own baths, the children were supposed to share. Macy pointed to the next door. "Closet."

And Clary pointed out the nearest one, its door open. "Is that another baby room? Did you have another baby, Mama?"

Her chest tight, Macy scooped up her daughter and held her tightly enough to feel secure, not enough to make her squirm. "No, honey. I—I fixed the room in case, but...it didn't happen."

Clary laid her hands on Macy's cheeks and stared deep into her eyes. "I'd like to have a little sister like Gloriana. Or a brother like Will only not so bossy. Or maybe a puppy. Yeah, I think I want a puppy. Like Scooter, only littler, since Scooter is really a dog, and a puppy is a little baby dog. When we find a new house, can I have a puppy, Mama?"

Dear God, she loved her daughter. All the shock, all the loss, and still her little girl could make her hopeful. She was such a miracle.

After spinning her in a circle, Macy smooched her belly. "You bet you can have a puppy, sweetie. Maybe even two."

Chapter 11

Macy awoke before dawn Monday, her heart fluttering, her skin damp with perspiration, her stomach twisted in knots. It took her a long time to open her eyes and gaze around the room. Clary was sprawled across her half of the bed and then some. The closet and hall doors were closed, the hall one locked. The door to her bathroom stood open, a dim light on inside. The air was still and didn't smell of anything it shouldn't. The house was quiet.

So why was her skin crawling, her hands starting to tremble?

The panic attacks started this way: a sense of overwhelming anxiety in those first moments of awakening, when she wasn't fully alert, when she was vulnerable to doubts and fears. On a good day, this was as far as it went. She'd drag herself from bed, take her medication and get busy, and before long the discomfort was gone.

On a bad day, it escalated. Sometimes she couldn't sit still. Sometimes she couldn't leave the house. Some days she cried until exhaustion set in. All those days she couldn't bear to let her Clary see her.

But it hadn't happened in so long. Months, since the doctor had adjusted her medication. She'd taken it faithfully. She'd stayed active. Now she'd had the something's-wrong warning twice in two days.

And she wasn't giving in to it. Throwing back the covers, she went into the bathroom, brushed her teeth and dressed in cropped pants and a button-down shirt. She applied makeup, spritzed on perfume, then opened the pill bottle hidden in a drawer and shook out a single tablet. After a moment, she let a second one slide out. The doctor had told her it was okay to double up for a day or two if she felt the need, and this morning she did.

She washed down one tablet with a cup of tap water then stared at the other one. Something seemed different about it. It was white, round, incised with letters and numbers, as always. It just seemed…lighter? Heavier? Smaller?

Grimly she washed it down, too. When she started worrying about the precise dimensions of her medication, she was definitely in the early stages of an anxiety attack. And she wasn't giving in, remember?

The first of the appraisers Lydia Kennedy had recommended was scheduled to arrive at 9:00 a.m. Macy got in a few hours' work before waking Clary, fixing breakfast and getting Brent and Anne started on finishing up the family room.

When the doorbell rang, instead of the stuffy older man Macy had expected, the woman was about her own age, blond hair in a ponytail and wearing a suit that would have been the height of propriety if it'd had an additional six inches or so on the skirt. After introducing herself as Rebekah Johnston, she followed Macy into the living room and stopped short.

Macy saw the room as she always had—filled with old things and far too uncomfortable for friendly visits. Rebekah, apparently, saw treasures. She walked around the room, reverently touched a few pieces and made notes in the folder she'd brought along. When she was done, she crossed the hall into the library, her gaze sweeping over the remaining books. "I know a collector—"

"We're donating the books to the local library. He can contact them."

After giving her an odd look, Rebekah examined the chairs, the tables and the rug, then made a few more notes before moving down the hall to the dining room. It was another room Macy tended to avoid when possible. The table was huge, seating sixteen, and the matching china cabinets at each end were filled with china, crystal and sterling. "You'll be keeping the family china."

Macy looked at the dishes: delicate in color and design, with an elaborate *H* centered on every piece, the letters decorated with vines and leaves. She tried to imagine using them, her and Clary sitting down to a meal, passing a platter to Stephen, letting Scooter lick a dessert plate clean, and didn't know whether to wince or laugh. "No, I won't."

Surprise flashed across the blonde's face. "You understand these dishes are well over two hundred years old. Augustus Howard had them commissioned before he began construction of Fair Winds. He brought them to the U.S. on his own ship, transported them up the river to Augusta and ensured their safe arrival here. They've never left the Howard family, not so much as one plate. Even the breakage has been minimal."

"I'm not a china sort of person." And not a Howard, either. As Stephen had pointed out last night, she and Clary were the only Howards left in Copper Lake, and that could be easily changed. She wasn't responsible for maintaining the legacy.

Rebekah looked as if she didn't know what to say, then a round of giggles from the family room reminded her. "What about your daughter? Shouldn't you preserve at least a portion of this for her?"

"Clary's not a china sort of person, either. She's three. She prefers dishes with cartoon characters on them."

"But—"

"This is only about half of the service, Rebekah. My mother-in-law has service for twenty-five, and service for another twenty-five is at Fair Winds, where it will likely stay. If Clary feels a need to possess some of it when she's grown, she can have that."

"But you're breaking up the set."

Macy could imagine Stephen's oh-so-logical voice saying, *They're dishes, for God's sake.* That was exactly how she felt. Of course some family heirlooms should be saved, but considering that two of the only four Howards Clary had known were murderers, Macy didn't feel the need as strongly as she otherwise might have. Her daughter would have photos, jewelry, a delicate chair and desk from upstairs. And, for the time being, her own Southern mansion filled with heirlooms.

And the history she would treasure was her family. Not how much money they did or didn't have. Not how long they'd lived in the state. Not whether they'd had power or influence, but whether they'd loved each other. Whether they'd loved her. How happy they'd been.

Radiating an antiques dealer's disapproval, Rebekah stepped into the hall, waiting for Macy to lead the way to the next room. It was Mark's office. She stopped just inside the door, close enough to step right back out if the need struck.

"Oh, my God. Is that desk a Littleton? Oh, wow, it is. I've read that he only made a half dozen of these and they're all in private collections. And it's in perfect condition! Absolutely perfect. This is amazing!"

Stopping on his way to the garage with a filled box, Brent mouthed, "You okay?"

Macy smiled, then brushed Clary's hair as she marched past. "C'mon, Uncle Brent. I'll open the door for you."

Rebekah examined the desk, touching it lovingly here and there, rubbing her hand over the ancient leather of the chair, marveling at the exacting simplicity of the credenza, the library table, the game table and chairs near the fireplace. Then she turned her attention to the bookcases. "These are…"

"They're Littleton, too. The room was built to accommodate them." Done so well that no one noticed they weren't built-in shelves. Each tall case unhinged into two shorter but still massive cases. The day they'd been moved safely into the house had been a happy one for Mark.

Had he gone out and murdered someone to celebrate?

The last rooms she showed Rebekah were the guest rooms upstairs. The furniture in the master suite was modern stuff, built with comfort in mind, but both guest rooms were furnished with pieces circa 1800. Another reason Macy had done the guesthouse herself, where the beds were wide enough and long enough and the mattresses actually had some give to them.

Still scribbling on her pad as they descended the stairs, Rebekah raised her hand only long enough to shake Macy's before going out the door. "I'll be in touch with you soon."

No doubt with contracts to sign, arrangements to get detailed appraisals, probably requests for provenance if it existed. It did. In the old days it had been ledgers detailing every purchase, bills of sale tucked between the pages. More recent generations had used file folders, then computers. So proud of what they possessed.

And all those possessions they'd amassed were supporting her and Clary and would continue to do so. Macy was grateful for that, but at the same time she couldn't wait to put the Howards in her past and do something for others. She could help fund Right Track. And the no-kill animal shelter Stephen had mentioned. She could do a whole lot of good for a lot of people, not for Mark or his grandfather but to honor the Howards who'd come before who weren't murdering bastards.

They weren't all murderers.

For Clary's sake, she needed to remember that.

The crew from Right Track were loading a dresser into a yellow moving van when Stephen and Scooter arrived after work. The ones who knew him greeted them; the new women, probably from the streets of Atlanta or Augusta, gave him a familiar look of suspicion. Most of the residents at Right Track had been used and abused by men—fathers, brothers, boyfriends, pimps. It took some longer than others to trust that not all men meant them harm.

He met Brent at the door, watching them maneuver the dresser into the back of the van then tuck blankets around it. The rest of the space was filled with sofas, chairs, dining tables and such. "This is their third load. Can you believe they cleaned out the house and the guesthouse except for the bedrooms we're using all by themselves? I'd be done in."

Sadness settled over Stephen as he watched them close the heavy door then load up, two in the truck, four in a pickup truck. "When you've been victimized, you tend to become strong in an effort to give yourself a chance the next time someone comes after you. They get lessons in nutrition at the center and have their own garden, and they make good use of the gym. If they're going down, they want to go down fighting."

Brent's expression turned troubled, only to fade when the slap of running steps echoed down the hall behind them. They both turned in time for Clary to leap into Stephen's arms then lean across to link one arm around Brent's neck. Stephen felt emptier inside. Some of the women at Right Track had been abused for as long as they could remember, but some of them had had wonderful childhoods. They'd begun life every bit as loved and pampered as Clary, until at some point things had gone horribly wrong.

Macy would love Clary with her dying breath, and so would Brent. Hell, Stephen had a deep urge to hold her tightly and never let go. But things could still go horribly wrong. With peer pressure she could end up on the streets, using drugs, drinking too much, selling herself for affection. God forbid, Macy could marry some pervert who liked little girls, or something could happen to Macy and Brent; Clary could wind up with a court-appointed guardian whose only interest was her money. Some greedy bastard could lure her onto the wrong path, away from her family, use her, take her money and leave her alone to die.

There were so many ways things could go wrong. But not as long as Stephen could do anything about it.

"Dr. Stephen, Uncle Brent, Mama said you could decide where we're gonna eat. She was gonna make a salad—" her little face scrunched up with distaste "—but she said we'll go wherever you want, and I wanna go to Aunt Mary's. Just so you know."

"Aunt Mary's?" Brent echoed.

"I think she means Tia Maria's. Mexican food, Little Bit? Is that what you want?"

Clary bobbed her head. "Tacos and salsa! But Mama said I had to let you choose, so when you do, remember tacos." She struggled down, greeted Scooter exuberantly, then skipped back down the hall with the dog at her side.

The family room was completely empty when Stephen and Brent followed her in. Just a long expanse of tiled floor, even the rug rolled up and carried out, flanked by empty shelves. The small dining table where he and Macy had shared their first meal was gone, too. The sense of space and emptiness made it hit home intensely: she was moving out. Out of the house, probably out of the town, even the state.

Unless he could change her mind.

He really wanted to change her mind. Yesterday morning—breakfast at Ellie's, playing at the park, the walk around town—had been a damn near perfect morning, except for the conversation. He could see himself making that a weekly habit. Going to church, staying for even the boring parts. Meeting friends for after-church meals. Picking up Clary's little friends for trips to the park. Concerts in the square on summer evenings.

Him, Macy, Clary and Scooter.

A family.

Macy was standing between the island and the counters with Anne. "Okay, guys, what do you want for lunch? My salad idea was completely blown out of the water—" Anne and Clary booed "—so we're letting you choose."

"Gee, I think I'd really like to have Mexican," Brent said. "Some tacos."

"And salsa," Stephen added. "Sounds really good."

Clary and Anne cheered as Macy rolled her eyes. "Two grown men, and neither of you can stand up to a three-year-old girl," she murmured as she passed them. "I'll get my shoes."

Anne headed to the guesthouse to get her purse. Clary watched from the glass door until she was out of sight, then turned and gave the men a bright smile and a crooked thumbs-up.

Both of them grinned foolishly back at her before she darted off with Scooter. Nope, neither of them could withstand her charm. More important, Stephen decided, neither of them wanted to.

"You want to load some boxes in the back of my pickup and Macy's van to drop off at the library after we eat?" Brent suggested.

"Sure." The quicker they got the boxes out of the house, the sooner he could stop toting them...and the sooner Macy would be gone. That dimmed his smile.

The women came out about the time they finished. Not slow to put on shoes or find purses, Stephen figured, but smart enough to avoid the heavy labor while they could. Macy retrieved her keys from Brent and closed the door, then stiffened and did a quick look around. "Where's Clary?"

"She was inside," Stephen and Brent said at the same time. "In the kitchen."

"With Scooter," Brent added.

Macy opened the door. "Clary? Come on, let's go."

Nothing but a faint whine came in reply.

"Clara! This is no time to play." Macy's voice was tense, her color pale.

When no call or giggle came in response, Stephen, Brent and Anne headed for the door, following Macy in. Scooter sat at the back door, his attention on the yard it barred him from, and whined again, fur bristling.

"Clary! Let's go, sweetie. We're all hungry."

"You two check upstairs," Brent ordered. "Anne and I will look down here."

Macy took the stairs faster than even Stephen's long legs could manage. At the top she went right, to the master suite, and he turned left. The girl's name echoed through the house, and something awful—primal fear, he thought—soured his gut. She'd been standing at the French doors, looking out after Anne. She'd given him and Brent the thumbs-up, then took off around the family room with Scooter, and now Scooter was standing at the door, staring into the backyard.

Not just standing there, he thought, recalling the dog's stiff posture and his hair on end. *Alerted* there. Scooter saw or felt or sensed something wrong outside.

He was leaving Clary's room with long strides just as a scream came from down the hall, a piercing cry, and commotion sounded in the corridor. Macy, face contorted in pain, raced from her own room and tore down the stairs, whimpering, "Oh, God, no, no!" Lungs constricting, he ran after her.

She skidded around the corner at the bottom of the stairs, banging her shoulder against the wall, losing one of her flip-flops. She didn't notice but ran to the back of the house. Brent appeared from Mark's office, face going stark at his sister's panic, and Anne came running from the utility room. "Macy, what—"

It seemed to hit the rest of them at once: the swimming pool. Dear God.

They raced together out the door and toward the pool, Brent jumping a row of shrubs to reach it first. He stopped abruptly, breaths heaving, and looked from the pool to Macy. Her cry peaked, and she clapped both hands over her mouth to stop the keening.

The surface of the pool was smooth, serene as ever. Nothing more than a leaf disrupted it; nothing but the intricate tiles down the sides and across the bottom showed through the water.

They stood silent, one horrible moment turning into relief. Then, remembering that the child was still missing, Stephen turned to scan the yard. "Clary! Where are you, Li'l Bit?"

A sweet face popped up over the back of a wooden chair in front of the fountain, in the far corner of the yard. "Here I am. Are we ready to go eat yet?"

Brent trotted toward her. So did Anne. Stephen stayed where he was, near Macy, who stared at the quiet pool. Her expression was still horrified. Tears leaked from the corners of her eyes, and a look of such anguish twisted her features. "I thought..." Her weak whisper trailed off. "I saw..."

"What, Macy?" When she showed absolutely no

response, he stepped closer, cupped his hands to her cheeks, forced her to look at him. "What did you see?"

Her eyes were sad and haunted, haunting. "I saw Clary. My baby. In the pool. I saw her, Stephen." Her hands gripped his wrists so tightly that her nails left impressions. "I didn't imagine it, Stephen!" she said in an urgent whisper. "I *saw* her! I saw...*something*."

He didn't try to reassure her, to dissuade her. He just pulled her snugly against him, his arms wrapped around her as if simple proximity could protect her, make her feel safe, keep her safe. He held her and smoothed her hair and whispered, "It's okay. She's okay. She's safe, sweetheart. You're safe."

His body absorbed her trembling with an ache. After a long moment, she raised her head, her face no more than an inch from his. "Stephen...am I crazy? Again?"

"No." He put as much conviction into the syllable as he could. He'd seen the terror. She'd truly believed her daughter was in the pool. He was no expert at psychology, but even he knew that visual hallucinations weren't typical of a diagnosis of depression and anxiety. She was stressed, no doubt about that. Misplacing things, sure. But seeing things that weren't there?

Though she'd thought that the day she'd seen movement in the guesthouse.

Nails clicked as Scooter trotted to them then rubbed against Stephen's leg with a whine. Stephen lowered one hand to rub his head, quieted him with a low word, wondering. Had Scooter been at the back door simply because Clary went out and didn't take him with her? That would be enough to make him pout, maybe enough to make him whine. But to make him bristle? Go on alert?

Had he sensed danger for Clary, alone in the yard

with the pool when she should have been with her people? Had he seen someone else in the yard? Had *he* seen something in the pool?

"Mama, are we gonna go eat?" Clary asked from her position on Brent's shoulders as he and Anne approached.

The shudder that rocketed through Macy convinced Stephen that all she wanted was to curl up somewhere safe with her daughter. She couldn't miss the innocence on Clary's face or the concern on Brent's and Anne's. Serious concern, serious worry about her mental status. But she drew a deep breath and, with an impressive sense of normalcy, she said, "Sure, baby. That was the plan, wasn't it?"

"Yay!" Clary clapped her hands over Brent's head. "Let's go!"

Chapter 12

Macy was so mortified with herself that she couldn't bring herself to care—yet—if everyone else thought she was crazy. She knew what she had seen: a small body, dressed in purple and pink, floating facedown in the pool. Her daughter, wearing the same colors, nowhere in the house. The terror that had practically brought her to her knees. The incredible sensation of having her heart ripped from her chest. The inability to move fast enough, to pray hard enough, to reach her soon enough.

That empty pool was the best thing she'd ever seen—and among the most frightening. The looks on Brent's and Anne's faces had solidified the ice inside her. They thought she was losing her mind.

She thought she was losing her mind.

But Stephen had answered her with such certainty. *No.* He had faith in her.

Or at least did an excellent job of pretending. Either way, it meant a lot to her.

They locked up the house again, leaving Scooter wandering. "He'll be on your bed by the time we back out of the driveway," Stephen said, apparently trying to defuse the tension with a totally normal comment. "Want me to go up and close the door?"

"He's welcome on the bed or anywhere else."

"Dr. Stephen, Mama said I could have a dog or a baby sister or a baby brother," Clary said excitedly. "Can you help get me one?"

Macy's cheeks warmed, though her embarrassment faded when Brent and Anne both laughed. When she dared a look at Stephen, he was grinning. Primly she said, "You asked for a sister or a brother, *then* decided you'd rather have a puppy. Remember?"

Her daughter tilted her head to one side, not quite understanding why Macy was pointing out the difference. "Yeah. So can Dr. Stephen help me get one? Like Scooter, only littler?"

"I can do that, Li'l Bit. As soon as your mom says it's okay."

"Yay! If it's a boy, I'm gonna name him Roscoe and if it's a girl, she's gonna be Bertha."

Roscoe? Bertha? Stephen mouthed to Macy, and she shrugged. Who knew where she'd heard the names?

They split up, Macy, Stephen and Clary in her van, Brent and Anne in their truck. Stephen drove, since her hands were still unsteady. She spent most of the trip clenching them tightly in her lap, remembering. Wondering.

"Mace."

She glanced his way at the sound of his quiet voice,

feeling a faint old comfort in the name. Her friends used to call her Mace, but Mark hadn't liked it. Said it sounded like something sprinkled on a holiday drink.

She'd given up the nickname for him.

"Why would anyone want you to think you're seeing things?"

Warmth flowed through her and melted the last bit of icy terror inside her. He did have faith in her—more than she had in herself. "I don't know."

"Who benefits from not having you around?"

"Nobody." Her fingers twisted painfully together. "Why do you believe me?"

He stopped at a red light and met her gaze. She could get lost in those hazel eyes of his. "You couldn't have faked that scream, that emotion. And Scooter. Something out there had his attention."

She smiled weakly. His faith in her was strong, but his faith in his dog was absolute.

"What happens to Clary if you're in the hospital again?"

"Brent would have custody, but she'd probably stay with Mom and Dad, just like before."

"Who controls the money?"

"Brent. Just like before."

"And if you—" Stephen swallowed audibly. "If you die?"

God couldn't let that happen to Clary, could he? Losing both parents before she was in preschool? Her own swallow was pretty loud. "Brent would have custody of Clary and control of the estate. But he would never…"

"No," he agreed. "He would never."

Brent loved her. Adored her. Her entire family did. They were closer than any other family she knew. Her time in the hospital had been as hard on them as her. Besides, if Brent had wanted control of her money, he'd had it for months.

As far as she knew, she didn't have any enemies. Well, there was Louise Wetherby, who was so accustomed to getting what she wanted. Could she want Fair Winds enough to terrorize Macy to get it?

And Lorna Howard. Mark's mother had been deeply disappointed in her for believing the authorities' tales about him. Could she have decided she didn't want her only grandchild or her son's fortune under the control of a woman who didn't honor his memory? Who'd never protested his innocence?

Macy couldn't believe either of them would do such a thing. She was sure they were capable, but not even Louise or Lorna would stoop to such levels.

She couldn't believe *anyone* in her life would do such a thing.

"Maybe it's Mark's ghost," she said with a sound somewhere between laughter and choking. "Maybe I'm being haunted for not standing up for him."

Stephen gave her a look.

"Fair Winds is haunted. Everyone who's spent time there knows it. Maybe our house is haunted, too. Maybe Mark's angry with me, so his ghost is punishing me."

As they turned into Tia Maria's parking lot, Clary piped up from the backseat. "Ghosts are just on TV and in books. They're not real. Grandma said so."

Macy took a deep breath to get a grip on her emotions. "And Grandma's always right, isn't she, sweetie?"

Lunch was a subdued affair. Brent and Anne both ordered margaritas, an attitude of relief as they drank them, and Macy ate too much queso and guacamole.

Only Stephen and Clary acted their usual selves, teasing, talking, telling silly jokes. He was very good with her daughter. Mark had loved Clary, but he hadn't been much of a hands-on father. That might have changed for the better as she grew older, but Macy suspected it wouldn't have.

Besides, what did love mean when it came from a serial killer? If he didn't value other people's lives, could he have truly loved anyone but himself?

Rubbing her temples, she wished she'd ordered a margarita, too. Maybe a pitcher.

After lunch, they delivered the boxes to the library, then Brent and Anne stopped to pick up more cartons while she and Stephen and Clary drove home. He and Clary went searching for Scooter, and Macy walked through the house and out onto the patio.

The pool still looked calm, undisturbed. Water dotted the flagstone around it from the sprinklers that had come on while they were gone. Had it been wet the last time she'd stood here? She couldn't remember. She hadn't thought to check, hadn't been able to focus on anything except that clear expanse of water where her daughter wasn't floating. The rescue hook was in its usual place. Everything was identical to her gruesome vision, except, dear God, for the body.

"What did you see?"

Startled, she stiffened, and it took a moment to relax even after Brent had slid his arm around her shoulders. "I would swear on my life it was Clary, floating face-down, not moving."

"Thank God it wasn't."

"But it looked like her. Brown hair, pink and purple

clothes." The image was clear in her mind. It would never completely fade.

"I know this is hard for you."

She stiffened again as she tilted her head to study him. His expression was so serious, so grim—a look she'd seen practically every day she was in the hospital. He'd driven the two hours from Charleston so often he'd joked he could do it in his sleep; he'd sat with her, held her, told her every little thing Clary had done or said. He'd been her anchor.

And now he thought she was hallucinating.

"I'm taking my medication, Brent. I'm keeping busy. I'm not losing control." She would have held out one hand to show him she was steady as a rock, but she knew it would betray her. As her mind had? "I'm not imagining things."

Except for the intruder in the guesthouse. The contract magically moving itself from the living room to the office. The cologne bottle doing the same upstairs. Now the body in the pool.

"The important thing is Clary's all right. We'll be done here soon. You can leave town in a few more days, and you can put all this behind you."

Frustration welled inside her. If she was breaking down again, leaving wouldn't cure it. But she wasn't breaking down. She *knew* what she'd seen. The terror couldn't have been any more real, the image couldn't have been any more real.... Except it wasn't real at all.

If she couldn't believe what she'd seen, could she be sure of anything else? Could she be sure she didn't have any enemies who would try to drive her mad? Could she truly trust her family? Could she know for a fact that Mark's ghost wasn't haunting her? Could she trust Stephen?

"Unless," Brent went on, "you've changed your mind about leaving." He nodded toward the house, and through the glass doors she saw Stephen swinging Clary in a circle in the empty dining space. They were both laughing and Scooter, chasing after her sneakered feet, barked in accompaniment.

Something like peace settled over her. She had questions about a lot of things, but she did trust Stephen. It was something innate, something rooted so deeply inside her that it hadn't been a conscious choice. It just *was*.

"You know I wasn't thrilled when you brought Mark home to meet us."

"I remember." He'd thought Mark was a rich kid with an overwhelming sense of entitlement. Mark had thought her family and their tidy little house were quaint and had wondered why someone with Brent's potential didn't do something besides lawn care. He'd made money at it, sure, but he could have made money doing something more, well, prestigious. Not performing a service that people didn't want to do for themselves.

"I wouldn't mind facing this one at family get-togethers. He's a good guy."

"I know." All other uncertainties aside, that was one thing she did know. "I was thinking yesterday that as soon as I settle, I could start donating money to some charities, and the first ones that came to mind were here in Copper Lake. You know, like I should start close to home and Copper Lake *is* home. And other than Mark's family, I like the town. It's a good place."

"And the cute little nerd vet makes it an even better place, huh?"

She elbowed him. "You've been talking to Anne."

"Of course. We talk about everything." Still embracing her with one arm, Brent led her away from the pool and across the lawn. "So you might stay here."

Stephen hadn't asked her to, but he'd hinted that he would like it. Besides, she couldn't choose a place to live based on a short-term relationship that could, despite her hopes, remain short-term. But she'd liked Copper Lake before she'd met him. She had friends here, people who didn't gossip about her, who knew what Mark had done had nothing to do with her.

"Apparently, I'm thinking about it."

"It wouldn't be a problem for you?"

"Not the town. Just the house. Fair Winds. A few people I can avoid."

"You wouldn't mind going from one of the wealthiest men in town to a vet who, I'm guessing, doesn't make a lot of money and doesn't care?"

She gave him a reproving look. "You know I don't care about money." It was easy to say when she had it, but she would give up every dollar to erase the past eighteen months of suffering and loss.

"I know." He wrapped his arm around her neck, pulled her close for a hug, then led her toward the house. "But you do care about *him,* don't you?"

Stephen was reluctant to go home that night. Brent and Anne had said good-night and retired to the guesthouse over an hour ago, and their lights had gone out soon after. After begging for her fifth *one last story,* Clary had fallen asleep in her mother's arms and snored lightly, while Scooter was doing the same on one of the chairs. Stephen and Macy were sharing the teak love seat on the patio. It was the only place left on the property, she'd joked, that would seat anyone comfortably.

She tried to hide a yawn, not easy when her arms were full of daughter. He took it as his cue to reluctantly say, "I should go and let you get to bed."

For just an instant in the dim light, panic crept across her face. "Sleep's overrated, you know?"

"I could—" He stopped himself from offering to spend the night. The old beds in the guest rooms were shorter than him by a head, and there wasn't even a decent couch left in the house to curl up on. He wasn't wild about bunking down on the floor because while sleep might be overrated to her, he needed it to function. But he'd do it if she asked.

She was looking at him curiously, so he changed his statement to a tentative offer. "You and Clary could go home with me." His house wasn't much more accommodating, though he did have a sofa Scooter would happily share with Clary and a bed *he* would happily share with Macy.

Not that they'd ever talked about sharing a bed, or done anything beyond a few amazing kisses. He wouldn't turn down more, of course. He wanted her. He missed her when he was away. He worried about her. He fantasized about her. He was pretty damn sure he'd fallen in love with her.

But he wouldn't pressure her.

He swallowed over the enormous lump in his throat. "I could, uh, sleep on the couch and you two could, uh, have the bed."

Her head was still tilted, her gaze still curious. Heat flooded his face and pumped into his body with his blood.

After a moment, she sighed. "You don't know how tempting that is."

Which even he understood translated into *Thanks but no, thanks*.

"This has been a tough day, and I…"

Wanted to retreat with her baby and forget any of it had happened. He understood that, too.

He stood and helped her up, and for a moment, they stayed there, the three of them in a silent embrace. He pressed a kiss to her temple, dropped another on Clary's head, then stepped back so Macy could lead the way inside.

Their footsteps echoed through the house. He wouldn't have thought it possible, but the place seemed even colder, less welcoming. It was the missing furniture and rugs, he told himself, all the softness removed, but that wasn't entirely true. It was also the threat. He couldn't name it, couldn't even say at the moment that it wasn't Mark's ghost, as she'd suggested, but he didn't like it. He would be happy the day he'd seen the last of it. Even happier the day Macy and Clary saw the last of it.

"Are you sure you won't change your mind?" he asked at the bottom of the stairs.

Macy's smile was meant to be reassuring, he figured, but it just made her look vulnerable. "We're safe. I'll set the alarm, and there are panic buttons in every room."

"Really? I haven't seen any." Not that he knew what a panic button looked like.

"On the nightstands. Underneath Mark's desk, the dining table, Clary's crib, the kitchen island. On the control panels themselves." She shrugged as if there were too many to mention. "Brent and Anne are right out back, and you know how loudly I scream. They'll hear me if I need them."

They'd been safe before lunch, too. Daylight, people in and out, and still...

"I can spend the night," he said. "I can manage that old couch or drag a chair in from outside."

This time her smile was stronger. "You need rest. So do I. I think I'm tired enough to sleep through anything."

He doubted that. After he left, she would put Clary to bed, then probably pace the room until she exhausted herself, and still she wouldn't rest. Whether there was a ghost or not, the house haunted her.

"Please, Stephen. I appreciate the offer, but I'm a grown woman. I'm emotional, but I'm not crazy. I'm not even alone."

"Okay." Reluctance shaded his voice. "You have my number."

"I do." She stepped closer and nuzzled his jaw.

"Do one thing for me."

She raised her gaze to his, so close he could see the shades of brown in her eyes.

"Let Scooter spend the night. He's not trained as a watchdog, but he's great about picking up on things that are out of place."

Finally her smile became a real one. "I guess it would be good practice for when we get Roscoe and Bertha. And Clary will be thrilled to wake up in the morning and find him here."

He kissed her, then bent to unsnap the leash. "You're staying here, buddy, okay? Keep an eye on my girls."

"Brent referred to the Right Track women as girls and one of them practically squared off with him. 'I'm nearly nineteen,' she said. 'Don't call me girl.'" She grinned.

"I am woman. Hear me roar—or, more likely, whimper like a puppy."

He chuckled then kissed her once more. Walking out the door was hard to do, but at least she'd agreed to keep the dog. It was a small comfort, but it was better than nothing.

Macy came awake suddenly. After wrestling a semi-conscious Clary into pajamas and tucking her in, she'd barely had energy to change into her own pajamas. When she'd crawled into bed, she'd been pretty sure she wouldn't sleep, but at some point, fatigue had won out.

Now she felt as if she'd never closed her eyes, never drowsed. The room was dimly lit by the bathroom light, and she could tell at a glance that nothing was out of place. Clary was stretched out on the far side of the bed, breathing evenly. The doors were closed, the desk chair propped against the one leading into the hall. Her bathroom door was just the way she'd left it, open wide enough to give light, not enough to be too bright.

So what had wakened her?

A low sound came from across the room, raising the hairs on her arms. Slowly she sat up, pushing back the cover. A shadow lurked near the hall door, big and fuzzy and—

Scooter, she realized and tried to swallow back a great laugh of relief. The feeling lasted for only a moment, though, because the dog was still staring at the door, still whining.

Her cell phone sat on the bedside table. Should she call Brent? Stephen? Awaken one of them from a sound sleep to tell them—what? That the dog wanted something? Not being a dog person, her best guess, given his concentration on the door, was that he needed to go out. Dogs sometimes did that in the middle of the night, didn't they? Take care of business, maybe chase a few scents around the yard before returning to bed?

It was so damn easy to overreact, she thought as she fumbled her feet into flip-flops. She'd been so nervous the past week. Her doctor had warned her this trip could bring a lot of emotions to the surface. Brent had cautioned her, too, and she'd been well aware of the risks entirely on her own. She'd been so fixated on being normal, so sensitive to any indication that she wasn't, that she didn't know how to react to anything anymore.

This wasn't a situation to overreact to. Scooter was a dog. Dogs sometimes had to pee at night. He was at the door, politely asking to go out, and by God, she would let him out without making a big deal of it.

"I'm coming, sweetie," she murmured. She pulled the chair from its place in front of the door, then opened the door. The dog shot off down the hall as if launched from a cannon. She could tell by the slaps of his paws that he'd reached the bottom of the stairs before she'd turned the corner at the top, and she smiled. Clary hadn't been potty-trained so long that these emergency *gotta-go-right-now!* episodes were forgotten.

In the faint light from the kitchen, she saw the golden glow that was Scooter, tail wagging furiously at the door, and picked up her pace. Shut off the alarm, unlock and open the door, *hurry hurry,* and the dog launched himself far enough to avoid the stone patio and land in the grass. Within a second or two, he'd disappeared into the shadows.

Arms folded across her chest, she surveyed the room while she waited. At 9:00 a.m., the second dealer would be here, this one looking at the smaller, collectible pieces—the Tiffany lamps, the ivory carvings in Mark's office, the paintings and sculptures and so on. Once he was gone, she would work on the two nurseries. She would keep the chair she'd rocked Clary in, some clothing and books given to Clary by Macy's friends, a few family heirlooms—an eighteenth-century sterling rattle, some ancient tatted bibs, a few crocheted dresses. She didn't want anything from the other nursery.

Scooter barked a few times, drawing her attention back outside. The lights on the back fence showed him walking, nose to the ground, occasionally stopping to look around. He followed a trail only he could see to the side of the pool, sniffed the hook a few times, then wandered a bit more. He came back to the house by a different trail and nosed the door a few times before he would step back and let her close it.

When he looked up at her, she would have sworn he was smiling, letting her know he'd done his part in keeping them safe for the night. "Aw, you're such a good boy. I'd give you a treat if I had any, but how about a good scratch?"

Though his ears perked up at the mention of a treat, he was satisfied with the rubbing and started down the hall when she was done. She set the alarm and followed him, nearly falling over him when he stopped in the living room doorway. "Scooter, you should—"

Her admonition faded as she followed his gaze. Light came from the room where it shouldn't, not electric but wavering, flickering flames. Tapers. Two of them. In candlesticks that could be traced back to Paul Revere. One on each side of the mantel, placed to cast the best illumination on the wedding portrait that hung above.

"Oh, God…"

With a low rumble, Scooter moved closer to her, nudging her trembling hand with his head. She tried to pat him, tried to say or do something, but all she could manage was staring at the scene.

Someone had brought those candlesticks from the dining room to the mantel.

Someone had lit the flames.

Someone had been in the house.

Someone…who wasn't her. She was sure of it.

"Clary!" She raced up the stairs to her room, flung back the covers and gathered her daughter into her arms. Thank God, her daughter was safe…but *someone* had been in the house!

"Okay, okay. We can go to the guesthouse. Better yet, we'll check into a hotel. I can call Jared at The Magnolia. He'll make room for us even if they're full." She paced to the closet, shifting Clary, mumbling now, to one arm and hip while yanking clothes from the rods. "I'll call Jared from the car…call Brent and tell him… Stephen."

Scooter appeared in the doorway and barked once, then headed back out of the room.

Stephen. He was only a quarter mile away. He would welcome them. He would understand. He wouldn't think she was crazy. He would hold her, comfort her, keep her and Clary safe.

Scooter came back to bark once more before trotting off again. Telling her to come on, quit wasting time, get out of this house.

She looked at the clothes she'd grabbed, two and a half outfits for herself, none for Clary, then dropped them on the bed. They could come back here and change in the morning, when it was daylight, when it was safe. She needed only two things besides her daughter and Scooter. She took her phone from the nightstand, grabbed her medication from the bathroom drawer and headed toward the stairs as Scooter barked a third time.

At the front door, she risked a look into the living room. The candles were still lit, their flames sending ghostly shapes across the canvas. "Gotta get out," she whispered, arms clenching Clary more tightly, but halfway out the door she remembered Brent. If he found them gone and the clothes tumbled on the bed, he'd panic.

Rushing to the kitchen, she scribbled a note and left it in a prominent place on the island, then rushed back to the door. She was all the way out when she thought about the candles. She couldn't leave them burning. They were a fire hazard. She didn't care about losing the house, but she couldn't endanger Brent and Anne or her neighbors.

She ran into the living room, blew out the flames, breathed in the acrid smoke that curled up from the wicks, then ran out again. Scooter, waiting patiently on the steps, barked, and she closed the door, locked it and hustled for the van. For such a short drive, she set Clary in the passenger seat, shushing her when she murmured and shifted. Scooter jumped into the front floorboard and rested his chin on Clary's leg. She sighed, patted his head and went on sleeping.

Once Macy drove through the Woodhaven gate, streetlamps were fewer and much farther between. Her fingers gripped the steering wheel so tightly they almost went numb, and her gaze kept shifting: street ahead, daughter beside her, road behind her. She braked to a jerky stop in front of the neat little cottage, yanked out her keys, ran around to the passenger side and lifted out Clary, then followed Scooter to the porch.

Her first knock qualified as polite. Ludicrous. She'd fled her house with her little girl in the middle of the night and acted as if she were making a routine visit. Scooter thought it silly, too, because he nosed the screen door open, banged the door with one paw and let out a great deep bark. She imitated his knock, curling her fingers into a fist and banging on the door, then called, "Stephen! It's me and Clary! Open the door, please!"

Lights came on in the bedroom, thin wedges spilling around the edges of the curtains, and she practically danced in place, anxious to get inside and into his embrace. A moment later, the lock clicked and Stephen pulled the door open. He was wearing boxers—black, she noticed, charmed in some small corner of her mind—and nothing else, not even glasses. His expression was dazed, worried and startled when she threw herself and Clary against his bare chest.

"Mace?" His mouth brushed her ear, and his arms automatically went around them, as if it were the most natural action in the world. She *felt* as if having them around her was the most natural. "What— Why— Are you guys okay?"

Scooter brushed around them and went into the kitchen, and the sound of lapping at water came a moment later. Normal, she thought again. Scooter was home and getting a drink. She and Clary were home and getting hugged by Stephen. Normal was such a shaky idea for her, one that she wanted so desperately that she didn't trust her voice to work. "C-can we st-stay here?"

"Of course you can."

His sleepy, husky voice drifted over her, and the sharp edge of tension gripping her began to dull. Whatever had happened at the house, now she could relax. Now she and

Clary were safe. The knowledge sent shivers through her, each ripple diminishing fear and anxiety, until at last her body went limp, taking support from his, her mind easing with the soft stroking of his hand down her spine, the soft murmurs. *You're okay. It's okay.*

When the shaking had stopped, he stepped back, moved his hands to her shoulders and met her gaze. "What happened?"

Her deep inhalation smelled of him and Clary and soap and triggered another loosening sensation of tension. She wanted to just breathe it in, just stand there, her, Clary and Stephen, and absorb the goodness of it, the rightness, but the muscles in her left arm and back were showing the strain of holding her baby for so long. She started to shift her to the other arm, but Stephen intercepted her, lifting Clary gently and laying her on the couch. He slid a small pillow under her head, tucked a quilted throw over her.

When he came back, he closed and locked the door and asked again, quietly, patiently, "What happened?"

Her first attempt at answering was little more than babbling, but after another deep breath, she folded her arms across her middle and feigned control. If you could pretend it, she thought, you could be it.

"Something startled me awake, and I realized Scooter was at the bedroom door, wanting to go out. I took him downstairs and let him out. When he came back in, he stopped in the living room doorway and that's when I saw candles burning on the mantel under the portrait."

His gaze narrowed so intently that she wondered for one heartbreaking moment if he doubted her, if his reassurances that afternoon had been merely an attempt to placate her, as her family often had. When he held up a finger and pivoted away into the bedroom, though, then came back with his glasses on, relief banished her own doubt. He'd just been trying to bring her into focus.

"Where did the candles come from? There have never been any on the mantel."

"The candlesticks were in the dining room. The china cabinet at the far end. Bottom cabinet. Paul Revere made them. The tapers must have been in there, too."

His eyes widened slightly. "*The* Paul Revere?"

"That's what the documentation says."

"Wow." That quickly the candlesticks' provenance was dismissed. Pulling one hand loose from where she hugged herself, he led her into the kitchen, flipped on the overhead light and seated her at the table. He took two mugs from the cabinet, looked at the coffeemaker, then took a bottle from another cabinet instead. After sitting next to her, he opened the scotch and poured some into each cup.

She gazed at it longingly. She'd never been much of a drinker, but a little liquid heat and courage was so tempting. Grimacing, she said, "I'm not supposed to drink with the medication I'm on. Not that it seems to be working so well lately."

"What is it?"

She pulled the bottle from the pocket of the gym shorts she wore with a T-shirt for pajamas and handed it over. He gave it a doctorly study, taking note of the dosage, the date it was refilled and how many pills were inside, then set it down and nudged the cup closer. "A few sips won't hurt."

The scotch was good, smooth, burned her throat and heated her core temperature to almost normal. It felt pleasurable enough that she took another drink. Even her fingertips and toes were warming, and her knees had stopped knocking. If it weren't for the subject, she could almost pretend this was just a man and a woman who were attracted to each other having a drink together in the middle of the night.

"What did Scooter do when you let him outside?"

The unexpected question made her blink. "He raced out the door, ran into the shadows near the back fence and presumably did his business there, then sniffed around the pool and all the way back to the house. Usual dog stuff."

He was quiet a moment before saying, "I should have told you, Mace, so you would've known but…Scooter doesn't go out at night."

Chapter 13

Her grip tightened around the cup, and she took a third drink, larger than the first sips. Her mouth thinned and shadows darkened her eyes. Stephen shrugged. "I suppose it could happen. I can't remember him ever doing it before, but that doesn't mean he can't. It's just his routine is to go out before bed, then sleep like a log until morning. Unless…"

"Something wakes him," she said flatly. "You think whoever lit those candles was in the house when he got me up?"

He hesitated to answer. She'd had enough scares already. But that was the point, wasn't it? She'd had plenty of scares by someone, ghost or human, who had access to her house. If one more fright put her on edge enough to keep her and Clary safe, it would be worth it.

As long as it didn't push her *over* the edge.

"More likely the guy woke him as he was leaving.

Scooter would have let you know if someone was actually in the house when he was awake. Maybe his point for going out was to make sure the guy was gone."

"But the alarm was set. I had to disarm it to let him out. I had to reset it when he came back in."

He summoned his calmest doctor voice. "Honey, if someone's been moving things, they've been in the house before. They have the code and the key."

"But—but who? I haven't just given out codes and keys to random people. There's no reason."

Random people. That was the problem. Whoever was doing this wasn't some acquaintance.

When she reached for the cup, he took her hand instead and pulled her over onto his lap. Her slender body was trembling again, nowhere near as badly as when she'd dragged him from a deep sleep, but enough to make him hurt for her. Enough to make him want to hurt whoever was doing this to her. "Who has access?"

She dragged her fingers through her hair before settling her head on his shoulder. "Me. Brent and Anne. Robbie Calloway. The alarm company. Possibly the cleaning service Robbie hired when I told him I was coming back." A defensive tone entered her voice. "Who has access to your house?"

"Me, Marnie and my landlady." He trusted Marnie with his life, the same way Macy trusted Brent.

But Stephen didn't really know Brent, and he hadn't talked as much to Anne as he had to Brent. His gut instinct was to trust them, but with Macy's sanity on the line, if not her life, he couldn't rule out anyone automatically.

"Okay. Robbie. Could he have a motive to hurt you, scare you, make you think you're crazy?"

"No. *No one* does." She lunged to her feet to pace, and he missed the warmth and weight of her body immediately. "I'm just an average woman, Stephen. I've got a daughter, and we've both got some money. There may be people who don't like me, but no one who cares enough to qualify as an enemy. No one feels that intensely about me."

"That's not true. *I* feel intensely about you."

Slowly she smiled, though the stress didn't leave her face. "But in a good way. No one dislikes me enough to want to hurt me."

She wanted to believe that. So did he. But the events of the past few days suggested otherwise.

Okay, so he knew Robbie and figured he could dismiss him. The Calloway family had multiple fortunes of its own, one with Robbie's name on it. He would have been careful about the access granted to the cleaning service, and as for the alarm company, Macy was just one more customer. There was nothing personal between them and her.

And this was very personal.

"What about Mark's mother and grandmother?"

She had stopped in the doorway to the living room and was watching Clary sleep. Her own shoulders were rounded, and when she faced him, exhaustion was etched into her face. "They both had keys. Lorna probably still does. But Robbie changed the code after Mark died."

Granted, Lorna could buy the code from a cash-strapped employee at the alarm company or even hire someone who could bypass it. But Lorna hadn't had contact with her daughter-in-law in a long time. Why harass her now?

Which led back to Brent and Anne. Brent knew how

fragile his sister was. He knew how much money she and Clary had. He was next in line for custody of his niece and control of both fortunes.

But he loved his sister—loved her in the never-ending do-anything-for-her way Stephen loved Marnie. If Brent needed money, hell, if he just wanted it, all he had to do was ask, and Macy would give it to him.

Anne loved her, too, and Clary. She was like a second mother to Clary. Macy credited both Brent and Anne with getting her through the ordeal of losing her baby and her husband with her sanity more or less intact.

Could Anne love Clary too much to let her go? Now that Macy was ready to settle elsewhere, was Anne afraid of losing her little girl?

It didn't feel right. None of it felt right.

Across the room, Macy was standing with her arms across her chest again. Earlier the posture had made her look vulnerable, as if she were trying to protect herself. Now she looked on the offensive, as if she knew the things he was thinking and didn't like them one bit. "No one I know would do this."

Someone she knew *was* doing it. Or Mark's ghost was hanging around. Or she was terrorizing herself.

Grimly he left the table and went to stand beside her, close enough to feel the chill emanating from her, to smell the faint fragrance of her perfume, the fainter scent of her fear. Together they stood and watched Clary for a moment, then he bumped his arm against hers. "You need sleep. Let me move Clary into the bedroom."

She laid her hand on his arm. "She's fine where she is."

He stilled, gazing down at her delicate fingers, the nails pale pink with white tips. Pretty, pampered hands, but strong enough to pick up her daughter and carry her where she needed. Strong enough to fight for her daughter. For herself.

She sweetened his next breath as well—less fear, more woman. He shifted his gaze to her face, also delicate, pretty. "Tell me you're not planning to sleep in that chair."

She shook her head.

"Tell me you're not planning for *me* to sleep in that chair." He managed something of a grin. "Though I will if you want."

Amazingly, slowly, she shook her head again.

Wow. He combed his fingers through his hair. He'd thought…wanted…wondered… But now… *Wow.*

A hint of a smile touched her lips. "I feel very intensely about you, too, Stephen. I want to sleep with you, but I also want to *sleep* with you. I want to be close."

He didn't have a clue exactly which meant have sex—sleep or *sleep.* He didn't care. If all she wanted tonight was to share space and warmth and know she wasn't alone, he was okay with that.

But when he followed her into the bedroom and turned from adjusting the door so they could hear any sound from Clary, Macy was stripping off her clothes. He stared long and hard. In a minute, he'd have to take his glasses off, and he wanted to remember her like this—naked, pale, sleekly curved, so damn beautiful and smiling at him with shy innocence, uncertainty, need.

You're getting lucky tonight, a voice crowed in his head. The cheerleader/homecoming queen/prom queen had chosen the nerd. He felt just like that nerd again as he removed his glasses and everything went fuzzy, as his knees went weak and his erection swelled hard. If he tried to speak, he was pretty sure his voice would wobble and squeak, so he didn't say anything. He just walked to her, cupped her face and kissed her.

He was devouring her, easing her closer to the bed, when she began tugging at his boxers. She got distracted, though, her delicate, strong fingers wrapping around him and wringing a guttural groan from him. Evading her hands while still feasting on her mouth, he shucked the boxers, managed to find the night table behind him and located a condom inside before they tumbled onto the bed together.

He didn't know how much time had passed. Two condoms' worth, the first too fast, of course, the second long enough to make a nerd proud if he weren't too tired to think about it. Then Stephen grinned. A true nerd was never too tired to take credit for and pride in his accomplishments. He'd made the Warrior Princess cry out, made her cling to him as if he were the only important thing in her world. Damn right he was proud.

Beside him she slept, her head on his shoulder, her arm over his middle. Her breathing was even and slow, her sleep so deep that when he brushed her hair from her face, she didn't even twitch. He wouldn't be surprised if she could sleep twenty-four hours. Sexual release was good for more than just sexual frustration.

But just as release had made her melt and go limp, he was now wide-awake, and his thoughts returned to her brother and sister-in-law. Macy had known Brent all her life; presumably it would be harder for him to harbor any great secrets without tipping her off.

Anne was another matter. She and Brent hadn't been married a year yet. How long had they dated? Where had they met? Was it good fortune that she seemed to love his family as much as he did?

There wasn't a correlation between length of time known and depth of love. Stephen had met Macy a week ago, and he knew he wanted to spend the rest of his life with her, be father to Clary, have more babies. He wanted to make Macy laugh and smile, to wake up with her every morning, to be exactly who he was and to let her be exactly who she was. He felt right with her. He belonged with her.

Anne could have had that instant strong connection, too. If her family was warm and loving, she would have been predisposed to want that kind of relationship with her in-laws. If her family was distant and dysfunctional, she could have been predisposed to want a normal relationship with her in-laws, to embrace a healthy family life with enthusiasm.

Unable to sleep and needing to do *something,* he carefully slid out from beneath Macy. She didn't murmur or cling; her breathing didn't change. She adjusted her head on the pillow and kept right on sleeping. He put on his glasses and boxers, then the thought of Clary made him add shorts and a T-shirt.

When he left the bedroom, Clary was still asleep, too. Scooter, curled up by her legs, lifted his head to watch Stephen, then laid it down again.

In the kitchen, Stephen picked up the mugs from the table, rinsed and left them in the sink, then he picked up the pill bottle. It was a popular medication, used to treat both depression and anxiety. It was a pill short; at some point, she'd felt the need to double the dose. Only six remained. And they weren't working, she'd said.

Wrapping his fingers tightly around the bottle, he

went into the office and logged online, looking up the medication. He scanned the information on the manufacturer's website, the side effects—hallucinations, hauntings and amnesia weren't among them—and looked at the enlarged photo of the tablet. It was round, white, with letters and a number on one side, the other blank.

With nothing else demanding his attention, Stephen opened the bottle and shook one tablet into his palm. Round, white, letters on one side.

But they didn't match the letters shown on the screen. When he turned the pill over, it wasn't smooth like the one on the screen. It had numbers. Maybe it was a generic, though the bottle indicated it was the brand name.

Next he searched for a description of the pill, and a result popped up an instant later. It was a medication for hypertension. No wonder it hadn't helped her anxiety. In fact, considering that the pharmaceutical company was adamant that patients should be weaned from the anxiety medication, she was damn lucky she hadn't had more than a few hallucinations.

Had it been an honest mistake? A pharmacy tech in a hurry sticking Macy's label on someone else's meds, the pharmacist not catching the error before the prescriptions were picked up?

Considering everything else that had happened, he didn't think so. Someone had deliberately replaced her anxiety meds with blood pressure medication.

And who had access? Brent and Anne.

God, it would break Macy's heart if her brother was trying to make her think she was crazy. Mark's betrayal had been bad enough. Could she survive being betrayed by Brent?

It must be Anne. It *had* to be, for Macy's sake. It would still hurt, but that was a recoverable hurt.

Grimly he returned the pill to the bottle, then did what he'd been putting off: he did a Google search for Macy and Mark. By morning he intended to know *everything* the internet had to say about either of them.

Waking up was a slow, easy transition from sleep to awareness. The sun shone through the window at the head of the bed, casting light and creating shadows. The bedroom door was closed, but Macy could hear two voices—Clary's cheerful little-girl and Stephen's deeper all-man rumble. A sweet, satisfied, broad smile stretched across her face. *Cute little nerd vet,* Anne and Brent had called him. A bumper sticker she'd seen somewhere said Nerds Try Harder. Stephen didn't need to try. He was perfect.

She rolled onto her side, facing his room. Unlike his office, it was sparsely decorated: one full bed made for snuggling, a dresser, a nightstand. White sheets and pillowcases, tan blanket, navy bedspread. It was a room where he slept, nothing more.

Except last night.

She didn't know what time it was, only that it was daylight and she could easily sleep another ten or twelve hours if she didn't have an appointment with the second dealer at nine. Besides, the aroma of coffee was faintly on the air, its fragrance rich and dark enough to start her heart pumping. It drew her from the bed and into her pajamas, folded neatly on the dresser—definitely not where she'd discarded them. With a finger-comb for her hair, she opened the door and her senses were assaulted with the scents of coffee and something savory-sweet.

Stephen and Clary sat at the kitchen table, identical mugs and empty plates in front of them. She was gesturing wildly, her favored way of talking, and he listened as if he really cared about flying dragons and knights of the realm. Considering his fantasy-book career, maybe he did.

He saw Macy first, and his serious gaze settled on her. She couldn't tell by looking at him that anything earth-shaking had happened last night, and for just one instant she wondered if the night had been out of character for her but far more the norm for him. Then he smiled, not even a full smile, but one with such—such *possession* in it—that her legs got wobbly and she had no choice but to sit with them at the table if she didn't want to fall flat on her face.

"Hey, Mama. Look, I'm drinking milk from a coffee cup. And we had pumpkin pie for breakfast. For *breakfast*. Dr. Stephen didn't have any cereal or eggs or sausage, and he says oatmeal is for aliens. Even Scooter won't eat it. And I told him, me, neither."

Her daughter's rambling settled over her like a familiar old blanket. This was exactly what she needed before she faced the house again.

Stephen brought her a mug of coffee, sweetened and creamed, and a saucer with a piece of pumpkin pie. Before she could speak, he did. "It's got eggs in it, and a vegetable, and the crust is kind of like bread. And it's all I had in the freezer that appealed to Clary."

"I love pumpkin pie for breakfast."

He smiled again, brushing her shoulder as he pulled away, as if he needed a touch, no matter how small. After refreshing his coffee, he said, "Clary, want to watch TV with Scooter?"

She slurped the last of her milk, swiped her face with a paper towel doubling as napkin and grinned. "You bet."

As they trotted off, Stephen called after her, "Watch out, though. Animal Planet is his favorite channel."

The TV came on a moment later. It always amazed Macy how the use of remote control devices seemed to be part of a kid's genetic code these days.

Stephen sat down to her right, and she automatically turned her chair in that direction. "I've got some things to do this morning, but first I need to ask you some questions, okay?"

Discomfort took the shiny edge off the morning, but she nodded. They'd avoided discussing who among the people close to her would have a motive strong enough to want her recommitted to the psychiatric hospital. She'd seen the guilt and trouble in his eyes while he considered whether it was her brother or her sister-in-law, but he hadn't pushed her and she had chosen instead to push something else.

Now, thin-lipped, fingers gripping the coffee mug too tightly, she nodded.

His voice automatically lowered to make certain Clary couldn't hear him. "Does Brent have any financial problems?"

"No. His business is very successful."

"Do he and Anne spend a lot of money?"

"No."

"But they both love Clary."

She nodded emphatically.

"How long have you known Anne?"

"About a year."

"And Brent's known her a few months longer?" He waited for her nod. "Where did they meet?"

Even thinking Brent or Anne could be the one haunting her made Macy's stomach roil. Talking about them, sharing personal things, made her face sweat. "At the hospital. Anne's sister was also a patient there. They'd bump into each other in the lobby, the restaurant, share their woes, and they fell in love." Yes, the hospital had had a full-service restaurant rather than a cafeteria.

"Do you know her maiden name?"

"Jones. Anne Jones."

For an instant, his eyes almost rolled. Macy knew what he was thinking: such a common name. Easy to hide behind, easy to remember if it wasn't really yours, far too hard to easily follow up on.

Then he schooled his expression, giving no hint what he thought of that. "What hospital?"

"Claremont House. It's in Columbia. The five-star resort of mental institutions."

"So Anne comes from money, too."

Feeling the hated fluttering in her chest, Macy took her cup and stood up to pace the small room. It was a nervous behavior that made other people look at her suspiciously, but activity helped her with control. "I don't know. Either that or really good insurance."

"How is her sister? When did she get out?"

"I—" Macy swallowed. "I don't know. Anne never talks about her to me." In fact, she'd never heard Anne mention family at all. It was as if once she'd married Brent, his family became hers and hers no longer existed. "I need to take my medication."

Silently Stephen rose and got the bottle off the top of the refrigerator, well out of Clary's and Scooter's reach, handing it to her.

She swallowed one pill with coffee, then shoved the

bottle into her shorts pocket. "You can't really suspect… Anne's like a sister to me, a mother to Clary. She would never do anything to hurt me. And Brent—it's just not in his character. He could no more terrorize me than you could."

He blocked her way, took the coffee, then put his arms around her. "I'm just trying to figure this out. Last night, when I opened the door and found you standing there, so scared and shaken… It's got to stop, Mace. Whoever's doing this has to stop."

She wondered which would be worse: being scared all the time, or finding out it was Brent or Anne manipulating her fear. She'd had her heart broken twice before. She didn't want to go through it again. She just wanted to be like everyone else in the world.

"You and Clary are welcome to stay here as long as you want, but I've got to get going."

He offered her the house key on his key ring, but she numbly shook her head. "We'll go home. Brent and Anne will worry—" She broke off, and her mouth tightened. "We'll go home," she repeated.

Stephen kissed them both goodbye on the porch, watched Macy load Clary and Scooter into the van, then walked to his car parked next to the house. After following them to their house, he drove out of the neighborhood and headed for the interstate that would take him to Augusta, then Columbia.

He'd spent most of the night on the internet and found countless sites that covered Mark Howard's death, his public life and his not-so-public activities, plenty of mentions of Macy, a fair number of Brent and virtually nothing about Anne. Of course, not knowing her maiden name hadn't made the search easier—wouldn't have made it easier now that he knew. The most he'd located about her was a blog belonging to a friend of Brent's who'd held a party to celebrate his and Anne's marriage. *His lovely new wife from Columbia* was the extent of her mention.

He wasn't proud of it, but he'd also checked Macy's cell phone. She'd left it lying on the night table when they went to bed. He hadn't looked at her phone book or call records. He'd simply scrolled through the pictures, hundreds of them, and forwarded two good shots of Brent and Anne to his own cell. With no more of a name to go on than Anne, he would need the photographs.

Once he merged onto Interstate 20, he kicked up the speed to ten above the limit and set the cruise control. Should he have told Macy why her anxiety meds weren't working? That he was going to the hospital to see if he could learn anything about Anne? He wasn't hopeful. If hospitals were prickly about patient confidentiality, psychiatric hospitals must be doubly so. But he wasn't looking for information on a patient. Just a woman who'd spent a lot of time there.

He decided for the dozenth time that not telling Macy was right. One more dose of blood pressure medicine wouldn't hurt her. Besides, she had to be at the house with Brent and Anne while he was gone, and there was no way she could hide his suspicions—her guilt—that long, if at all. She would surely say something to someone, and whichever one was responsible for switching the pills—maybe both of them—might take more direct action. It was best that she remain in the dark awhile longer.

And if he didn't learn anything on this trip?

Then it was time to call the police. Ellie Maricci's

husband, Tommy, was chief of detectives now that A. J. Decker had been promoted to fill the retiring chief of police's spot. Tommy was a good cop and had subtlety down to an art. Marnie had worked with all of the detectives at one time or another, and she respected Tommy a lot.

The drive to Columbia and to Claremont House took nearly three hours. The place was gorgeous. Built of stone and surrounded by terraced gardens, it looked like an Italian villa lifted from Tuscany and placed on this spot of wooded land. The roof was rust-colored tiles, huge windows lined four floors and marble steps led up from a rose garden and down to the pool, up to patios and down to lush expanses of grass.

Access to the main portion of the building was easy: he simply walked in the door. A receptionist sat at a desk centered on a large patterned rug in the middle of a vast marble floor. A bouquet of pink roses stood at each end of the desk, their shade a perfect match to the pinks in the contemporary paintings on the walls.

A broad corridor bisected the lobby running north-south, and two smaller ones ran east-west from each end of the lobby. Discreet signs indicated gift shop, restaurant and snack bar down one hall, administrative offices down another. A grand staircase led to the second floor, guarded by a suit full of muscles at the bottom.

Stephen wondered how luxurious the patient rooms were—not that it mattered. It was still a hospital room, its occupant still in a place she or he didn't want to be. Macy must have hated every moment in her gilded prison.

A very expensive prison. She'd commented that Anne's family either had money or very good insurance, but from what Stephen understood, insurance rarely paid as well for psychiatric treatment as for medical care, and this place must have cost a fortune. Was Anne's sister still here? Was that another reason, in addition to Clary, Anne wanted Macy out of the way? Because with Brent's renewed access to the Howard fortunes, she could pay for her sister's care?

Or did her sister even exist?

He approached the woman at the receptionist's desk. She was about his mother's age, with narrow glasses and a well-fitted suit, and she gave him a warm smile. "Can I help you?"

He pulled out his phone and located the photo of Anne. "I'm picking up my friend here. She was visiting her sister, and her car wouldn't start. Her name is Anne Jones. Have you seen her?"

He watched the woman study the photo closely before shaking her head. Not so much as a faint hint of recognition. "I haven't, but I only came on an hour ago."

"I'm surprised you don't recognize her. She practically lived here last time her sister was in."

She shook her head again. "I can have her paged if you like."

"Um, no, thanks. I'll just wait around here like she told me to." He smiled awkwardly, shoved his cell and his hands into his shorts pockets and walked off to look at a monster-sized painting on the far wall. After a furtive glance at the reception desk, he turned down the hall and went into the gift shop.

The woman working there was a clone of the first: older, well-dressed, friendly smile. He smiled back, then spent a moment or two wandering the aisles on his way to the checkout counter. She looked up and smiled again. "Can I help you find something?"

"Maybe someone." He showed the photo again. "My friend Anne. She brought her sister by today, and I guess they're running late since we were supposed to meet half an hour ago."

"Oh, honey, you should know by now that the entire world's running late. No one seems able to keep to a schedule." She pulled a pair of narrow red glasses dotted with yellow flowers from a pocket and slid them on, then took the phone. "Ah, *that* Anne. I haven't seen her…oh, in a good long while. You say she brought her sister today?"

Swallowing hard, Stephen willed his hand not to tremble. "Yeah, for a—a follow-up visit."

"Oh, poor thing. And here I thought you meant we were getting another dedicated volunteer. I didn't even know Anne had a sister, and certainly not one who needed…ah, Claremont care." Her face pinked, and she gave over the cell and began backing away to a stack of boxes behind her. "I'd better get back to work. You tell Anne that Betty in the gift shop says hello."

Stephen didn't move, his brain trying to process the new information and all the questions he wanted to ask, but Betty was studiously ignoring him while she unpacked the top carton. The arrival of two customers made the decision to leave for him. He walked out, a dozen feet down the hall and into the snack bar.

It was small and offered mostly prepackaged items, a limited menu of hamburgers and hot dogs, plus fountain pop. A half dozen staff members sat at the tables, having a late breakfast or an early lunch, but the clerk, in her early twenties, was unoccupied, leaning against the counter and inspecting the bright pops of color that covered her fingernails.

"Hi," he greeted her, inhaling deeply the scent of fatty meat and steamed buns. "Coke and a hot dog, please." As she pulled on plastic gloves, he added, "Slow morning, huh?"

She gave him a look. *Good job of stating the obvious, Noble.*

"Have you worked here long?"

Another look. Apparently small talk wasn't part of the job. But after plopping a wiener on a moist bun, she said, "Couple years."

"A, uh, friend of mine used to volunteer here. I—I was thinking about maybe doing the same if there are, uh, any positions open. Anne Jones. You know her?"

He wasn't sure if she was thinking about it or simply ignoring him so he showed her the digital photo. She grunted. "Not really. Seen her around." She set his hot dog and Coke on a small red tray, took his money, then glanced around the dining room. "If you're interested in volunteering, you should talk to that guy. Duncan West. He's in charge of volunteers."

Stephen followed the line of her pointing finger out glass doors to a patio shared by both the snack shop and the restaurant next door. Duncan West sat alone at a table for four. He wore a white dress shirt with pale gray trousers and was reading on an iPad while he ate.

"Uh, thanks. I will." He carried the tray to the condiment station and squirted mustard onto the hot dog. So Anne had volunteered at Claremont House instead of simply visiting her sister there, and she hadn't talked about her sister with the people she worked with. Information, but nothing to justify accusing her of anything but having a giving spirit and guarding her sister's privacy.

But damned if Stephen didn't still believe she was guilty.

Drawing a deep breath, he went out the door and walked over to the lone occupied table. "Duncan West? I'm Stephen—" a slight hesitation, then he offered his middle name instead of his last "—Keith. I understand you're in charge of volunteers around here. I'd like to talk to you about that."

Chapter 14

The second dealer, an elderly man by the name of Bartlett, was so pleased with everything Macy had shown him that she'd half expected him to want to carry it all away with him. He pronounced every piece excellent, exquisite or extraordinary and told her he could sell every one of the paintings that very day to customers who kept him on the lookout for those artists. He'd even known of a small museum that would pay handsomely for the wedding portrait.

That one, she'd said drily, wasn't for sale. She still intended to destroy it.

Mr. Bartlett had left the house shortly before noon. They'd taken a break for lunch in town, where they'd run into Anamaria and her sister-in-law, Jessica, who had promptly invited Clary to join their kids for a play-day at the library. Macy had agreed because the child needed a break and time with kids her own age. Besides, this afternoon the primary thing on the schedule was getting Mark's office and the nurseries packed up.

"Where is Stephen?" Brent asked when they returned to the house.

"He had things to do." What things, she'd wondered all morning, and did they involve her? Conceit to think that his entire life revolved around her now when a week ago he hadn't known she existed. But she couldn't shake the unsettled feeling that she was the reason for his absence.

As she set her purse on the counter, Brent wrapped his arm around her. "Hey, I've been meaning to tell you. You're a grown woman. You don't have to sneak out in the middle of the night to visit your boyfriend."

Her face turned deep red, making both him and Anne laugh. "You're such a *good* girl," Anne said, pinching her cheek on the way past.

"You know, he could have just spent the night here."

Macy didn't mention that the point had been for *her* to get out of the house. She didn't need to, since Anne scrunched up her face. "New lover in worthless husband's bed? Eww."

Her cheeks burned hotter, and she felt the need to pull her shirt from her throat to ease the constriction. Problem was, the scoop-neck tank was nowhere near her throat.

Anne laughed again and hugged both of them. "No more teasing about cute little nerd vet. Let's get to work. Where do you want me?"

Three rooms on the agenda, and Macy couldn't bring herself to set foot in two of them. Something must have shown in her expression because Anne's own expression turned serious, her voice gentle. "I'll take care of the baby's room, okay?"

All she could manage was a grateful—and guilty— nod. Stephen was wrong for even considering bad things of Brent or Anne. They were good people who loved her and showed it every day. She would accept it was Mark's ghost haunting her before she'd believe it could be either of them.

When she walked into Clary's room five minutes later with an armful of packing material, she realized how tense she'd been by the sudden ease that flowed through her. Her shoulders and neck relaxed, her gut unknotted and the taut lines across her forehead went away. The room smelled of her daughter, powdery, sweet, innocent, and she swore if she closed her eyes, giggles and soft snores would echo off the walls.

She was sorting baby clothes when a distant ring sounded. Her hand automatically went to her pocket, where her cell phone sat silent. A moment later Brent called up the stairs, "You just got a hang-up, Anne."

"Thanks, sweetie." Anne passed the open doorway on her way to the stairs. "Can you toss it up to me?"

"What if it breaks?"

"Are you doubting my ability to catch? Or yours to throw accurately?"

Macy smiled as she started folding a pile of spit-up- free clothing and stacked them in a box, then immediately her mouth slipped into a frown. What if Stephen wasn't wrong? What if it *was* her brother or her sister- in-law, or both of them working together? What if they'd decided she wasn't fit to have Clary on her own? If they'd decided they would rather have her daughter and their money than have Macy in their lives?

Could Brent sell her out for money? Could Anne?

If either of them were guilty, she would be devastated. But devastation healed. She'd been there before with Mark, with the baby, and she'd made it back. Well, almost back. She would recover, but she would be, oh, so much sadder for it.

The cell phone rang again, this time just down and across the hall. Anne answered quickly, sounding as breezy and carefree as ever. That was one of the things Macy admired about her. No matter how grim life was, she always sounded as if it were good. *If you could pretend it, you could be it.*

"Yeah, sorry about that," Anne was saying. "I left my cell at the house when we went to lunch. What do you need?"

Where *was* Stephen? Macy hadn't thought to ask him how long his business would take. It was amazing how much she missed him. The very last thing she'd expected when she'd driven up from Charleston last week was to fall in love. She wasn't sure she would ever do that again in this lifetime. But here she was. And she was hopeful in ways she hadn't known possible when she'd fallen in love with Mark.

Anne passed the room, blowing out a harsh breath, then headed downstairs. The sound of her voice, tight and controlled, floated back up, but her words were indistinguishable. Macy hoped she wasn't getting bad news about her sister.

If she existed. If anyone outside the Irelands existed in Anne's life.

Damn it, she *hated* this! She wasn't a suspicious person. She gave her trust and didn't take it back until it was proved a dozen times over that it wasn't deserved. She *wouldn't* let doubt taint two of the closest relationships in her life.

"Macy?" Anne called from below. "Could you come down here a minute?"

Her muscles knotted, her heart fluttered and sweat broke out across her forehead. She tried to tell herself she was overreacting; it was just the near-constant stress, all the reminders of Mark and the true evil she'd lived with. There was no reason to panic.

But that was the hell of panic attacks. There *was* no reason.

She forced her fists to unclench from the tiny pink silk dress she held, laid it aside and rose from the rocker. Because she was shaky, she held the railing all the way down the stairs, then walked to the back of the house. Finding the kitchen empty, she pivoted toward the office door, stopping at the threshold as she heard the low rumble of the garage door opening.

"Where's Anne?" she asked of Brent, who was loading a batch of files into a carton.

"She'll be here in a second. How's it going upstairs?"

"Okay. Here?"

He gestured toward the sealed cartons stacked in the middle of the room. "Did you know this desk has three hidden compartments?"

"I'm not surprised. A lot of old furniture does."

"Nothing hidden in any of them."

"Because Mark's greatest secret was hidden in his soul."

"If he had one," Brent agreed.

Macy's gaze was drawn to the credenza, and she shifted uncomfortably. Brent had gathered all the photographs in the room there, two dozen or so, mostly portraits though also a few snapshots. One in particular stood out to her, a picture of Mark when he was a teenager, standing beside his grandfather, both of them grinning ear to ear as if they had known something no one else in the world knew.

And they had. He was fourteen the first time he'd killed. Probably half the bodies unearthed at Fair Winds had been his work.

Queasiness swept through her. A handsome kid, a strong impressive man, the majesty of Fair Winds rising behind them. Monsters and the place that spawned them.

Something rippled across the surface of the photo. Just a reflection, she told herself. A dust mote caught by the sun. But the rippling continued, chilling her blood, drawing her across the threshold, first one step, then two, more. Her hand shook as she reached for the frame. The wood was hot, the glass shimmering, the picture changing, transforming.

"Macy?"

Brent's voice sounded distant, but she couldn't answer. Her jaws were locked tight, her teeth clamped together, goose bumps giving birth to goose bumps all up her spine. *Monsters.* But not two. Three. Superimposed right next to Mark was Anne with her ready smile, her compassionate eyes. An unholy trinity of evil.

"Oh, dear God," she whispered just as Anne's voice came from the dining room.

"In here. Now."

Footsteps shuffled, a shoving sound, a muffled curse. Macy looked at the photograph again and saw nothing but what had always been: Mark and his grandfather, grinning at the camera. The glass was normal glass, the wood just wood. She turned slowly, seeing Brent still behind the desk but on his feet, a stunned and bewildered look on his face, and she turned more and saw Stephen, dazed, disheveled, barely able to sit upright in the chair nearest the desk. A man stood a few feet behind him, his white shirt rumpled and stained, his face vaguely familiar, and Anne was in the doorway.

Anne, her sister-in-law, her friend, her daughter's second mother, holding a gun on them all.

"Anne...what the hell—?"

She smiled tightly at Brent's shocked words. "Yeah, that was my first thought, too, when this idiot called and said he'd kidnapped our cute little nerd vet. What the hell."

"He was *asking* questions about you!" the man protested.

"Any fool can ask questions. It's putting the answers together in the right way that matters, and this fool couldn't have done that." Disgust crossed her face. "We had a plan, Duncan. All you had to do was stick to it. You didn't have to drag Stephen into it. You didn't have to drag yourself any further into it than you already were. But you panicked."

Macy looked from Duncan to Stephen. His eyes were glazed, and his rumpled hair showed blood crusted and drying at the crown of his head. He shook his head several times as if trying to clear it without success.

From somewhere upstairs came Scooter's barking, and she realized she hadn't seen the dog since they'd returned from lunch. He'd probably gone to snooze on her bed while they were gone, and Anne had closed the door, shutting him in. At least he'd be safe up there.

"What's going on, Anne?" Brent demanded. "Who is this guy?"

"He works at Claremont," Macy said. "In administration, I think."

The man shot Anne a look as if her recognition justified his kidnapping Stephen.

Claremont, Anne, a kidnapping, a gun… Oh, God, Stephen had been right. Anne had wanted everyone to think Macy was insane. She wanted possibly her daughter and definitely their money, and she was willing to do anything to get it. Marry Brent. Befriend Macy. Mother Clary. Lie and deceive and torment.

Murder. Just like Mark.

Brent's shoulders slumped, and a look of such anguish crossed his face that Macy's heart broke for him. "You want the money? You married me so you could get access to my sister? To her money?"

"You think I'd go to this much trouble for Macy's inheritance? Invest more than a year of my life for her piddling little fortune?" Anne shook her head with mock disappointment. "I want Clary's money. And Clary."

Anger surged through the numbness that had fallen over Macy. "You can't have my daughter."

"Oh, sweetie, I can." Anne's voice was so normal, her sympathetic look so familiar. She could even convince Macy—had almost convinced her—that she was losing her mind. "You made Brent her guardian in the event that something happened to you, and Brent made *me* her guardian in the event that something happened to him. So if you die, and he dies… Your mom and dad have already said they can't raise her, and they know how much I love her, and Mark's mother doesn't really give a damn. Who's going to fight me for her?"

Stephen stirred, grimacing as if the movement nauseated him. "My sister. I called her before I left the house this morning." The words were slow, slurred. Had Duncan been satisfied with cracking him over the head with something, or had he also drugged him?

"What could you have told your sister?" Duncan scoffed. "You didn't know anything."

"I knew that Anne had substituted blood pressure medicine for Macy's antianxiety drug. I knew enough to be suspicious of her." Stephen lifted his head and swayed unsteadily, swallowing hard but maintaining eye contact with Duncan. "I knew enough to go straight to you, didn't I?"

Such a huge sense of relief washed over Macy. Her pills hadn't stopped working because she was losing control again! Anyone with anxiety disorder would be likely to start having problems again if they stopped their medication.

She bared her teeth at Anne's partner in a semblance of a smile. "How's your blood pressure, Duncan? Just about high enough right now to make your brain explode, I'd imagine."

He bared his teeth back. "It's fine. I told one of the doctors at work I lost mine, so he refilled it for me, no questions asked." Turning back to Stephen, he said, "So you told your sister. Big deal. What can she do?"

The answer seemed beyond Stephen at the moment, so Macy responded for him. "She works for the local police department. She'll prove my medicine was tampered with."

Alarm stiffened his body, turning his cheeks and throat deep red. "Damn it, Anne!"

Irritation crossed Anne's face, an expression Macy had never seen there before. What an incredible actress she was. If she'd set her sights on Hollywood instead of the Howard inheritance, she could have made a fortune of her own. "Shut up, Duncan. It's part of the plan."

As Anne's irritation deepened, Macy thought he might be on the hit list, too, but didn't realize it. He'd provided Anne with information on Macy when she was committed and with the medication to make the switch, but once she'd reached her goal and no longer needed his help, he was a liability.

Slowly Stephen got to his feet, wavering so far left, then right, Macy didn't know how he kept from falling. He awkwardly placed one hand on the desk, then followed it around the corner toward Brent. Carefully he planted one foot in front of the other, ignoring Duncan's mutter about staying where he was. When he rounded the next corner, he gave Brent a goofy smile. "Do you mind if I trade chairs with you? That one's not very comfortable."

Brent moved toward him as if to help, but a sharp word from Anne and a jerk of her head made him back off. He joined Macy, leaning against the credenza for support, rage and sorrow radiating from him. "I'm so sorry, Macy," he whispered. "So damn sorry."

"Me, too," she murmured.

Stephen had almost reached the plush leather chair when his knees buckled, his face drained white and he sank to the floor out of sight. "Stephen!" Macy took a step in his direction, but Brent caught her arm, kept her by his side.

"Oh, for God's sake, what did you give him?" Anne asked.

Duncan shrugged. "I don't know. Something to keep him knocked out for the drive here. It'll clear out of his system. It always does."

In the small space under the desk, Macy saw Stephen's huge tennis shoe moving. Hastily she pulled her attention back to Anne and one of her earlier comments. "It can't be part of the plan for Stephen's sister to find out someone switched my medication."

"She won't find that out. I kept your pills, of course, when I switched them with Duncan's. Once we're done here, I'll switch them back, and all anyone's going to notice is that a) your pill bottle is almost full and b) there's no evidence in your system that you've been taking them. They'll think you took yourself off your medication. Mental patients often do that, you know, and then they're right back in whatever pit they crawled out of. I, of course, will be here to tell the police how you'd been sinking back into that horrible depression that had resulted in your committal the first time, how I had warned Brent, how you both were in denial. How I came home from picking up Clary after her playdate and found such a tragic scene awaiting me. Stephen, Brent, you, all dead at your own hand."

"I don't own a gun," Macy said flatly.

"But you found one. Really, you did. This was your husband's. It was hidden in the guesthouse. Duncan found it while he kept watch on you until Brent and I got here."

So she really had seen someone out there. And of course, Anne had given him the code and the key so he could sneak in and rearrange things. "Clary in the pool?"

Anne smiled. "Actually, that was me. I'd brought a doll dressed in her clothes. When I went to get my purse from the guesthouse, I tossed it in. When you screamed, I dragged it out, hid it under some bushes and dashed into the house to pretend I'd been searching for her."

Stephen's foot clunked against the desk and Anne scowled at Duncan. "Get him off the floor and into the chair."

Grumbling about not being hired muscle, Duncan hauled Stephen's shoulders out from under the desk, then half lifted, half dragged him into the chair. His hair looking tamer than she'd ever seen it, Stephen met her gaze, fear in his eyes, but something more. Hope. Satisfaction.

Oh, God, the panic button! Just last night she'd told him there was one under Mark's desk. He must have pressed it, which meant the hidden cameras had been activated and the police had been notified. Leave it to him, drugged and probably concussed, to remember the small detail that might save their lives.

If Anne didn't get too impatient.

Taking advantage of the cover provided by her and Brent's bodies, Macy felt behind her, searching for the heaviest picture frame there. "Anne, I loved you like a sister. I was so happy when you and Brent got married. I would have given you just about anything if you'd only asked."

Anne tilted her head to one side. "Would you have given me your daughter?" After a moment, she said, "I didn't think so. Don't worry. She doesn't remember what happened to her father, and I'll make sure she completely forgets about her mother. She'll be the best-loved little girl in the world, and I'll teach her to be strong and independent. She won't grow up weak-minded and weak-willed like you."

Weak-minded? Weak-willed? Her fingers brushed a frame and heat warmed them. It was the photo of Mark and his grandfather, she knew from the strange sensations in her hand. She hefted it, unusually heavy for its size, and clenched hot wood and shimmering glass, and without a word, without further thought, she flung it across the room at Anne.

Startled, Anne jerked the gun up and pulled the trigger as the frame sailed end over end. The bullet struck it with a heavy clunk, but the frame's course didn't alter. It followed its arc, connecting solidly with her face, glass shattering. The impact made her shriek and stumble backward, falling against the door frame, small cuts bleeding all over her face, dripping into her eyes.

The next voice was the sweetest Macy had ever heard—after Clary's, of course, and Stephen's.

"Damn. Nice throw, Macy," Lieutenant Tommy Maricci of the Copper Lake Police Department said from the doorway. "Mrs. Ireland, we'd better get you and your friend out of here before she does some real damage."

Stephen freed himself from the paramedics as quickly as he could. His head wound was cleaned, and whatever sedative he'd been given had worn off for the most part. They advised him to go to the hospital, but he refused. He'd get checked out later, but there were things he had to do first.

Anne and Duncan West had both been taken away in handcuffs, him under his own power, her strapped helpless to a gurney. Tommy Maricci and A. J. Decker were in the living room with Brent, the crime scene people were gathering evidence in the office and from the trunk of West's car, and Macy was standing at the French doors, staring out into the yard.

She responded when he approached, but not with fear. Without looking, without him speaking, she knew it was him, and she leaned back into him as he put his arms around her. "Thank you," she murmured.

"For what?"

"Remembering the panic button. Suspecting Anne. Going to Claremont."

"Getting my head cracked open didn't do much to help."

"It forced her to move up her schedule." She rested her head against his shoulder, and he let his chin sink into the silky mass of her hair. "You saved our lives."

"That picture frame throw helped. I didn't know you had an arm like that."

Finally she tilted her head enough to meet his gaze. "Would you think I was crazy if I said I had help?"

He considered it. Ghosts didn't exactly fit into his view of the world. But he didn't know everything. "It makes sense. Despite what he was, Mark loved you and Clary."

She nodded, hair tickling his jaw. "I may have to stop hating him and just…let go."

He nodded, too. Hating took so much energy, and there were so many better things she could do with that energy. Like loving *him* and starting all over again, just her and Clary and him. "Mace— Hey." He scowled as his right arm was jerked away from her body and found Marnie holding him by the wrist.

She barely glanced at him. "We need a sample of your blood to see what medication you were given."

Before he could react, the tech had the tourniquet on and was approaching with a needle. Tensing, Stephen turned his head the other way and squeezed his eyes shut, at least until a soft giggle made him open them. Macy was smiling at him. "You don't faint, do you?"

"He has before," Marnie answered. "Usually if you distract him and you're fast enough, he's okay."

"Huh. Just like Clary."

Since he was feeling about three years old, Stephen stuck his tongue out at her.

She laughed again. "Want me to kiss you when it's over and make it better?"

Now there was a suggestion he could get behind. He couldn't answer, though, not with the tech withdrawing the needle and Marnie slapping a bandage on his arm, then bending his elbow tightly.

"Hold that for a minute," she said brusquely, then turned her attention to Macy. "I'm Marnie, his older sister, and you, obviously, are Macy. While I regret the drama you underwent today, I do wish you had beaten your sister-in-law to death with that picture. He's the only brother I have." She nodded once for emphasis then walked away.

"Wow. That counts as overwhelming emotion for Marnie," he murmured.

"She loves you." Macy slowly turned in his arms to face him. "So do I." Stretching onto her toes, she kissed him, then brushed her fingers through his hair. "I feel bad."

"For loving me?"

She made a face at him. "Poor Brent got his heart broken, and I got mine healed. I know you haven't asked me to stay or anything, but I do love you, Stephen, and I'm not going anywhere. Well, away from this house because it totally freaks me out, but not away from this town. Not away from you. Unless…" She swallowed hard. "Unless you'd rather have someone a little less prone to drama—"

He stopped her words with a kiss that heated too hot

too fast and made him a little unsteady on his feet. Holding on to her for balance, he rested his forehead against hers. "I have a suggestion. Let's get me checked out at the hospital, get your brother checked into a hotel, get Clary and Scooter settled at home, and I'll leave absolutely no doubt in your mind how much I want you in my life. Sound like a deal?"

Her smile came slowly and sent heat straight through his body, making him rethink the order of his suggestions. "Sounds like the best deal ever." She took his hand, draped his arm over her shoulder and looped her free arm around his waist, encouraging him to lean on her as they started toward the door. "Tell me, Stephen. Do your stories have happy endings?"

His fingers tightened fractionally on her shoulder. "This one does, Mace."

* * * * *

A sneaky peek at next month...

INTRIGUE...

BREATHTAKING ROMANTIC SUSPENSE

My wish list for next month's titles...

In stores from 21st June 2013:

❑ Carrie's Protector – Rebecca York

& For the Baby's Sake – Beverly Long

❑ Outlaw Lawman – Delores Fossen

& The Smoky Mountain Mist – Paula Graves

❑ Triggered – Elle James

& Fearless – HelenKay Dimon

Romantic Suspense

❑ The Colton Ransom – Marie Ferrarella

Available at WHSmith, Tesco, Asda, Eason, Amazon and Apple

Just can't wait?

Visit us Online

You can buy our books online a month before they hit the shops! **www.millsandboon.co.uk**

0613/46

Special Offers

Every month we put together collections and longer reads written by your favourite authors.

Here are some of next month's highlights— and don't miss our fabulous discount online!

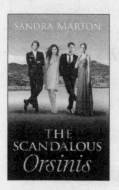

On sale 21st June

On sale 5th July

On sale 5th July

Save 20%
on all Special Releases

Find out more at
www.millsandboon.co.uk/specialreleases

Visit us Online

0713/ST/MB422

Join the Mills & Boon Book Club

Want to read more **Intrigue** books?
We're offering you **2 more** absolutely **FREE!**

We'll also treat you to these fabulous extras:

- **Exclusive offers and much more!**

- **FREE home delivery**

- **FREE books and gifts with our special rewards scheme**

Get your free books now!

**visit www.millsandboon.co.uk/bookclub
or call Customer Relations on 020 8288 2888**

FREE BOOK OFFER TERMS & CONDITIONS
Accepting your free books places you under no obligation to buy anything and you may cancel at any time. If we do not hear from you we will send 5 stories a month which you may purchase or return to us—the choice is yours. Offer valid in the UK only and is not available to current Mills & Boon subscribers to this series. We reserve the right to refuse an application and applicants must be aged 18 years or over. Only one application per household. Terms and prices are subject to change without notice. As a result of this application you may receive further offers from other carefully selected companies. If you do not wish to share in this opportunity please write to the Data Manager at PO BOX 676, Richmond, TW9 1WU.

The World of Mills & Boon®

There's a Mills & Boon® series that's perfect for you. We publish ten series and, with new titles every month, you never have to wait long for your favourite to come along.

Blaze.

Scorching hot, sexy reads
4 new stories every month

By Request

Relive the romance with the best of the best
9 new stories every month

Cherish™

Romance to melt the heart every time
12 new stories every month

Desire™

Passionate and dramatic love stories
8 new stories every month

Visit us Online

Try something new with our Book Club offer
www.millsandboon.co.uk/freebookoffer

M&B/WORLD2

What will you treat yourself to next?

Ignite your Imagination, step into the past...
6 new stories every month

INTRIGUE...

Breathtaking romantic suspense
Up to 8 new stories every month

Captivating medical drama – with heart
6 new stories every month

MODERN™

International affairs, seduction & passion guaranteed
9 new stories every month

n o c t u r n e™

Deliciously wicked paranormal romance
Up to 4 new stories every month

RIVA™

Live life to the full – give in to temptation
3 new stories every month available exclusively via our Book Club

You can also buy Mills & Boon eBooks at
www.millsandboon.co.uk

Visit us Online

M&B/WORLD2

 *Mills & Boon® Online*

Discover more romance at
www.millsandboon.co.uk

 FREE online reads

 Books up to one
month before shops

 Browse our books
before you buy

...and much more!

For exclusive competitions and instant updates:

Like us on **facebook.com/millsandboon**

Follow us on **twitter.com/millsandboon**

Join us on **community.millsandboon.co.uk**

Visit us Online   Sign up for our FREE eNewsletter at
www.millsandboon.co.uk

WEB/M&B/RTL5